"I was trying to avoid this," he said

The detective drew a photograph from his pocket and held it out to her.

Jillian gulped for air, the room spun and for a second she thought she might faint. She stared at the tattered photo in Adam Ramsey's hand. "It looks…" She hauled in another lungful of air. "He looks…like Rob."

The man in the picture was wearing a gray suit and standing beside a dark-haired woman in a white dress. Did Ramsey think Rob had an affair while he was married to her? Or did he think the woman in the photo had something to do with his death?

It couldn't be. Rob would never… Jillian plucked the picture from Ramsey's fingers and turned it over. Someone had written "Our wedding day," and a date. A quick sense of relief washed over her. "If you're thinking what I think you are, you're wrong. My husband died in April of that year. This is dated the following May. And that writing definitely isn't his."

She looked up at Ramsey. "I have to admit the man does resemble Rob, though. Where did you get this photograph?"

His lips formed a thin line. "That's confidential."

"Fine. Keep it confidential." She handed back the photograph. "I'd like you to leave now."

"Okay," he finally said. He took something else from his pocket and gave her what looked like another photograph. Glancing down at it, she saw the same man and the same woman—and a little boy.

Dear Reader,

Sometimes when I finish writing a book, a particular character won't let go. That's what happened with Jillian Sullivan, who first appeared as the best friend of Dana Marlowe, the heroine in *Daddy in the House*. A young widow with a daughter to raise, Jillian begged for a book of her own. All the wonderful letters I received from readers said you felt the same, and before long I had another story idea percolating.

Because Jillian's husband's murder had never been solved, her story meshed perfectly with another idea I had about cops who work on cold cases—cases that may be years old but remain open. The hero who leapt to life was Detective Adam Ramsey, a divorced, multi-decorated law enforcement officer. His partner's death and the end of his marriage sent him on a downhill spiral that resulted in his reassignment to cold cases. It's Adam who discovers *The Man in the Photograph*—a piece of evidence that sets him and Jillian on a course that will change their lives.

Beneath the surface, these two are more alike than they know. I think we're *all* very much alike, in that we all want to love and be loved. Love transcends boundaries—between husband and wife, parent and child, friends and lovers.

Jillian and Adam's experience together is an adventure—both heartbreaking and exhilarating. I hope you'll enjoy reading about it as much as I enjoyed writing it!

Linda Style

P.S. I love hearing from readers. You can write me at P.O. Box 2292, Mesa, Arizona 85234, at LindaStyle@LindaStyle.com, or reach me through my Web site at www.LindaStyle.com.

Books by Linda Style

HARLEQUIN SUPERROMANCE

923—HER SISTER'S SECRET
977—DADDY IN THE HOUSE
1062—SLOW DANCE WITH A COWBOY

The Man in the Photograph

Linda Style

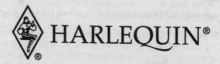

TORONTO • NEW YORK • LONDON
AMSTERDAM • PARIS • SYDNEY • HAMBURG
STOCKHOLM • ATHENS • TOKYO • MILAN • MADRID
PRAGUE • WARSAW • BUDAPEST • AUCKLAND

ISBN 0-373-71084-4

THE MAN IN THE PHOTOGRAPH

Visit us at www.eHarlequin.com

Printed in U.S.A.

DEDICATION

For Jay
My hero—and inspiration

ACKNOWLEDGMENTS

Writing a book is more than just writing; it's research and more research. My special thanks to: Paul Bishop, twenty-year veteran of the Los Angles Police Department, currently supervising the West Los Angeles Sex Crimes and Major Assault Crimes units, twice honored as Detective of the Year, and author of six novels.

Mark and Caron Style, who generously shared their Costa Rica knowledge and experience, and

Virginia Vail, for lending her Spanish expertise.

Since this is a work of fiction, I have taken liberties in some areas for the sake of story. Any errors are mine.

Thanks always to my family for your love and support and most of all—your patience!

PROLOGUE

Los Angeles Police Department

DETECTIVE ADAM RAMSEY slammed a fist on the metal table next to him. "I want the case, Mac. I deserve the case."

A woman was being questioned on the other side of the one-way glass, and Chief James MacGuire stood sentinel by the door, thick legs apart, arms crossed over his barrel chest. "You're too close to it, Ramsey. Besides, the feds are on it. It's out of our hands."

"Screw the feds. I'm the one Bryce called for help. I was his partner, for God's sake. Seven years we were partners. You can't shut me out, dammit." His fist came down again, making the table bounce.

Adam felt his chest constrict, his breath coming hard, as the anger raged in him, overriding the pain.

He'd been on vacation with his about-to-be ex-wife when his partner, his best friend, had called him for help. He hadn't known about it until two days later, when he returned to his apartment—alone—and listened to his phone messages.

He hadn't been there. If he had... Guilt swept through him now. If he had, maybe his partner wouldn't be dead.

Chest heaving, Adam leaned forward, both hands on the metal table, head bowed. "I didn't even get to see him, Mac."

"I know," the chief said, crossing to Adam and placing a hand on his shoulder. "None of us did. His parents wanted the closed casket. It was best." He stared at the woman on the other side of the glass. "The transfer is a good thing."

Adam's head snapped up, his anger spiking again. He shrugged off MacGuire's hand and squared his shoulders. "That's bogus. I didn't ask for a transfer. Why me? Why now?"

"You're the best man for the job, that's why."

"I'm the best man for *this* job. I knew Bryce better than anyone. He doesn't make mistakes. Not this kind."

MacGuire turned away, as if looking at Adam was too difficult. After a long silence, he said, "Bryce *did* make a mistake. A fatal one. He got made—his cover's blown. The feds are on it. That's all I can tell you. Leave it alone, take the transfer and do good things."

"I want to listen to the tape again."

"The feds have it. You know that."

Adam swung around, shoved a hand through his hair. "I keep thinking there's something…something he said that might give me a clue." He laughed wryly. "The last thing he said was that he knew he could count on me."

Adam took a breath and glanced at the woman behind the glass, seeing her, but not really seeing her. She was crying, tears streaming down her cheeks because her husband had been killed when his truck ran off the highway.

He knew exactly how she felt.

But he was a law enforcement officer. LEOs were strong and used to this kind of thing. They didn't cry.

CHAPTER ONE

Four years later

THE BLACK SEDAN WITH dark-tinted windows cruised to a stop across the street from Jillian Sullivan's suburban Chicago home.

Holding open her front door with her backside, Jillian reached for her daughter's rolled-up sleeping bag and suitcase. "I'm taking your things over to Dana and Logan's van, so hustle," she called to Chloe, then let the door slam behind her.

Summer wrapped around her, Midwest moist and hot. As she lugged Chloe's gear across the wide expanse of lawn, toward her neighbor's van in the driveway next door, her gaze drifted again to the black sedan.

The windows were so dark she couldn't tell if the person behind the wheel was a man or a woman, and he, or she, hadn't made a move to get out. Odd.

"See that car?" Jillian said to Dana as she dropped Chloe's things on Dana's driveway. "It drove up a few minutes ago and the driver hasn't budged."

Her best friend glanced over, then chucked a duffel bag into the van. "Well, I doubt he's casing the house while we're still here." Grinning, she elbowed Jillian.

"Hey. Maybe it's the hunk you had your eye on at the market this morning."

Jillian slapped her forehead. "Of course. Why didn't I think of that?" Why, oh why, had she even mentioned noticing the guy? All that did was give Dana another excuse to needle her about dating again. Though her friend hardly needed an excuse.

"Hey, I told you, you're ready. And after four years, it's about time."

"Not ready enough to be picking up men at the market, that's for sure." Despite what her friends seemed to think, she was just fine with her life as it was. With three hair salons to run and an eleven-going-on-twenty-year-old daughter to raise, she had little time for anything else.

She'd told her friend about him only because he'd been the first man she'd given real notice to in a very long time—and it wasn't because he had a great hair-cut.

Jillian glanced at the car again. "Maybe the driver's sick or something."

"Or waiting for the Hansens to return from golfing?" Dana crossed her arms. "Look, Jillian. Are you worried about how Chloe will be on this trip with us?"

"No, but two weeks is a long time. She's never been away for more than a few days before."

"A long time for Chloe? Or for *you?*" Dana's knowing smile broadened.

"And after that, vacation will be over and she'll be back in school."

"So indulge yourself for a change. Do something wild and totally irresponsible with the two weeks."

"I already did when I let my friends talk me into taking off so much time from work. It'll be tough to top that."

Dana shoved back her blunt-cut brown hair and looked at Jillian in exasperation. "Everyone should have such problems. Be happy you're in the position to do it." She reached for Chloe's suitcase and wedged it between two others. "The girls will have a great time. And I'm hoping they'll be a big help with little Remy."

"Hah. Dream on." As sweet as Dana's two-year-old son, Remy, was, it wasn't likely the two preteen girls would spend much time baby-sitting. Chloe and Dana's daughter, Hallie, had been practically attached at the hip ever since Jillian and Chloe moved from L.A. to the Beverly suburb four years ago to be near her mother-in-law, the only family they had left after Rob died.

"I know. It's more likely they'll spend their time squealing over music by some boy band. But one can always hope."

"Well, if Chloe is any problem at all, just call and I'll—"

"Chloe will be fine." Dana gave Jillian a reassuring hug. "Now, I've got to get a few more things from inside and then we're off. Is that everything? Is Chloe ready?"

"I'll check." While Dana headed into her garage, Jillian glanced at the car across the street once more before she sprinted across the overgrown grass and up the front steps of her old Tudor home. She went inside to see what was taking Chloe so long.

"Mo-om, I can't find my 'NSync CD," her daughter wailed from her room.

"Chloe, forget the CD and get down here right now, or the Wakefields are gonna leave without you."

Seconds later Jillian's look-alike daughter came clomping down the stairs, her waist-length strawberry-blond curls secured by a clip. All skinny arms and legs, she was already only a few inches shy of Jillian's five-nine. Chloe hated being so tall just as Jillian had hated it when she'd first sprouted up but not out.

The doorbell buzzed. "I bet it's Hallie," Chloe chirped, making a mad dash to the living-room window. She lifted a corner of the sheer curtain and peeked out. "Nah. It's just a salesman."

"Chloe, come on. You were supposed to be ready fifteen minutes ago. You can't keep people waiting all the time."

Chloe scowled and struck her defiant pose, legs apart, hands on boyish hips. "*You* do it all the time."

"Oh, no, you don't, Miss Sassy Mouth. *I'm* not the one keeping my best friend waiting. *My* habits are not up for discussion."

"Never are," Chloe muttered, and yanking open the closet door in the foyer, hunkered down next to the ever-growing pile of junk, tossing out one item after another, clothes, boots, soccer ball.

"You might need that backpack if you go hiking."

"I'm not going at all if I can't find my CD."

Jillian closed her eyes and counted to ten. She couldn't let their squabbles get to her. Not today. Not when her little girl was leaving.

"Look, get the rest of—"

Two loud knocks rattled the front door. Damn. She'd forgotten about the salesman, and apparently *he* couldn't read her No Solicitors sign.

Nerves taut, she turned to her daughter again, drew on her practiced calm and said evenly, "Chloe, get the rest of your things. You're going right now whether you've got all your CDs or not."

Chloe stalked off in a huff while Jillian, adrenaline still pumping, swung open the door.

"Whatever you're selli—"

It was the "hunk" from the market.

She took in his clothes—black sports jacket over a rumpled Los Angeles Lakers T-shirt and faded jeans. Running shoes. "You're not a salesman," she said.

Her mind flashed to that morning when, standing side by side at the organic-vegetable stand, they'd reached for the same eggplant. Their fingers had touched, skin grazing skin, her breath caught and their eyes had met and held. In that moment she'd felt a rush of awareness—which had come as a complete surprise.

Now his assessing gray eyes did a slow-motion sweep from her tangled hair to her bare feet and silver toe rings. Her blood warmed along the path of his gaze.

"You're right. I'm not a salesman."

Lord. The first guy I've even looked at in years and he thinks I'm coming on to him and follows me home. Gripping the knob, she slipped outside and pulled the door halfway shut behind her so Chloe couldn't hear them.

"If I gave you the wrong impression at the market,'' she said, ''I'm really sorry. I was in a hurry and sometimes when I'm in a hurry I get preoccupied, and when I'm thinking of other things it might look like I'm thinking of something else, I mean something that might've given you the wrong impression.'' She stopped for a breath.

The ghost of a grin played at the corners of his mouth. ''Mrs. Sullivan…'' His expression quickly sobered.

She blinked. *He knows my name? Oo-kay. My name. L.A. T-shirt.* And he was following her. Yeah. She got it.

He flashed a police shield. ''Mrs. Sullivan, I'm Detective Adam Ramsey.''

She felt a fleeting disappointment that the attraction she'd experienced when she first saw him had been only on her part. And *that* was stupid. Utterly stupid.

''LAPD,'' he added.

''I gathered. Were you following me earlier?'' She squared her shoulders. ''Or did you just happen to be in the same place I was?''

His only response was a dazzling white smile. He stuffed his badge into a pocket, then glanced past her into the house. ''I'd like to talk with you. May I come in?''

She didn't step aside ''Have you found my husband's murderer?''

''No.''

That was it? she thought. No explanation or apology? The LAPD had put her through living hell during their investigation of her husband's murder. When they'd come up with nothing, they'd focused on her, as if *she* was the criminal. As far as she was concerned, they'd botched the job and the killer had literally gotten away with murder.

"I suppose that four years after the fact it's a bit much to expect that someone somewhere has done his job."

"Sorry, I can't comment," the detective said, "but I would like to talk with you about the case."

She glanced over her shoulder to see if Chloe was coming. "Can it wait until my daughter's gone?"

He shrugged. "Sure I'll come back in an hour, okay?"

"Mo-om. I still can't find the CD, and I promised Hallie I'd bring it."

The door yanked open from behind and Jillian turned. Chloe stood there scowling, as if the missing CD was Jillian's fault. But when Chloe's gaze swung to the cop, her blue eyes lit up.

"Well, then," Jillian said to Chloe, "I guess Hallie will just have to be disappointed, because *you* didn't bother keeping track of it."

"Are you my mom's date?" Chloe asked, as if Jillian hadn't spoken.

Jillian, lowering her voice to a stage whisper, said, "Chlo-ee. If I were dating, you'd know it. Now, *get* ready."

The detective extended a hand past Jillian to her daughter. "Pleased to meet you, Chloe. I'm Adam and I'm here to see your mom on business."

Color blossomed on Chloe's cheeks as she reached out and shook his hand. "My mom didn't tell me anyone was coming over." She speared Jillian with an accusing glare.

The detective smiled, another disarming, full-fledged job that made Jillian all too aware of…him. Tall, six-four at least, broad-shouldered and blessed with a thick shock of sun-bleached, sandy-brown hair. Her first impression was validated. The guy was gorgeous. Too bad he was a cop—like her so-called father.

"It was a surprise," he said. "Your mom didn't know I was coming."

"A surprise I really don't need," Jillian countered, trying to ignore how nice he was being to Chloe.

"Yeah." The detective rubbed a hand over his chin. "So, I'll come back later."

She could hardly wait.

"Have a great time on your trip, Chloe," he said with a smile and a wave.

Together Chloe and Jillian watched the detective stride across the street and climb into the car.

"Wow, Mom. He's cool! I think you should absolutely date him."

"Thanks for the assessment, Ms. Matchmaker, but if you don't mind, I'll pick my own dates. He's not my type."

"No one's your type." Chloe frowned and pursed her lips, as if her mother's lack of a social life somehow reflected on her.

"That's a discussion for another time. Now get the rest of your things."

Chloe stomped off.

Jillian sighed. These days a discussion with her

daughter about anything quickly became a battle that Jillian never won. It was too soon for her little girl to go through this adolescent stuff!

Five minutes later Jillian was outside giving Chloe a crushing goodbye hug, and then her daughter was off for the next two weeks. Two long weeks.

"Love you," Jillian called out as she waved goodbye, her words gobbled up in the rumble of the engine. She continued watching until the van disappeared around the corner.

Heaving a sigh, she headed inside through the door to the kitchen, poured some raspberry iced tea and leaned against the refrigerator, periodically rolling the icy glass over her forehead. Maybe she should take a real vacation while Chloe was gone. Go to California and visit old friends. Or somewhere different altogether.

She gazed around the old country kitchen, with its worn maple cabinets, the faded Formica countertops and dated "harvest gold" appliances. The place looked awful, but with the move and all she'd had to do after Rob's death, home improvement hadn't been high on her list of priorities. Hell, back then she'd barely passed survival on Maslow's hierarchy of needs.

After that, she'd been busy getting the first hair salon up and running, and then she'd expanded to two and then three salons, which had taken even more of her time. But now she had no excuses. She had both the time and the money.

The more she thought about it, the more she realized the whole place needed renovating—and it *would* give her something to do while Chloe was away. But she couldn't change Chloe's room unless her daughter was involved in the process.

Jillian's excitement mounted. If Chloe was interested, they could redecorate her room as soon as she got home.

Deciding, she rummaged through the junk drawer for paper and pen, then sat on a stool at the counter to make a list of what needed to be done. She'd prioritize and get started immediately.

After she got rid of one Detective Adam Ramsey.

As if summoned by her thoughts, the bell rang. Her insides knotted. He was here to talk about Rob's murder. Something she didn't want to talk about. She just wished to hell she hadn't noticed him at the market and pegged him as an eligible bachelor or something, when he wasn't.

And now that she knew who he was, she wasn't interested, anyway. She went to the foyer and pulled open the door.

His smile produced tiny wrinkles near the corners of his eyes. He might be older than she'd thought. Late thirties, maybe.

"You're early. You said an hour."

"Right on both counts. Would you like me to leave and come back later?"

She'd like him to leave and *never* come back. He made her feel…jittery and a little uncertain, when she was not a jittery, uncertain person. A bit scattered sometimes, but that was different.

She motioned him inside and into the living room on her left. "What's on your mind, Detective?"

"May I sit?" He gestured toward the couch.

"Go ahead," she said, even though she didn't want him to get too comfortable.

The taupe faux-suede sofa seemed to diminish in size as he settled. In fact, the whole room felt smaller with him in it, the air thicker, hotter. Instead of sitting herself, she leaned against the side of the easy chair and crossed her arms. She noticed tiny beads of sweat forming on his tanned brow.

"Aren't you a little warm with that jacket on?"

"I am, but—" he lifted one side of his jacket up "—the gun makes some people nervous."

"Anything involving the LAPD makes *me* nervous."

He frowned, but seconds later his expression softened. "I understand. In your shoes I might feel the same." He glanced at her feet. "Well...that's if you were wearing shoes."

He smiled, then leaned back, one arm slung across the top of the cushion beside him. His charm was disarming.

"I'm sorry to bother you. I'm new on the case, so it's important to bring myself up to date."

As he talked, his gaze panned the room. She knew he was studying everything, even her. Just like her father had when she'd finally met him after her mom died.

She hadn't known her father was a cop, hadn't known lots of things about him. Her delight at discovering she had a real live father was squelched as fast as it had come, and the disastrous experience of living with him tainted her perception of any man in the same profession. The treatment she'd received later at the hands of the LAPD hadn't helped.

The way this detective was looking at her now made her wish she'd worn long pants, instead of the skimpy shorts. Self-conscious, she let her hands fall to her thighs as a cover of sorts. "Why do you want to bring yourself up to date? Isn't it too late for that?"

"Too late?"

"Yes. Your department told me if they didn't have a lead within the first week or so, the likelihood is that the case will never be solved. Four years ago I was told they'd closed the books on it."

He nodded. "The part about getting information quickly is true, but recent forensic advances have allowed us to solve some old cases that we weren't able to get conclusive evidence on at the time."

"I've heard. But don't you usually have to have some new evidence or something to open a case again?"

"An unsolved homicide is never closed, Mrs. Sullivan. We work it until all leads are exhausted, then if still unsolved, it becomes a cold case. But now, with the improved methods, we're getting new leads on old cases. Which is why I'm here."

Dread ripped through Jillian at the thought of reliving the most terrible time in her life. She took a deep breath. "I don't understand. I told the police everything four years ago. I'm sure you'd be better off going to your files for the information, because my memory of events is pretty hazy now."

"The answers to my questions aren't in the file."

She stared at him for a moment, then asked, "Such as?"

"How involved were you in your husband's business? Did you know much about it?"

Her heart sank. He *was* going to go into it all over again. "Of course I did. I took care of the accounts. But you already know that—your predecessors confiscated our books and never returned them. I had one helluva time trying to get the taxes done that year." She moved from the chair arm onto the seat.

He looked surprised at the comment but continued, "How about business partners?"

"Rob worked alone. He owned his truck and contracted with several companies. He did regular runs most of the time."

"And...the night he died?"

"No different from any other. He worked alone," she repeated. Then added more softly, "And he died alone." She felt a renewed pinch of sadness.

"Maybe you can tell me a little about your husband's friends, longtime friends he might've known before he met you. Friends he might've kept in touch with?"

Her nerves twitched. Was he saying Rob might have told a friend something he hadn't told her? Furious, she bolted to her feet and in three seconds was at the door. She turned to face him. "Four years ago, Detective Ramsey, I lost my husband. My daughter lost her father. We've finally managed to get on with our lives and we'd like to continue to do so."

She paused, struggling for self-control as she realized how easily their lives could be turned inside out once more. "I've answered all those questions before and frankly, I don't wish to do it again. The information is already in your records. So unless you can give me a compelling reason to do so, I refuse to put myself or my daughter, especially my daughter, through that pain again."

Ramsey dropped his chin to his chest and ran a hand across the back of his neck, then rose to his feet. She thought he would leave, but instead he stopped right in front of her. He was close enough to alert her senses, make her suddenly, acutely aware of him as a man, just as he had that morning.

Which seemed dangerous somehow. Threatening.

"I'm sorry for your family's loss, Mrs. Sullivan. I understand how you feel, and I don't want to cause you any more pain. But I do have a good reason for asking."

His eyes warmed, and for a second he looked as if he really did know how she felt, as if he, too, knew about loss. Still. "And that reason is?"

He cleared his throat. "I'd like to have your husband's body exhumed for further testing. It would speed things up if you gave your permission to do so."

Adam winced at the shock he saw in the woman's eyes. Sometimes he just didn't get the words right. *Damn.* "I'm sorry. I didn't mean to surprise you with that."

Her chest heaved. "Well, you did."

"Are you okay?"

"I'm fine." She took another deep breath and flipped an avalanche of red-gold curls behind her shoulders. "Why didn't you just say what you wanted in the first place? You could've saved us some time."

She spoke her mind, he had to give her that. "Why don't we both have a seat again while I explain why I think it's necessary?"

Her tongue glided over a full bottom lip. Apparently she was considering the request.

After a moment she said, "I don't want to know why you think it's necessary. I can tell you right now I won't agree to it."

"At least hear me out."

She was quiet, which he hoped was a good sign. He needed her to agree. If he could get this done swiftly, without having to get a court order, he might be able to prove his theory, and if he proved his theory, he might be able to solve the case—and his partner wouldn't have died in vain. And maybe, just maybe, he might be able to get his own life and career back on track.

But he couldn't tell her he had a score to settle. Because there was still the other question—had she been part of her husband's illegal business? Though now, after meeting her, it seemed unlikely.

"Two minutes," he said. "Give me two minutes, and if your answer is still no, I'll accept it and go back to L.A."

Her gaze met his. Her eyelashes were almost the same light color as her hair. Her eyes bluer than... well, blue. Her smooth brow was furrowed in a

frown, as if giving him any time at all couldn't
be good.

Hell, how could she refuse a guy two minutes?

She moved back into the living room. Turning toward the window, she clasped both hands behind her
neck and tipped her head from side to side, as if working out some kinks. The gesture exposed an inch of
creamy skin between her white shorts and red sleeveless top. His body instantly took notice.

She lowered her arms and turned to face him.
"Okay. Two minutes."

He didn't let her see his relief. Now all he had to
do was follow through. Rivulets of sweat trickled
down his neck.

She surprised him by asking, "Would you like
some iced tea?"

Her voice was low and sultry and to his ears, her
question about iced tea could've been a line from an
old Bogart-Bacall flick. *If you want me, just whistle.*

"Sure, thanks." An infusion of liquid might keep
him from keeling over in heat prostration—and maybe
extinguish the flames of testosterone licking at his rational thought. But he doubted it. He'd been watching
her for three days and couldn't help liking what he
saw. Well, no problem there, as long as he kept it in
perspective.

Something he hadn't done with his ex.

As soon as she left the room, he yanked off his
jacket and adjusted his gun so that it was behind his
arm and less visible. He couldn't do anything about

the holster, but if the gun bothered her, he'd take it off rather than put the damned jacket back on.

"I'm sorry it's so hot in here," she said, returning with a tray holding a pitcher of tea and two glasses. She set it on the coffee table. "These old homes don't have central air, and since we usually only need it for a few weeks during the summer, I couldn't see the point of converting the whole house."

She was nervous. He could tell by the way she ran on. Maybe she did have something to hide. He shrugged. "It's hot everywhere. Just one of those summers, I guess."

After filling both glasses, she left the room again to find an electric fan. He'd already downed his tea by the time she returned.

She plugged in the unit and adjusted the oscillation. Then she refilled his glass and sat opposite him on the overstuffed ottoman, her posture reminding him of a little kid, her knees together and her bare feet splayed. After a sip of tea, she held the glass in both hands and leaned forward, allowing the fan to blow the hair away from her face.

"Oh, that feels good."

In that single moment she transformed from a little girl into a woman, and he was mesmerized by the graceful way she moved—drawn not so much by her look as by something intangible.

Oh, she was certainly pretty. But California had an abundance of pretty women, most about as deep as Norton's Creek back home, and he was no longer impressed with looks alone.

But this woman was different; her quick, sharp assessments had surprised him, her candor intrigued him. She possessed a physical ease he found seductive as hell.

And was he concerned about being seduced? Not at all—as long as it was only in his mind.

Then, remembering something someone had said about great sex beginning in the brain, he knocked back the rest of his tea.

CHAPTER TWO

"So, TELL ME," JILLIAN SAID. "Tell me in two minutes why you think I should allow you to defile my husband's final resting place."

Adam nearly choked on his tea. Stalling, he swiped the back of his hand across his mouth and mentally called up all the usual ways to convince people to do what he wanted. He didn't like any of them. Doubted they'd even work on this one.

He quickly scanned the room, searching for some other hook to get her to agree. The family photos he'd noticed earlier were everywhere. Husband and wife, father and daughter, photos of the three of them.

A happy family, a happy marriage.

An anomaly that didn't exist in real life. At least not in his. "I'm looking for something that could link your husband's killer to your husband, some prior association or relationship that might have been overlooked before."

She arched a brow. "Your department, Detective Ramsey, determined the murder was a random act. The crash was caused by a sniper, since there were empty cartridges found near the scene. Are you saying you don't think that's the case? Has something changed?"

"I'm saying that conclusions were drawn from the evidence and the tests available at the time, and that now, with better testing methods, we might be able to draw different conclusions. I think it's worth a try."

"But..." Her face went pale. "When the truck went over the cliff, Rob's body...the explosion destroyed almost everything. Identification was made in other ways." She stopped, then put her fingers to her lips and closed her eyes. A moment later she asked, "Can you even do DNA testing on what's left? Wouldn't they have done it back then if it was possible?"

Seeing her discomfort, he was suddenly sorry he had to press. But it was his job to press, and for the first time since Bryce's death, he was going to do it right.

"My biggest problem in working this case is that I haven't been able to locate all the test results done back then. Which leads me to believe some tests weren't completed."

"The police collected evidence and preserved it. I know they did. Your department should still have all that. If you need to do new tests, why can't you do it on the evidence you have?"

Because that's missing, too. Only, he couldn't tell her that. This time, telling the truth wasn't going to engender confidence in the LAPD, especially since she was skeptical already. But beating around the bush wasn't getting him anywhere, either. "Because we can't. The old evidence is unavailable."

She sat quietly for a moment, then glanced at her watch and looked up at him. "I'm sorry. Your two minutes are up.'' She dusted her hands together and rose to her feet.

Damn. He clenched his teeth to keep from saying something he shouldn't.

Hovering over him, she said, ''That's your cue to leave, Detective Ramsey.''

She must've seen his irritation because she added, ''You said after two minutes you'd leave and wouldn't bother me again. I hope you're a man of your word.''

He felt duped. She'd had no intention of hearing him out. Not really. ''Ah, but you took up some of my time with your own questions. I think it's only fair that you give me the time we agreed on.''

''And exactly how much of your time do you think I took? Ten seconds? The truth is, Detective, you haven't given me any good reason to allow an exhumation. In fact, I still don't know why, after all this time, the police are suddenly interested again. Do you have new evidence you're not disclosing?''

Keeping his voice even, he said, ''It isn't a matter of *interest*. It's a matter of taking a killer off the streets. How much time has elapsed is irrelevant.'' He shook his head in disbelief. ''Don't you want to see your husband's murderer behind bars?''

Silence. Except for the soft whir of the fan shifting warm air between them.

He leaned back in his seat. ''I asked for your permission out of respect for your family, Mrs. Sullivan. Fact is, I don't need your permission to get your husband's body exhumed. I can get a court order.''

She stiffened and looked away. When she turned to

face him again, her eyes flashed with steely determination.

"*Fact is,* Detective, I know you wouldn't have come here on a Saturday morning on a four-year-old cold case if you hadn't needed something from me. *Fact is,* I can hire an attorney to stall or halt any court order you attempt to get."

Adam gritted his teeth, slapped both hands on his thighs and launched himself to his feet, then reached for his jacket. "I thought you'd be eager to help, Mrs. Sullivan. I wish I'd been right about that."

He stuffed a hand into the inside pocket of his jacket, fingering the glossy surface of the evidence that had started him on this quest. Would it convince her? Or would it screw up his plan? If she truly had no involvement in her husband's side business, the new information he possessed might be enough to convince her to help him. If she'd been involved, or still was, and she thought he was going to uncover her part in it, she might agree just to make him stop asking questions and go away.

"At least think about it."

"I have, Detective. And now I'd like you to leave."

"Yeah," he all but growled, unable to disguise his irritation. His new partner was right. His people skills were rusty.

A few years ago, he would've had her agreeing to most anything. Admitting his own expertise in that area wasn't cockiness, just the plain truth. He'd been good at his job. The best.

But that was then and this was now. After scraping bottom, it was hard to get back to the surface.

"I was trying to avoid this," he said, "but I see I can't." He drew the photograph from his pocket and held it out to her.

Jillian gulped for air, the room dipped, and for a second, she thought she might faint. She stared at the tattered photo in the detective's hand. "It looks..." Her voice quit. She hauled in another lungful of air. "He looks...like Rob."

She was too stunned for her thoughts to gel. The man in the picture was wearing a gray suit and standing beside a dark-haired woman in a white dress. Did Ramsey think Rob had had an affair while he was married to her? Or did he think the woman in the photo had something to do with his death?

It couldn't be. Rob would never... Obviously the photo was taken before Jillian and Rob had met—except she'd known her husband for thirteen years, and this man appeared older than Rob did back then. He looked more like Rob at thirty-eight, his age when he died.

Jillian plucked the picture from Ramsey's fingers, flipped it over. Someone had written "Our wedding day," followed by a date.

A quick sense of relief washed over her. "If you're thinking what I think you're thinking, you're wrong. My husband died in April of that year. This is dated the following May. And that writing is definitely not his."

She pulled her gaze from the photo and looked up at Ramsey. "I have to admit, the man does resemble Rob, though, and I can see why someone might mistake them for one and the same." She paused. "I've heard we all have a twin somewhere, so maybe it's really true.''

He frowned, then locked eyes with hers. ''That photo is reason enough to exhume your husband's body.''

''I don't think so,'' she said quickly, mostly because she couldn't think of anything else to say. She still couldn't marshal her thoughts enough to fully sort out what he was suggesting or why. ''Where did you get it?''

Ramsey's lips formed a thin line. ''That's confidential.''

Fine. She didn't want to know anything more, anyway. It didn't matter where he got the picture or what he thought it meant.

An hour ago she'd felt safe and secure, and within minutes, he'd changed all that. She wanted that feeling back again. She wanted to forget about him and his ugly photograph.

Yet at that precise moment, she had an awful feeling that nothing would ever be the same again.

''Fine. Keep it confidential.'' She handed back the photograph. ''I'd like you to leave now.''

But what she wanted apparently didn't matter. He just stood there looming over her, his expression vigilant and intense, his chest expanding, then contracting with each breath he took.

''Okay,'' he finally said. ''But first...''

He drew something else from his pocket and handed her what looked like another photo.

Her heart pounding, she retreated a step. She didn't want to take it, didn't want to look. But like a driver passing the scene of a horrible accident, she was unable to stop herself. She reached out and took the photo from his hand.

The same man and the same woman, who appeared to be Latino, as well as a little boy, no more than two, were standing by a boat.

They were smiling—and just looking at them made Jillian's eyes hurt. With trembling fingers, she turned over the photo.

Jack, Corita and Bobby Sullivan Jr. Mirador. June 2000.

"Where's Mirador?" she asked.

"It's in Costa Rica."

"Oh." She had nothing more to say.

"Your husband also went by the name Jack, didn't he?"

She closed her eyes, hoping this was all a bad dream and that when she opened them, Detective Adam Ramsey would be gone.

But when she did, he was still there, waiting for a response.

Robert John Sullivan Jr. Rob's mother had called him Jack to differentiate between her son and his father. Jillian had met Rob after his father had died and Rob had started going by his given name. But the people to whom he'd been closest had always called him Jack. Sometimes so had she. She felt faint and placed a hand against the wall for support.

Ramsey reached out.

She waved him away. There had to be an explanation, most likely a simple one. As firmly as she could, she said, "It's obviously a mistake. Maybe the dates are wrong. Maybe someone who looks like my husband wanted to disappear and has taken his name. Or…or someone who wanted to assume a new identity picked the name from the obituaries and made himself look the same. I've heard of that being done…on television or somewhere. There was a program…*20/20*, I think…''

Her voice sounded not her own, and she feared she wasn't making sense. The next thing she knew, Ramsey was at her side, urging her to the chair. He poured a glass of tea and brought it to her.

What did he think? That her husband was somehow still alive? Was that what this was all about? Well, it couldn't be.

Could it?

She shook her head and waved the glass away. ''I can see where you're going with this…and I know what it looks like. But you're wrong. Very wrong. My husband's world revolved around his family. He loved us and he loved his life with us.

''That man may resemble my husband, Detective, and he may have the same name, but that's where any similarity ends.''

''There could be mitigating circumstances.''

''Like what?'' she spat, angry and hurt and confused and hating the man pressuring her to do something abhorrent. ''Jack would never have willingly left us, his family. Not without a gun to his head.''

''Another possibility,'' Ramsey said softly.

Tears welled in her eyes, but she forced them back. ''The man in that photograph has no gun to his head. So…so I think that possibility can be ruled out. Now, please go." She thrust the photo at him. "Please take this and leave me alone."

"Okay." He set down the glass and went to the door where he stood for a moment before saying, "I'll be in town for another day, then I'm heading back to L.A." He laid a card on the small table by the door. "The number where I'm staying is on the back of the card. I sincerely hope you'll change your—"

"Please...go."

"I'm sorry, Mrs. Sullivan. Truly." Then he opened the door and left.

Jillian sat on the couch for the longest time just listening to the click of the fan oscillating from side to side, wishing she'd had the presence of mind to look more closely at the photos. Surely there was something there to prove the man couldn't be Rob.

Hell, the fact that the pictures were taken after his death should be proof enough of that. Shouldn't it?

Her confusion coalesced into anger. Detective Ramsey had lied to her! He'd said he wanted to do further testing to uncover something new about her husband's murderer, when what he really wanted was to exhume the body in order to prove that it wasn't her husband who'd died in the crash. Did he believe she'd been lied to by the police? That everything they'd told her had been a lie? What else could she think?

Because some empty bullet casings were found near the highway where Rob's truck went over the cliff, the LAPD had concluded that a sniper had shot at Rob and caused the accident. Two years of so-called investigation and they had no other evidence, no reason to suspect anything other than one deranged person playing God with people's lives. And they couldn't track him down.

After years of frustration about Rob's senseless death, knowing his killer would never be caught, Jillian had found peace within herself. She had a daughter to raise, Rob's daughter, and she couldn't do it well if she was railing at the world about something she couldn't change.

Detective Adam Ramsey was wrong. Dead wrong. But then, he didn't know Rob. He didn't know that her husband would never have left his family, not for anything. After thirteen years together, she'd known her husband as well as she knew herself.

But someone impersonating Rob *was* within the realm of possibility, wasn't it? Hard to imagine that kind of thing ever happened outside of the movies, but it did happen.

Still…myriad questions swirled through her brain. If this was indeed an impersonation, who *was* the man in the photograph? Every bizarre scenario one could possibly imagine rose to her fevered brain.

Rob could've picked up a hitchhiker who'd killed him, run the truck over the cliff with his body inside and was now impersonating him. What if someone had hijacked the truck and in the crash *he'd* died, but Rob had been thrown out and wasn't dead? What if he was wandering around with amnesia and used the only name he knew to start another life?

As surreal as it sounded, things like amnesia did happen, too. Four years ago, Dana and Logan's daughter, Hallie, had suffered amnesia after a simple fall. Temporary amnesia, fortunately, but it could have been much worse. So, while amnesia or other phenomena were unlikely, they weren't outside the realm of possibility.

Yet, no matter what scenario she posed to herself, the most horrible question of all remained. What if Rob had *wanted* to disappear? And if so, who was the man who'd died in his truck?

No! She couldn't even think it, not for a second. Rob had been her savior, her husband, her surrogate father and her best friend.

A runaway at fifteen, she'd been living on the streets of East L.A., homeless, hungry and desperate— so desperate she'd been ready to prostitute herself to get money for food. The night she'd first tried had been the night she'd met Rob.

He'd taken her in, cleaned her up and saved her from self-destruction. Ten years older, he'd been kind and patient and loving and never once asked for anything in return.

When she'd offered herself in gratitude, he'd jokingly called her "jailbait." He hadn't touched her, said he wouldn't until she was eighteen and they were married.

He'd been a man of his word.

He was a good man, an honorable man, and at that point in her life, he was the *only* honorable man she'd ever known. Rob had taught her to trust again, and she was indebted to him. If she agreed to have his body exhumed, wasn't that the same as believing he wasn't the man she thought he was?

If she doubted him now, everything they'd had together would be tainted by that doubt, and she'd start second-guessing the only meaningful relationship she'd ever had.

She couldn't let that happen. He was Chloe's father, for God's sake.

Chloe. Thank heaven she wasn't home.

Jillian knew she had to pull herself together, or she'd be a basket case by the time Chloe came home.

But could she? Could she forget that there was a man out there impersonating Rob? A man who, no matter how remote the possibility, could *be* Rob?

No. The only way she was going to stop thinking about it was to *do* something!

Jillian headed for her bedroom, where she ditched her shorts and top for a pair of faded jeans, a gauzy white shirt and chunky sandals.

Meadow Brook Nursing Home, where Rob's mother now lived, was only a few miles away. Within minutes she pulled into one of the dozen empty spaces and exited her new red Mustang convertible, the only concession she'd made to conspicuous consumption now that she could afford it.

After two strokes, her mother-in-law had never been the same. One day Harriet was her old spunky, cantankerous self, making Jillian's life a living hell, and the next she was frail, faded and forgetful. Many times she didn't even remember Jillian.

"Hi, Mary Ann." Jillian greeted the receptionist on her way in, then waved to some of the residents. "Hi, Jim. Mrs. Kramer."

She headed toward the lounge, breathing in the strange combination of air freshener and disinfectant—lilac and Pine-Sol. Harriet was sitting in a wheelchair amid half a dozen other residents. Her silver hair, accented by one dark swoop down the left side, was easy to pick out among the sea of gray.

"Hi, Harriet. How's the world's greatest gin rummy player?" The older woman looked up at the sound of her name, and Jillian bent to give her mother-in-law a hug. Harriet was wearing her I-can't-place-you smile.

Undaunted, Jillian said, "Your granddaughter is a real pill, Harriet. I had one heck of a time getting Chloe out the door today. She went with the Wakefields to their cabin for the remainder of the summer vacation, so she won't be able to visit for a couple of weeks."

At the mention of her granddaughter, the old woman's eyes lit up. "A girl her age should be having fun and not be so serious all the time."

Jillian chuckled and pulled a chair up to the card table. "It's called adolescence, and I wish they'd invent a formula or something so we could just skip that whole stage and go right to mature."

"Maturity ain't so hot, either," said another white-haired resident on Jillian's left.

"Is my son here yet?" Harriet asked. "He'll play rummy with me when he gets here."

"No," Jillian said softly. "He's gone now. Remember?"

Her mother-in-law's hopeful smile switched to a frown. "Yes, of course I remember. I remember when he left in that truck of his. Dangerous thing, I told him. He should be careful, but then, he never listens to his mother."

Jillian wondered what Harriet's reaction would be

if she knew the police wanted to exhume her son's body for testing. She'd be horrified, no doubt. A year after Rob died, Jillian had wanted to replace the temporary headstone for a permanent one with a meaningful inscription, but Harriet had made her promise she'd never disturb Rob's grave in any way, not even for that.

Jillian had discovered then that Harriet had deep-seated beliefs about death, and disturbing a grave meant you'd disrupt the person's afterlife. Apparently she'd passed her beliefs on to Rob, because he'd told her the same thing.

"My boy will be back soon," Harriet said to the aide standing by the door.

Jillian's heart turned over. For Harriet, time seemed compressed, and she talked about the past and the present as if they were the same. Jillian had never gotten used to hearing Harriet talk that way. And now, since the visit from the detective, Harriet's habit had an eerie prescience.

"That's nice," the aide said.

Harriet eyed Jillian. "There're cards in the drawer over there. Are we going to play rummy or not?"

"Sure." Jillian got up and crossed to the table for the cards.

"You mix 'em up and deal," Harriet said. "I don't do that so good anymore."

"You do just fine, Harriet. But okay, I'll start." Jillian sat down again and shuffled the deck. The cards, somewhat tacky from use, kept sticking.

"Harriet," Jillian began slowly, deciding how best to phrase the questions she felt compelled to ask. "Do you remember when we buried Rob?'' One by one, she dealt out the cards.

Harriet gathered her hand and fanned it out, pondered briefly, then switched a few cards around. "Of course I remember. It was the worst day of my life. Don't *you* remember?''

"Yes. Yes, I do.'' Jillian sighed, ready to go on with her questions, but Harriet stopped her by raising a gnarled finger.

"The police still don't know nothin' about my son,'' she said to the aide. "Did you know that?''

The aide shook her head.

"Have you heard about all the new scientific advancements these days?'' Jillian asked. "With improved testing, I understand they can find out information they couldn't before. Maybe if they did more tests—''

"You sound just like that detective.'' Harriet waved a hand in dismissal, then laid down two sets of cards, three of a kind. "He asked too many questions. I told him he'd have to talk to Jack.''

Jillian stiffened. Ramsey had been here, too, and he hadn't said a word to her about it. Or had he come here after he'd talked with her?

But why? Did he think Harriet could get Jillian to agree to exhume Rob's body? Or was he looking for other information?

Harriet plucked up another card and inserted it into the fan of cards still in her hand. "Jack told me not to talk to anybody.''

Jillian made her play. "Well, I'm sure he wouldn't mind if you talked to me.''

"Nope. I said I won't say anything and I won't."
She plunked down another set of cards, dropped a discard on the pile and, smiling, she looked up. "Gin."

Jillian felt distinctly unsettled when she left Meadow Brook a half hour later, the demons of doubt nipping at her heels. Everything she believed in had been forged from her relationship with Rob. If she couldn't believe in that, what could she believe in?

Back at home, with all manner of drama playing out in her head, she sipped her coffee while listening to the early-evening news on television, hoping the noise would drown out the horrible thoughts corrupting her good sense.

She could not, *would* not, doubt Rob. Because if she did, everything she'd come to believe about love and trust would crumble. Rob had been an honorable man. Doubting his veracity was a betrayal of the worst kind.

Yet...that *what if* question kept rearing its ugly head. She needed to see those photos again.

"I'VE GOT NOTHING," ADAM told Rico on the phone.

"Hey, hold on a minute. Someone's here."

"Yeah, sure. What else do I have besides time?" Adam dropped onto the bed and leaned against the padded beige headboard in the beige motel room.

He had all the time in the world. Because nothing was urgent in cold cases, which made up the bulk of his assignments these days. And according to the chief, the situation wasn't likely to change unless he could prove himself.

For a guy used to being in the trenches, working

cold cases depressed the hell out of him. And Enrico Santini, his new partner who'd come on board only a year ago, had taken the brunt of his dissatisfaction—until one morning when the kid had laid into him, telling Adam that if he wanted to tank his career and spend the rest of his life wallowing in self-pity, that was his choice. But Rico wasn't going to put up with his sarcastic jabs anymore, wasn't going to keep covering his ass or let Adam's attitude screw with his head or his job.

You're the problem, Ramsey. If you're going down, you're gonna do it alone, Rico had said—right before he'd contacted the employee-intervention program.

Despite the scuttlebutt that the fresh-from-the-academy propeller-head was a go-by-the-books wuss, Adam figured Rico had more guts than most to take on a multidecorated senior officer. The kid, all full of shiny ideals about the way the world should be, reminded him a little of himself when he'd started on the force more than a dozen years ago.

Now, after three months in therapy, a whole lot of determination and a new lead, Adam was on a course to set things right. Four years was too long to be in limbo.

Now, with the new information connecting Sullivan to Bryce on the night he died, he was going to uncover who was responsible for his partner's death and make the scumbag pay.

He couldn't fix his broken marriage, but he was better off for it. A cop who couldn't focus on more than one thing had no business being married.

"I've got some stuff for you to check out when you

get back tomorrow," Rico said when he returned to the phone.

"Yeah? Like?"

"Nothing huge. You'll see when you get here."

Adam had come to respect his new partner's eye for detail and his powers of deduction. The kid thought things out, while *he* charged through life like a bull, a just-do-it, act-on-instinct kind of guy. Despite their rocky start, they made a helluva good team.

"What're you gonna do about the widow?"

"Nothing. Not yet. I'm hoping she'll have a change of heart, call tonight and agree. If not, I'll get the order myself. It'll take longer, but maybe I can squeeze an old debt to hustle it through."

He quickly ended the call before he got a lecture from Rico on the way the court system was supposed to work. Calling in old debts didn't fit with the kid's altruistic philosophy. Just as he hung up the receiver, the phone rang again.

"Yeah. What'dya forget?"

"Mr. Ramsey?"

His adrenaline kicked in.

"Detective Ramsey, this is Jillian Sullivan."

As if he didn't know. As if he wouldn't recognize her voice in an instant. "What can I do for you, Mrs. Sullivan?"

"I want to see those photos again."

"I've got a plane to catch early in the morning."

"How about now?"

Man, oh, man. Someone somewhere was smiling on him. "My place or yours?"

She was quiet for a moment. "How about splitting the distance? A café or something."

"Sure. It's your town, you make the call and tell me how to get there."

They made plans to meet at a diner at six-thirty. She said she had a birthday party to attend afterward.

He knew why she wanted to see the photos again. She wanted to make sure she was right—that the man in the photo *wasn't* her husband.

No matter how much you trusted someone, once the seeds of doubt were planted, they were tough to ignore. He knew that only too well. He felt a twinge of regret that he'd sowed those seeds in Jillian Sullivan.

But in his business, people sometimes got hurt. That was reality. So why did this one lodge so solidly in his craw?

Hot, sticky and irritable, he showered and shaved, pulled on a pair of jeans and a white Polo shirt. He used his ankle holster for his gun, wanting to do whatever he could do to make her feel more comfortable and more agreeable to his suggestion.

It was six-twenty when he pulled into Joe Bailly's parking lot. An early-evening breeze dusted him as he headed toward the door. He hoped for some quiet corner where they could talk privately, but the place was crowded and a jukebox blared.

"How about the patio?" he said to the hostess, who led him outside to a table with an umbrella. The heat wasn't as stifling as it had been earlier, and it was quieter outside, although he could still hear the faint beat of the music piped in from somewhere. He picked a spot where he could see anyone who entered the patio.

Five minutes later he saw her striding toward him in a figure-skimming scarlet dress that was so hot it could've set the place on fire. He couldn't take his eyes off her. With each confident step, her long strawberry-blond hair swished from side to side keeping time with the primal beat of a rock-and-roll song.

As she neared, he could see large silver hoops glinting at her ears, and dark red toenails peeking from barely-there black sandals. He'd never been so aware of a woman in his life.

It was a damned good thing he was going home in the morning.

Reaching him, she gave him only the briefest acknowledgment, and when he made an attempt to stand, she said, ''Don't bother.''

She sat down opposite him. The waitress took their drink orders, Jillian's for one of those fancy iced coffees and his for a cold glass of draft beer.

''You mind if I order dinner and eat while we're talking?''

''And if I did?'' She crafted a wry smile.

He shrugged and gave her a smile of his own. ''I'd order anyway. Maybe you'd like to join me?''

''I'd like to look at the photos again. Did you bring them?''

''I did. And I apologize if I seemed insensitive earlier.''

Her eyes rounded, as if she was surprised at the admission.

''I've been told I'm too results oriented,'' he said,

"that sometimes I have a tendency to go for the gold and forget common courtesy. I'm trying to change. So please accept my apology, have dinner with me and we'll start again."

Jillian had to admit the man rattled her sensibilities, yet something in her yearned to say yes. Instinct, however, told her to stay as far away from this man as Jupiter.

"Thanks for the invitation," she said, "but I think I'd better save my appetite for the party."

He shrugged. "Suit yourself."

The waitress came back with their drinks and took his order for a steak sandwich, French fries *and* onion rings. Just as the waitress was leaving, he asked, "You *sure* you don't want something to eat?"

She smiled. "Yes, I'm sure." What a strange man—he seemed so concerned, so genuine and sincere. And just as strange that she was so drawn to him.

Just then a man and woman with two children were led to a table on the other side of the patio. As they passed, one little boy dropped his ball. Adam caught it on the bounce and tossed it back to the child with a smile. When the kid caught it, Adam gave him a thumbs-up.

His ease with children surprised her. But then she remembered he'd been just as at ease with Chloe.

"You like kids?" she asked.

He nodded. "They remind me of my nephews."

"Really? How many do you have?"

He let out a breath. "I lost count at six or seven."

"So you're from a big family, then?" She didn't

know why, but she'd thought of him as someone without much family.

"Maybe by some folks' standards. But in the Ramsey family, anything less than half a dozen is small. We were six. Four girls, two boys. All my sisters are married and pressuring me to get with the program."

"And you don't like the program?"

He eased back in his chair and looked directly at her. "Hey, I think it's great." A beat later he added, "For other people."

So. He wasn't married. And didn't want to be. She reached for her drink and took a sip. All this small talk was just a way for her to put off the inevitable.

Her reexamination of the photos.

CHAPTER THREE

"HELP YOURSELF TO SOME FRIES," Adam said after the waitress brought his food. He shoved his plate toward her.

She smiled and shook her head. "No, thanks. I don't need the calories."

He leaned back in his chair, his eyes dancing over her. "You don't look like a woman who needs to worry much about that."

He smiled then, his wide, dazzling smile, and she felt a sudden burst of desire low in her belly. The sensation surprised her.

He took a bite of his sandwich, and after he finished chewing, he said, "Must be some birthday party."

"Why do you say that?"

"Well, you got all dressed up for it."

"Oh." She didn't know what to say. Certainly not that the party was all women and she didn't know why she'd chosen this dress in particular.

Or maybe she did. "I'm not. Not really."

He took another bite of his sandwich and studied her as he chewed. Then he said, "Sorry, I forgot. You're a California girl."

"Which means?"

"You have the look."

The look. She didn't think so, but that he'd noticed at all sent another shiver of desire through her.

"Then I guess it's okay for me to say you have the cop look," she returned.

He glanced down at his clothes. "No uniform, no visible badge or weapon. What?"

"It's not what you're wearing, it's the way you walk and talk and how you check everything out. Your RoboCop attitude."

"You're an expert in body language?"

"My father was a cop." At his look of surprise, her gaze narrowed. "You didn't check me out?" She didn't believe that, not for a second.

Instead of answering her question, he asked one of his own. "You said *was?* Is he retired?"

"He's dead."

"Sorry."

"We weren't close. And he died a long time ago."

"LAPD?"

"No." Time to get to the real purpose of this meeting. "If you don't mind, I'd like to see those photos now."

His hand went to his back pocket, and in that flicker of a second, an awful doubt filled her. Did she really want to do this? She'd wanted to prove to herself that the man in the photo couldn't be Rob, and up till this very moment, she was sure she'd find something to cement that belief. But what if she found something else? Something she didn't want to know.

"Excuse me a minute." She shoved her chair back and bolted to her feet. "I'll be right back. I've got something in my eye."

As she brushed past him, he caught her hand.

"Here, let me see." Still holding on to her, he stood. "I'm usually pretty good at this kind of thing."

He lifted her chin, and at the touch, she felt suddenly breathless. As he reached up with his other hand, she blinked and said, "Wait." She stepped back to put some space between them and blinked a couple of times. "I think it might be okay. Yes. It's fine now."

"You sure?"

She nodded and they both sat.

His expression was puzzled. He nudged his plate toward her again.

This time she took a fry and poked it into her mouth. Then she grabbed another and when she finished that, she sampled an onion ring. Before she finished chewing, she reached for her drink and gulped that down, too.

He gave her a lazy grin, as if to say he'd pegged her right, that she didn't worry about calories, after all. But he was too gallant to mention it.

She blotted her mouth with the corner of the napkin and then wiped the grease off her fingers. "The photos, Detective?" she reminded him, using curtness to cover her emotions.

He kept his eyes on her as he pulled out a small envelope, took both pictures out and laid them on the table between them. It was still light enough for her to see the photos clearly. Her hand shook as she picked up the wedding photo, held it up and searched for something to prove it wasn't Rob. Couldn't be Rob.

But what? Most of the things she thought of wouldn't show in a photo, especially when he was wearing a suit. The hairstyle was a little different, yet the part was on the same side...a cowlick in the same place. Not particularly unusual. She picked up the second photo.

The little boy looked so much like the man in the photo, and the man looked so much like Rob, it was uncanny.

Ramsey was saying something to her, but suddenly she couldn't hear a word over the roaring in her ears. She pulled herself ramrod straight and slapped the photo down on the table in front of her.

"Well, that served no purpose." She glanced at her watch. "I'd better leave now or I'm going to be late."

She shoved to her feet, and the chair scraped noisily against the wood floorboards as she pushed it back. Her legs felt wobbly.

"Thank you for meeting me, Detective Ramsey."

And with that, she turned and fled.

MONDAY MORNING, BACK in L.A., Ramsey nudged open the Special Investigations unit door with one foot, then shouldered it the rest of the way. He crossed to his desk and set down the coffee and the egg-and-cheese-filled tortilla he'd picked up for breakfast on the way to work, then circled it to sit.

"Any luck?" Sam Houston, also known as Tex, asked from his corner of the room.

"Me, have luck?" Adam responded around a mouthful of *tacquito*. "How're you doin', Tex?"

"Good as can be expected." Tex waited a second before he added, "Considering."

Tex wasn't fond of his current gig—working cold cases—any more than Adam was.

"Yo." Rico Santini charged into the room, his face lit up as if he'd just been promoted. "Wait till you see this."

He dumped a pile of papers on Adam's desk, nearly spilling the coffee. "Hey, kid, take it easy." Adam rescued his coffee and cuffed Rico on the shoulder. "Your enthusiasm so early in the morning isn't shared by all."

Tex grunted in agreement. At forty-five, he was the oldest detective in their unit. Adam fell in the middle at thirty-five and Rico Santini, a mere twenty-seven, was the baby.

Adam doused his breakfast with more hot sauce, stuffed the rest of the tortilla into his mouth and washed it down with scalding coffee. He picked up one of the papers Santini had dropped on him.

"What am I looking for?"

The kid's black eyes shone. "You tell me. That's the whole purpose of this."

No rush, of course, thought Adam. After he got the body exhumed, and if the information turned out as he suspected, there might be a need for speed then.

A rogue thought sideswiped him. If the guy in the photo turned out to be Sullivan, how would the "widow" react? Stupid thought. He knew from what she'd said, the guy all but walked on water.

He didn't know what it was like to have a woman feel that way about him. Not even when he'd been married. He felt a twinge of envy, which surprised him. More than that, it annoyed him.

Hell, he didn't know if the guy was dead or alive, crook or not. He didn't know if the man's wife knew something or nothing. Just thinking about her in a personal way was crazy. Unprofessional.

Especially since she lived in Chicago and the only place *he* was going to see Jillian Sullivan again was in court.

Adam continued shuffling through the papers, but his thoughts were focused on the lady in red. It was obvious she liked the color, since every time he'd seen her, she'd worn something red. Even her car was red. But what he remembered most was the dress. That dress was stamped indelibly in his mind. Even now, he could see her walking toward him, her hips swaying seductively....

Damn, the lady confused him. How did a class act like Jillian Sullivan get mixed up with a guy like her maybe-not-deceased husband? But then, he had no real proof that Jack Sullivan was involved in anything. Yet.

It was still just a hunch, because the sting Bryce had been working on was so sensitive, so high profile, even their own guys weren't in on it. But since he'd been back on track, Adam had pieced together enough information to know that the project involved the SWBI—Southwest Border Initiative—and was to crack down on drugs coming over the border into the U.S. from Mexico. What Bryce's part was, he didn't know, other than he'd been deep undercover.

The photos Adam had received, which had come with a letter, were like manna from heaven. They gave him the evidence he needed to move forward. All he needed now was for his vacation request to go through and for Jenna, the unit's administrative assistant, to type out the "gun letter" he'd sweet-talked her into doing for him. He might need it while he was traveling to prove he was a cop and that it was okay for him to have a gun. Once all that was nailed down, he'd be on a plane to Costa Rica.

He went back to the files on the Sullivan case Santini had given him and didn't emerge until he'd read every word.

He didn't like the way the case stacked up.

Jillian Sullivan had been right that he hadn't checked her out before he'd headed to Chicago. After receiving the letter and the photos, he'd punched up Sullivan on the computer and, discovering the connection, had run the backgrounder on Jillian. But he was too antsy to wait for the information to come back before he left. So he'd skimmed the file for the basics—where she lived, where she worked, who she hung out with, relatives' names and addresses, of which there'd been only one, her mother-in-law. All the easy stuff.

He read his notes again. There were three strikes against her. Number one—four years ago she'd paid $300,000 cash for her house. Okay. Could've been the insurance money. Still, it was a hefty bit of insurance for a truck driver. Number two—she'd started three upscale salons after moving to Chicago, and all of them were doing exceptionally well. Number three— she was debt free. How the hell could a person her age manage all that in such a short time?

Either she was one helluva businesswoman or she'd found a pot of gold.

JILLIAN RAN A THUMB over the smooth glass on the family photo, her gaze lingering on her husband. He'd always lamented not being rich enough to give her the things he felt she deserved. Mostly he regretted being "just a truck driver."

A tear squeezed from her eye. Ironic that he'd died in his truck.

But those photographs! She didn't know *what* to believe. Was the man her husband? Yet there was no logical reason to think that. And the idea of amnesia was too bizarre.

She threw herself across the bed. What now? She'd spent the past two nights trying to decide what to do and still hadn't come up with anything. How could she prove to herself the man in the photograph wasn't Rob?

She couldn't do what Ramsey wanted. Because every time she thought about it, something told her it was very wrong to dig up a man's final resting place. Harriet would be devastated, and doing it without telling her was the same as lying. And lying went against Jillian's personal code of ethics. Doing it for her own peace of mind wasn't a good enough reason for her. There had to be another way.

She glanced at the clock. It was 8:00 a.m. and she hadn't slept more than a few hours all night. She had to do something before she went crazy. Studying Rob in the family photo again, it hit her. Of course! All anyone had to do was locate the person in Ramsey's photos and they'd know the man wasn't Rob.

Did Ramsey plan to do that? Maybe she should call

to find out. But it was only 6:00 a.m. in California, and even if he was there, he wouldn't be at work yet.

Still, she was too wired to do nothing. She scrambled off the bed and flew downstairs.

There were other agencies that located people. Patti Krakowski, the manager of her first shop and now manager of all three, had been adopted as a baby and had done a search for her biological parents. Maybe the agency she'd used could locate the guy in the photo if the LAPD wouldn't.

She got out pen and paper and started a list of all possible sources that might be of help. She thought of calling Dana's husband, Logan, but his company only did high-level top-secret investigations, and she didn't want to spoil their vacation, anyway. More important, if she could avoid it, she didn't want Chloe to know anything about this.

Next she went to her computer, got on the Internet and typed in *Locate people.* Within seconds of hitting Search dozens of sites popped up.

Wow. It looked daunting. But she rubbed her eyes and started checking out each site. Before she knew it, it was almost 10:00 a.m.

She punched in Patti's home number. No answer.

She called the shop. Patti wasn't there, either. She had to be in transit, so she left a message with the receptionist at the First Mane Event to tell Patti she'd stop by later to see her.

Adrenaline surged through Jillian's veins. She had a plan and it felt damn good. Find the man in the photo, identify him, and that would be that.

She grabbed her purse and pulled out Adam's card.

Her hand trembled with nerves as she punched in the number.

"Ramsey here."

"Detective Ramsey, this is Jillian Sullivan."

"Ah, the lady in red." His voice, a rich baritone, had switched from business formal to familiar. "I tried getting in touch with you earlier, but your line was busy."

"Is something wrong?"

"No. Just checking up on you because you seemed upset when you left the other night. I wanted to make sure everything was okay."

He must've called when she was on the Internet. "Your sensitivity training kicking in, RoboCop?"

He laughed. "Something like that."

His laugh was warm and natural, and it coaxed a laugh out of her. Hearing he'd called to see if she was okay, such a simple act of caring, touched her most basic needs—and made her realize she'd been alone for a very long time.

How odd to think the one person who'd sparked her interest was the wrong person in every way. Not only was he a cop, he'd made his feelings about home and family perfectly clear. *Great. For someone else.*

"What's on your mind?"

"I was wondering what efforts your department plans to make in trying to locate the guy impersonating Rob?"

The line was silent. She wondered if they'd been cut off.

Then he said, "I'm not sure what you're asking, Jillian."

"I'm wondering why you don't just go to this Mirador place and talk to the man in the photo. Get his fingerprints. Wouldn't that be all the proof you need?"

More silence. Then he replied, "No. But it might be the proof *you* need."

"Excuse me?"

"The LAPD is looking for your husband's murderer. If there's an impersonator out there, it only means something to us if the tests show the imposter had something to do with your husband's death."

"And if his murderer is the imposter?"

She heard a sigh on the other end of the phone and envisioned Ramsey rubbing the back of his neck, scrubbing a hand across his solid chin. "I'm sorry, Jillian. We can't pursue that piece until we have the other information. And even if it turned out the guy in the photo was the murderer and is impersonating your husband, it opens another can of worms altogether. Lots of paperwork and red tape. Not to mention money the department would have to approve."

"Oh," she murmured, disappointed.

"I have to follow procedure. The first step is to get DNA testing done, which on a cold case, can take months. If I need to get a court order to have the remains exhumed, it'll take even longer. Sorry to say, it's not top priority."

Months? She wanted to know now. It seemed important for her to know now, but she didn't know why. Even if she agreed to the exhumation, it would take too long. "Isn't there something else you can do?"

"No. I'm sorry."

She sighed.

"Is that the only reason you called?"

His voice was husky with meaning. She tried not to think about it, but couldn't stop her thoughts from going elsewhere. She knew right then why she wanted to know now. She was, as Dana had said, *ready*. "What other reason would I have?"

"I thought you might have had a change of heart. That maybe you'd decided to give us the okay on exhuming your husband's body."

God, she was an idiot.

"If I change my mind, Detective Ramsey, you'll be the first to know."

"PATTI? YOU AROUND?" Jillian peered into the stockroom at the First Mane Event, renamed after she'd opened the second and third salons. The scents of perm chemicals and peroxide tangled with that of citrus shampoo and hair spray, which always caught in the back of her throat.

Hearing the low-level hum of hair blowers and the voices of a half-dozen stylists chatting with their customers gave Jillian a sense of comfort she hadn't felt since her so-called vacation started.

Three days and she missed work already. She missed Chloe already. In eleven years, they'd not been apart for more than two days.

Patti emerged from behind some shelves in back, and spying Jillian, she stopped in her tracks. "What on earth are you doing here?"

"I just stopped by to chat."

"And you expect me to believe that? Get real, girl-friend." Patti walked to her station, which was empty at the moment, snatched up a broom and took a few swipes at the locks of hair on the floor.

"So, how's the e-mail guy?" Jillian asked to divert attention from herself.

"Just fine, thanks. More important, I heard you had a hot date with some gorgeous guy."

Jillian opened her mouth to protest but Patti shushed her with "Uh-uh-uh-uh! Sherry *saw* you at Joe Bailly's on her way to the movies Saturday night. So don't try to deny it."

"It wasn't a date. And the only thing that was hot was the temperature."

Patti looked at her askance. "Sherry thought otherwise. But date or not, if you make the right moves, who knows what can happen?"

"I don't make moves, right or otherwise."

Patti, whose hair this week was such a dark red it was almost purple, peered over the top of her black-framed glasses and gave Jillian a "tsk-tsk, poor-thing" shake of the head. "You gotta get out more, babe. Start flashing that great bod of yours around town a little. Start getting laid."

"Yeah, that's just what my daughter needs—a sex-crazed mom who brings home a different guy every night. Good plan."

"Okay. Okay. So is there a reason you're here? Because if it's just to check us out, I'm insulted. And if it's not and things are fine, I really don't want to see your face until your vacation is over."

"All right, two things. I need the name of the agency you used to find your birth parents because…a cousin of mine wants to find someone. And second, I wanted to tell you I'm thinking about taking a trip.''

Patti's mouth fell open, and after a sputter or two, she said, "Cool. Where to?"

"I haven't decided. At first I thought California. I still have some friends there. Then I thought, why not go somewhere exotic, like Jamaica, or Cozumel?" Jillian waited a beat, then said, "Costa Rica, maybe."

Patti's head snapped up. "You serious?"

"Well, it's not that surprising, is it? I mean, you guys are the ones who convinced me I absolutely *needed* a vacation. Besides, Chloe's gone for two weeks, so I'm as free as the wind."

Her friend frowned. "Yeah, but hell, no one figured you'd really do it."

Jillian sighed. "Am I that predictable?"

"Not at all. Just a workaholic." Patti gave Jillian a brief hug. "I say, more power to ya, sweetie."

"Well, I haven't even decided if I'm going for sure. But if I do, I just wanted to make sure everything was all set with the shops and supplies and all. I'd call in every so often."

"Oh, no, you don't. If you're going on a vacation, then it has to be a real vacation. Nothing's going to fall apart while you're gone. We can handle it. Trust me."

"I know you can. I just don't know if I can handle you handling it."

Patti laughed and, after giving Jillian the name of the agency she used to find her parents, practically shoved her out the door.

Later at home, Jillian struck out on agencies to do

the work for her; all had a backlog of cases and couldn't promise to get to it anytime soon. The agency Patti had used was now out of business.

From there, she progressed to private investigators, and while talking with one P.I., she realized that once they located the guy, she'd still have to see him herself. Which meant going to Costa Rica or wherever they found him.

It wasn't as though a P.I. could bring him back for her to identify. Especially if the man was evading the law. If he knew someone was on to him, wouldn't he take off?

A day alone had given her some perspective. Not only did she need to know if the man was impersonating her husband, she needed to know that the man *wasn't* her husband. How else could she get on with her life?

She didn't believe for one minute that Rob was capable of such deceit. But she couldn't write off the possibility that, as Ramsey had said, there were mitigating circumstances. And if by some wild fluke Rob was alive, if he had amnesia, or God knows what, Chloe would still have a father. And *she'd* have a husband. *She'd still be married.*

To a man who had been everything to her.

She *had* to do something.

She picked up the receiver again and called long-distance information. "Yes, I'm looking for a number in Mirador, Costa Rica."

THE NEXT AFTERNOON, after she'd changed planes in Houston for the second leg of the flight from Chicago to San José, Costa Rica, Jillian popped a dramamine pill into her mouth to ensure she wouldn't get airsick. When the 747 reached the appropriate altitude, she pushed back her seat to sleep for the duration—if she could stop thinking about the crazy thing she was doing.

Do something wild and irresponsible. She'd called Dana's bluff on that one. Most definitely. And it felt scary and wonderful both at the same time.

That she'd been able to find a phone number in Mirador for a Jack Sullivan had come as a total shock. She'd only called information to cancel out a remote possibility, but to have it confirmed instead...

And then she'd called the number just to see if it worked and if anyone would answer. When a man's gravelly, sleep-filled voice said, *"Hola,"* she'd gasped and slammed down the receiver. There hadn't been time to register if the voice sounded familiar or not.

After the numbness had worn off, she'd made her decision. She'd called Logan and Dana to make sure Chloe was fine, and then told them she was taking a trip and would call when she arrived to let them know the number where she'd be. They were thrilled for her. She'd then called Patti and Meadow Brook to let them know the same.

With all that taken care of, she'd called a travel agent whose number she'd plucked from the travel section of the newspaper, and he'd taken care of her flight and lodging arrangements. He'd even given her the name of a person who would meet and assist her once she arrived in San José, and who would be her guide to Mirador. How much safer could one get?

The flight attendant approached and asked what she'd like to drink. She ordered orange juice, which she drank quickly; then with renewed determination and a fair share of personal satisfaction that she'd made a sound decision, she nestled into the narrow seat and closed her eyes, welcoming sleep. She'd hardly had a wink since Detective Ramsey had first shown up on her doorstep.

She was just drifting off when she heard the flight attendant ask someone else, "And what would you like to drink, sir?"

A deep, familiar voice replied, "I'll have what this young lady is having," and, for one brief second, she thought she was dreaming.

CHAPTER FOUR

JILLIAN'S EYES SNAPPED open. Adam Ramsey was standing next to the aisle seat. Looming over her, he smiled—a lazy sort of smile, as if bumping into her on a plane bound for Costa Rica was an everyday occurrence.

"Hello there," he said in a friendly tone.

She nodded. "Detective."

"Mind if I sit here?" He gestured to the empty aisle seat.

Somewhere between Chicago and Houston she'd moved to the middle in her row of three because she'd felt a draft sitting next to the window. The other two seats were empty, and she had no reason to refuse his request.

"Suit yourself."

"Thank you, don't mind if I do."

When he settled, he turned to her with a quizzical look. "I'm surprised, Jillian Sullivan. I had no idea you'd be on this plane. Fancy that."

"And vice versa. Let's see, what were the words... something about following procedure, and your department couldn't afford a trip like this, and if they did, there was all that paperwork to get it approved, which would take forever, and then there was a little matter of red tape because it was a different country, not to mention your office wasn't looking for an imposter but a murderer. Or did I misunderstand all that?''

He tipped his head in acknowledgment. ''What an excellent memory you have. You're assuming, of course, that I'm on this plane for business and not pleasure.'' He grinned.

After a pause, she said, ''You're right. I made that assumption. If that's incorrect, why don't you enlighten me? Are you on vacation? Or is it that everything you told me before was a lie and you're going to Mirador to find the man who's impersonating my late husband?''

''May I say I thought your idea was brilliant and decided to forgo the paperwork and follow up on it myself by taking a little vacation time?''

Not one to beat around the bush, she asked, ''If you're not traveling to Mirador in any official capacity, what can you do?''

''I'm going for the same reason you are. To find the man in the photograph.''

''Well, I doubt we're on this plane for the same reasons, Mr. Ramsey. I believe *you* want to find the man because you think he's my dead husband and that he's done something criminal and went missing because of it. *I* want to see who the imposter is because his taking Rob's identity could affect my family and my business.''

''You haven't, for even a moment, entertained the thought that he might be your husband?''

She chewed on that for a second. ''Of course I've

had the thought. Especially since you mentioned…
those mitigating circumstances. In truth, it's plagued
me ever since. So, to get any peace of mind at all, I
have to know. Because if by some bizarre twist of fate,
Rob is still alive…''

A lump grew in her throat. She took a breath. ''If
he *is* still alive, it would be a miracle, and I'd do
everything I could to help him.''

Adam gave her an odd look, as if she'd said something very perplexing.

''That's all pure conjecture, though,'' she added. ''I
highly doubt the possibility, but I need to know so I
can sleep at night.''

He was staring at her mouth, and she had an urge
to moisten her lips with her tongue. Her skin warmed
as she realized how easily his gaze unnerved her. She
didn't *want* to be unnerved by this man.

''Hmm,'' he said. ''Since we're going to the same
place for the same purpose, perhaps we should join
forces?''

Taken aback at the suggestion, she managed to say,
''We're going to the same place, period. We don't
have the same purpose.''

''Yes, we do. We're both trying to find the same
person, and since we'll need to rent a car to get from
San José to Mirador, it would make sense to do it
together, don't you agree?''

She pursed her lips. She hadn't planned on renting
a car. On the map, Mirador looked to be fairly close
to San José. ''I thought I'd take a cab.''

''You speak Spanish?''

"I can get by," she lied. "I took it in my freshman year."

He pulled his briefcase onto his lap, opened it, and after thumbing through some papers, he pulled out a map. "See this dot over here? This is Mirador. See this line here? Those are mountains. Not far in miles, but still at least a day away. If you could even *get* a cab to take you that far, it would cost a fortune."

"The travel agent didn't tell me that. But he made arrangements for a guide to show me around. I'm sure the guide can take me, or advise me where to catch a bus or something."

Adam shook his head and grinned.

Did he know something she didn't?

"Well, if you change your mind about going together, let me know. I plan to head out early in the morning."

"I've taken care of my arrangements, Detective, but should you need help yourself, just let me know." She flashed him a superior smile.

He shrugged. "Have it your way, and could you please call me something other than Detective? Ramsey, Adam, hey you—any of those'd work."

With that, he stood up and set his briefcase on his seat. "Gotta stretch the legs and see a man in the back," he said. "I feel like I've been doing yoga for the past hour. You'd think whoever designed these seats would take into account that everyone in the world isn't short."

"I know what you mean," she said as he walked away. She did know, but to her there were worse things about being tall than no legroom in a plane. As a gawky long-legged kid, she'd been mercilessly teased by other kids in school. And when she'd gone to live with her father, he'd focused on her height just as cruelly.

The plane shuddered and the warning light above her head flashed on. She grabbed for her seat belt as the turbulence increased enough to toss her to the side. At the same time, Adam's briefcase lurched off the seat and fell to the floor, papers spewing everywhere.

Amid the rattles and bumps, she reached down, grabbed a handful of papers, brought the briefcase up to the seat again and stuffed the papers inside. Then the turbulence subsided as quickly as it had come.

She grinned to herself, imagining Adam's big body wedged into the tiny washroom. He'd be lucky not to get stuck inside. She reached to close Adam's briefcase and saw some photos sticking out of an envelope.

The photos? The infamous photos? She couldn't resist taking one more look. Maybe—

As she picked up the envelope, a letter dropped into her lap. The writing looked the same as that on the back of the photos.

She stared at the letter, then glanced away. It wasn't right to read someone else's mail. But if the writing on the photos was the same...

She glanced down the aisle where Adam had gone. He was standing in the back talking to one of the flight attendants, and he didn't look in any hurry to return.

She glanced at the letter again. If she didn't pick it up but got a glimpse of it as it lay there, she couldn't be accused of actually reading someone else's mail, could she?

No. She should shove the thing into his briefcase and forget it. But her gaze was glued to the paper, and slowly the words came into focus, instantly melding into sentences.

To the Los Angeles Police Department
I'm writing to you with hope that you can locate my husband, Jack Sullivan, in Los Angeles.

Jillian's adrenaline surged. She snatched up the letter and began to read in earnest.

I am terminally ill and have left our son with a friend in a village near Mirador. My husband went to Los Angeles on business and was supposed to return weeks ago. He hasn't returned and I fear something bad has happened to him. I hope you can find him soon because my friend cannot take care of the boy for very long. I have no family and my son will be all alone if his father doesn't return. Please help me, I beg you. For my little boy's sake.

Sincerely,
Corita Sullivan

"Find something of interest?"

Jillian jerked her head up. Adam hovered over her. Her cheeks flamed. "Your briefcase fell during the turbulence," she said guiltily. "The photos came out. I thought since they were out, I might as well look at them again, but then this letter... I didn't..." Her voice froze in her throat.

"You didn't what?"

Her face got hotter by the second. "I didn't plan on reading it, but it was there and I couldn't help catch the words and then I couldn't stop."

He reached down and snatched up the letter and photographs, stuffed them inside the briefcase, then shut and locked it.

"I'm sorry that happened," she said. "But it did, and now that I'm thinking about it, I'm wondering why you didn't tell me about that letter in the first place."

Now her anger spiked. How could Adam give her only half the information? "Why did you lie to me and let me believe this man was still in Mirador? Now I discover he's in Los Angeles and I've wasted my time and money on a wild-goose chase."

Adam spoke softly. "*You're* mad at me because you read my mail and didn't like what you read? Excuse me, but I think your indignation is slightly skewed."

Yes, it was wrong of her to read his mail. But she couldn't change the fact that she had, and she didn't like the way she was feeling because of it. "You lied to me. You've lied to me from the second you walked into my home."

He shook his head. "This is my job, Jillian. I didn't lie to you without reason. I have to follow procedure."

"Even if that procedure could harm someone in the process?"

When he looked confused, she said, "What about that little boy the woman mentioned in the letter? Were you just going to leave him without a mother or a father? Leave him to fend for himself?"

"My job is to solve this case, which means finding your husband's murderer."

"But this woman asked for the LAPD's help. How can you just blow it off?"

"Well, there you go making those assumptions again. If it's any consolation, the department has done everything it can to locate Jack Sullivan in L.A. So you can pretty much rest assured he's not there. If he's anywhere, Mirador is our best shot."

"Oh." She looked down, twisted the fabric on her T-shirt. "Why didn't you just say so?"

"Because you didn't give me a chance." He swung the briefcase to the overhead bin. Then he sat back down and heaved a sigh.

Still miffed that she'd read the letter, Adam realized it really didn't matter now, since she was on her way to Mirador, anyway. Not showing her the letter had been simply a safety precaution. The less she knew, the better. He didn't want the information leaked to Sullivan, inadvertently or otherwise.

But it wouldn't do him any good to make an enemy of her, either. "Okay. Look...I'm just doing my job, following procedure, which doesn't always make me Mr. Nice Guy. For that I apologize, but in the end, I have a job to do."

"I thought you were on vacation."

"Would you like something to drink?" It was the flight attendant again, making another run with the drinks cart.

He ordered a beer and she ordered wine, and they sat in silence until she said, "I apologize for reading your mail. All I really wanted was to see the photos again and...well, I know that's no excuse, and I'm sorry.''

He caught her gaze. ''Apology accepted, but not necessary. I understand. And to answer your question, I thought as long as I'm on vacation, I might as well follow up on the lead. Unofficially.''

She held up her glass. ''Truce.''

He clicked his beer can against her glass. ''Truce.'' For however long it would last. He still didn't understand her reasons for not wanting her husband's body to be exhumed, and he wasn't one-hundred-percent certain she wasn't involved in some way. Why hadn't she told him she was going to Mirador when she'd phoned him?

The most obvious answer was that she wanted to warn Sullivan. Yet that didn't really make sense, because if she was involved, she could have made contact from Chicago; she wouldn't have needed to make the journey. And besides, his gut told him that she hated leaving Chicago, was loath to be so far from her daughter.

Still...he wasn't sure he could trust his gut. It had failed him regarding his ex, certainly. He would've given the world to Kate if he could have, and then he found she'd been cheating on him. And if that wasn't enough, she'd taken him to the cleaners in court, as if *she* was the wronged party. No, he didn't have a whole lot of faith in his gut anymore. At least not where women were concerned.

And he sure as hell wasn't going to let his gut have any say in his mission this time.

"So, when we arrive, what's your plan, Detec— Adam?"

"Since it'll be too late tonight after we arrive to do much of anything, dinner and a good night's sleep are in order. Then in the morning I'm off for Mirador." He angled his head toward her. "The invitation still stands. You're welcome to come along if you'd like."

She smiled. She had a great smile, one that reached her eyes. Nice eyes, too. Bluer than a perfect sky— and whenever he met her gaze, he couldn't seem to look away.

"What?" She raised a hand to her face.

"Are you wearing colored contacts?"

She pulled back. "No. I don't have a vision problem. Why?"

"I've never seen eyes quite that color before. Blue, yes, but never such a...blue blue."

"Chloe's are the same color."

He nodded. "Yeah, now that I think about it, I remember that. She seems like a great kid."

Her eyes warmed at the mention of her daughter. "She is. Most of the time. Right now, though, it's a little hard to tell. Adolescence has a way of masking someone's better qualities. And with her father gone, it's even harder for her. I think having a father around at her age is so important."

"What about relatives, or friends?"

"Well, my neighbor, my best friend's husband, Logan is kind of a surrogate father for Chloe. In fact, Chloe's with Dana and Logan and their two kids at their cabin right now. They'll be there until a couple of days before school starts." She paused, appearing thoughtful. "Logan is wonderful, but that's still not the same as having her own father."

Yeah, he could understand that. He couldn't imagine how his own childhood would have been without his father.

"It's been four years," Jillian went on, "and Chloe was young enough that, if it weren't for the pictures and stories I've told her, I don't think she'd even remember him. It's like there's this huge hole in our lives."

Wow, he thought. Four years later and she still loved the guy. He heard it in her voice, as well as her words. If she only knew. But she *didn't* know. Or maybe she did and didn't care, because he'd filled her needs. Something *he'd* obviously not done for Kate, because if he had, she wouldn't have looked elsewhere.

But why the hell did *he* care if Jillian Sullivan still loved her husband?

Her being here now offered him the opportunity to do a little fishing, and he'd be a fool not to take advantage of it. If he got her to talk, she might tell him something important. Any tidbit of information might be the one piece to crack the case wide open.

"I know the feeling," he said. "Even though there were six of us, my dad had this amazing way of focusing on each kid. I remember feeling like I was the only person in the world who mattered when he was talking to me. He was always incredibly interested in everything I had to say. He was just the greatest dad. I wish I'd had the opportunity to tell him that before he died." Adam paused and smiled ironically. "He used to say, 'Wishes have no substance. It's what you do that counts.'"

"I'm sorry. When did he die?"

"Last year. But my mom's going strong. She loves being a grandmother—I think it's her calling."

"Your parents...your family sounds terrific. If Rob hadn't died, well..." She breathed a sigh. "He was on the road a lot, but he was home enough to still be a wonderful father to Chloe."

Adam drummed his fingers on the armrest. Every time he heard her say how fantastic this guy was, his blood did a slow simmer.

"Does the rest of your family live in L.A.?" she asked.

"Nope. Most still live in Kentucky where I grew up. In or around Henderson."

"Kentucky? I'm surprised. You don't have a Southern accent."

"I've been gone awhile." He smiled. "Henderson is on the Illinois-Kentucky border. Some think it's more Midwest than Southern, anyway. What about your family?"

She took a moment to answer, then, "My mom died when I was eleven. I went to live with my dad then, but I didn't know him before that—he abandoned my mother when I was still a baby. He was a small-town cop and we didn't get on very well, to say the least, and...well, I left when I was fifteen."

"Where'd you go? To live with another relative?"

"No. I went to L.A. by myself."

"You ran away?" He was stunned, especially when

he thought of his own sisters at that age trying to manage on their own in a strange city.

She frowned. "I never really thought of it as running away, but yes, I guess that's what I did."

"And your dad, being a cop, called out the troops?"

She shook her head and gave a wry laugh. "No, like I said, we didn't get along. I'm sure he was relieved I'd gone. From then on, I was on my own and learned quickly how to take care of myself. I never saw him again until his funeral." She looked down. "That was seven years ago."

A knot grew in Adam's chest. No kid should have to be on her own at fifteen. Especially not in L.A., though he saw it happen all too often. He looked at Jillian with new eyes. That history would explain her involvement with a scumbag like Sullivan.

"If your business success now is any indication, you managed to take care of yourself very well."

She let out a long sigh. "I guess. But if I didn't have Chloe, it wouldn't mean anything. And I'd trade it all in an instant for the chance to be a family again."

Right. She'd said that before and it grated on him. While he might understand her desire for family because her own had been so lacking, some things just didn't make sense.

He looked squarely into those bluer-than-blue eyes. "I'm not sure I get it. You wanted a family and yet you ran away. And your dad just let you go off and shift for yourself when you were still a minor. What kind of parent would do that?"

She shrugged. "Well, that's what happened."

It was clear she didn't want to talk about it anymore.

He changed the subject, and their talk, much of it about education, was mostly in generalities.

Finally she tipped her head back against the seat and said, "If you don't mind, I'd like to take a nap for the duration. I haven't slept very well lately."

"Good idea. Think I will, too." But he doubted he'd get much sleep. He was too wound up, and far too focused on the woman beside him.

Their conversation had given him a little insight about Jillian Sullivan. Except when she was married, she'd been making her own way since she was fifteen. No wonder she wasn't afraid to jump on a plane to go looking for some guy she believed might be impersonating her dead husband.

She was a walking contradiction, a mixture of little girl and woman. Naive to the world at large, yet experienced in other ways. But she was her own person, no question about that.

And, he had to admit, he liked that about her—even if she was annoyingly stubborn at times. But none of that changed his purpose. He was on a quest, with or without her.

If she decided to tag along, it might be the best way for him to keep track of her. On the other hand, she could be more trouble than he needed. Either way, he was going to get his man.

JILLIAN FELT A BUMP and awoke with a start.

"We're here," a deep male voice beside her said. "Touchdown in San José."

She glanced over at Detective Adam Ramsey, still sitting next to her. She'd spent a long time trying to fall asleep and hadn't actually succeeded until twenty minutes ago, and then she'd crashed hard. And now she was tired and cranky—and more nervous than she thought she'd be.

He folded up his newspaper and stuffed it into the seat pocket in front of him. "Finish the crossword puzzle?" she asked. Anyone who even attempted the *New York Times* crossword deserved a commendation. She'd tried once or twice and given up, deciding her inability was due to some right-brain deficiency—or was it left brain? Someone told her once that she fell into the artistic category, whichever side of the brain that was.

"Yep. Piece of cake."

"Not for me. Too detailed for this non-college-educated person." After learning about Adam's educationally rich background—an undergraduate degree in American studies, a graduate degree in criminal justice, then police training—she felt even more deficient. She'd always wanted to go on to college, but instead, got her education on the streets. Once she moved in with Rob, he'd insisted she finish high school, which she had.

Hair-design school had been Rob's idea, as well. Though it wasn't the college education she'd longed for, she'd latched on to it like glue. Education in any area was better than none at all.

Then, after Rob died, making her business a success had become a way to repay him for his direction and advice and to make him proud of her—even if he wasn't around to see it.

"Education has nothing to do with crossword puzzles," Adam said. "What's needed is patience. Something you don't seem to have much of." He chuckled.

Really? Did she lack patience? She'd never really thought about it, but maybe it was true. She wanted instant results from the things she did, and worked hard to make things happen—even though they rarely happened the way she hoped.

She looked at Adam. Interesting that he'd even noticed that about her, especially when she wasn't even aware of it herself.

The plane taxied to a stop, and the flight attendant reminded passengers to fill out the Customs declaration form if they hadn't done so already. Adam was kind enough to help Jillian with hers, after which he pulled her carry-on luggage from the overhead bin.

The instant she stepped outside, Jillian felt as if she'd walked into a sauna. If she'd thought a Chicago summer was hot and humid, it was nothing compared to this. They disembarked on the tarmac and were headed for the terminal.

The building was minuscule compared to O'Hare or John Wayne in L.A., the only two airports she'd ever been in. "Is this it?" She walked in tandem with Adam, pulling her small suitcase on wheels. His case also had wheels, but he seemed to prefer lugging it in hand.

"You got it, blue eyes."

"But it's deserted. Where are all the people, airline personnel?"

"Hey, it's not O'Hare, that's for sure. And it's evening midweek. So, where's this guide supposed to meet you?"

"Here, I thought. He's probably waiting inside. If he doesn't mind, maybe we can drop you at your hotel. Where are you staying?"

"Same place as you, as long as you're offering me a ride."

"You don't have reservations? Who travels out of the country without reservations?"

He grinned. "When I left, I wasn't sure if I'd be staying in San José or heading out as soon as I got here. I figured I'd find something somewhere. August isn't exactly high season."

She shoved damp hair off her already perspiring forehead. "I think I understand why."

Before they entered the building, a man dressed in a brown uniform appeared and asked questions about their baggage. As soon as they were inside, Jillian glanced around for a person who looked as if he could be a tour guide. The name she'd been given was Ernesto. A few people milled about, but most were either military types or uniformed airline personnel. She didn't see an information desk anywhere.

They were directed to Customs. "Maybe he's waiting by the baggage claim. He might be thinking I'd have additional luggage."

"You don't?"

"This is it," she said as they followed the arrows, flashed their passports at the gate and then went on to the baggage claim area.

"A woman with one piece of luggage. I'm impressed."

"I didn't figure I'd be staying more than a few days."

He laughed. "Length of time never made an iota of difference to any woman I've ever known."

And she'd bet he'd known more than his share. The thought sent a peculiar shaft of—what? Jealousy?—through her. But that was ridiculous. Why on earth would she give a damn how many women he'd known?

She'd never had any desire to be one of many. Hell, for four years now, she'd had no desire at all.

Not until she'd noticed Adam at the market.

When they arrived at the baggage claim area, she still saw no one who remotely resembled a tour guide.

"Look," Adam said, "maybe you better find out exactly where this hotel of yours is, since your guy doesn't seem to be around."

They found a spot to sit, and she fished out the envelope containing the information from her small backpack. "Here it is. La Paloma. I guess we'll have to take a cab."

"Or rent a car. I planned to do that for tomorrow, anyway." He pointed to a desk with the names of all the major car-rental companies emblazoned across the front.

Just then, a small shuttle bus with "La Paloma" on the side pulled up. "Or—look!" She tapped him on the arm excitedly. "A shuttle. We can take that. It'll be faster since it's right here and I need to get to the hotel to make some calls before it's too late."

He frowned as if considering what to do. "Okay. I can rent a car at the hotel. That's probably better, any-way." He got up and held out his hand to help her up, too. "Let's ask when the shuttle is leaving. Maybe we'll have time to change some money first."

"Can't we do that at the hotel?" She wouldn't be changing much, since she wasn't planning to stay long.

"Sure. Whatever the lady wants."

Ten minutes later she was standing at the reception desk of La Paloma arguing with the clerk, whose English was as poor as her Spanish, about her reservation. He had no record of it, apparently. Furthermore, the hotel was booked solid because of a chartered planeload of tourists who'd arrived earlier in the day.

While Jillian fumed, Adam simply stood on the sidelines with a smirk on his face. She stomped off to a pay phone to call the idiot travel agent who'd set it all up, but she soon realized she didn't have the right change and she wouldn't know how to make a long-distance call in Spanish, anyway.

Adam had followed her, and she turned to him in exasperation. "You can jump in anytime, Ramsey. Any ideas?"

"I thought you'd never ask." He grinned and walked back to the reception desk.

She grabbed her things and hurried alongside him. "He already said he didn't have any rooms."

"*Señor,*" Adam said as they reached the desk. Then he rattled off something in Spanish and the two men engaged in a lengthy discourse, none of which she understood.

Her blood pressure rose. Adam, the jerk, could've told her he spoke the language, and he could've helped her earlier. Well, she wasn't going to give him the satisfaction of asking what he'd said to the desk clerk.

Adam turned to her. "He knows of another hotel that might have rooms for us, and he's going to call there to make sure, so we don't make the trip in vain. He said it's not fancy, but it's his brother's place and he's fairly sure he can get us rooms there."

"I thought this wasn't high season."

"Right. But apparently this is the time of year when some travel companies charter planes and book packages for people who can't afford high-season rates."

She crossed her arms over her chest. "Well, I guess it doesn't matter as long as we can get rooms somewhere."

Then Adam, in his impeccable Spanish, rattled off another sentence to thank the man, who then smiled and immediately got on the phone.

Okay, she had to ask. "Why didn't you tell me you spoke Spanish fluently? You might've helped me out earlier, you know."

"You never gave me a chance." He grinned. "You were too busy taking charge." After a brief pause, he said, "And I kinda liked watching you do it."

Even though his teasing was at her expense, she liked that he wasn't serious all the time. She grinned back. "Well, next time, don't wait so long. Okay?"

Fifteen minutes later they were standing in the lobby of the shabbiest hotel she'd seen since living on the streets of L.A. Good Lord. As she glanced around at the faded wallpaper, the peeling paint and cracked-tile floors, her stomach plummeted. Not a very auspicious start to her venture, she thought.

"Guess Raphael's brother doesn't get much business," Adam said, glancing around. "Might've been an elegant hotel in the past."

"The ancient past."

He looked at her and chuckled. "You okay with this?"

It was only for a night, maybe two, at the most. Then she'd be on her way back home. "*No problemo!* As long as there's no red light in my window."

Adam laughed outright. "Okay, *señora,* let's check in."

Adam walked her to her room minutes later, and they made plans for dinner. His room was three doors down from hers, which she found odd. She doubted the other rooms were even occupied and wondered if Adam had asked that his room not be next to hers.

Hmm. Maybe he wanted to make sure she didn't overhear anything he was doing. Well, it didn't matter to her what he did. Inside her room, the first thing she did was call Dana to let her know where she was and how to reach her. Chloe was outside at the moment, so Jillian said she'd call later or in the morning to talk to her.

Next she called the travel agent. Not only did she have no guide, no hotel room and no arrangements to get to Mirador, she got no answer at the agency, apart from a recorded greeting. She left a scathing message, including the hotel's number for the agent to call her back. Her clothes were sticking to her clammy skin by the time she hung up. She needed a shower.

She thought about calling the number in Mirador

that she'd called from home, but decided against it. Too many hang-ups might tip the guy off that someone was on to him.

The water pressure in the shower wasn't exactly needle hard but even so, she relished the cool water against her skin, the slippery feel of soap as she lathered up. Suddenly the water pressure reduced to barely a trickle. She cranked both knobs one way and then the other. No response.

"Damn!" She banged on the wall near the showerhead. Nothing. Hoping to rattle something to make it work, she kicked the wall, nearly slipped, but caught herself by grabbing the faucet. Then she heard a resounding clunk, and a gush of water, red with iron or rust from the pipes, blasted out like a burst dam—in her face and in her mouth and drenching her hair. She furiously twisted the knobs, then finally shut it down.

Oh, man. From the second she'd seen Ramsey on the plane, she'd had a bad feeling about this trip. A really bad feeling. And it was getting worse by the second. She sighed.

Well, at least she'd gotten the soap washed off.

A knock on the door startled her. Quickly she grabbed a gauze-thin scrap of fabric that supposedly passed for a towel and wrapped it around herself. "Yes. Who's there?"

"Message for you, Señora Sullivan."

"Can you stick it under the door, please?" She hoped it was a phone message from the travel agent with some good news. She plucked the paper from the floor. It was a brief note from Adam in bold printed letters saying he'd be back in a few minutes and would meet her in the lobby at seven for dinner.

The snack she'd been given on the plane wasn't enough for a gnat and she was starving. She had no idea where Ramsey planned to eat dinner, but she hoped it wasn't far.

She blotted her hair and tossed on a red sleeveless top, loose tan cotton pants and sandals. When she went to plug in her hairdryer, she discovered the plug didn't fit with her grounding prong. *Huh.* Why was she not surprised?

Near seven, she went to the elevator, punched the down button and waited. There were no lights to show the floor numbers and there was no light on the button, either. She waited. Nothing. Finally a woman walked by, shook her head and said in broken English, "Not work very much."

O-kay. So this was how it was going to be.

As Jillian took the stairs to the lobby, she thought how unprepared she was for everything here, not least of all the language barrier. Going with Ramsey to find the man in the photograph was looking to be a better deal all the time.

Four flights later, sweaty again and feeling as if she hadn't even showered, she showed up at the desk to meet Adam.

He wasn't there.

CHAPTER FIVE

So FAR, SO GOOD. Adam paid the man for the car rental, made arrangements to pick up the vehicle in the morning and then headed back to the hotel. Once he had the car, he would pick up the overnight cargo he'd sent, which contained his dismantled gun and a satellite phone.

Jillian Sullivan might be able to take care of herself in Chicago, but she was definitely out of her element here. She had no idea their mission could be dangerous.

It would be better if he could convince her to go back home. Even better if she hadn't come at all. But hell, it'd never occurred to him that she'd take matters into her own hands.

Another strike against his gut instincts. Having met and talked with her, he should've known she'd do something like this. But he'd never even suspected. The woman was unpredictable. That in itself was dangerous.

Plus, he liked being around her. Liked it far too much. Which was another reason he wanted her to go home.

Their undesirable hotel accommodations, and the wreck of a car he'd had to take might work in his favor. The discomfort might have her champing at the bit to go back to Chicago. If not, though, he'd figure out some other way to send her packing.

He walked the few blocks back to the hotel, checking for a decent restaurant—but not too decent. He didn't want her to get comfortable. He passed a hole-in-the-wall bar-restaurant and decided that would be where they'd eat.

She was waiting in the dimly lit lobby when he walked in through a side entrance. The low light camouflaged a multitude of what would be building-code violations in the States. Even so, seeing her standing there next to a bedraggled potted palm with a large ceiling fan rotating overhead put him in mind of a scene in the movie *Casablanca.* Any minute now he expected to hear a piano playing "As Time Goes By."

She hadn't seen him come in, so he sidled up next to her. "Hi."

"Oh!" Her hands flew to her chest and her eyes rounded like dinner plates. "Omigosh, you scared me half to death sneaking up on me like that."

"I didn't sneak. I *don't* sneak."

"Well, I couldn't even hear your footsteps."

He gestured at the guy behind the desk. "I didn't want to disturb Sleeping Beauty over there." He stared at her. "New hairdo?"

She scowled. "Yes, I'm trying the drowned-rat look. What do you think?"

He pulled back and positioned his hands to frame her head between the square he made with his fingers. "Not bad. But...I think I like the other way better." The way that reminded him of the honey-haired angels on the frescoes in the church he went to when he was a kid.

But Jillian Sullivan shouldn't be reminding him of angels. Because, while she might look like one, there was every chance she was anything but.

She shifted her weight to one side and crossed her arms. "My hair blower wouldn't work because the outlets here are different, and the shower…oh, never mind. In this heat my hair will dry within the hour."

"I guess taking a spur-of-the-moment trip didn't give you any time to do outlet research." He smiled. "Good thing you had a current passport."

She pursed her lips. "I'd wanted to take Chloe on a trip last year and got it then. Unfortunately the trip never materialized. This is my first time out of the country. I've lived in California and Chicago, and that's the extent of my travels."

She hadn't been anywhere? Almost everyone he knew had been somewhere, if even just vacationing in a camper as his family had done one summer at his mother's insistence. They'd hadn't had much money, but had still covered a good portion of the U.S.

"You don't like to travel?"

"Never had the opportunity. Before my mom died, we lived in a room in the back of the little grocery store where she worked. The owners deducted the low rent for the place from her paycheck. She felt lucky—there wasn't much work to be had where we lived. Needless to say, there wasn't any money for luxuries."

He'd never have guessed from talking with her or from looking at her that she'd had a deprived childhood and no real family. "Where exactly did you live when growing up?"

"A town in Southern California called El Mirage." She laughed. "It was really small, not much more than a bus stop with a gas station and a grocery store. Just a mirage in the middle of the desert." She laughed, then pointed across the street. "Oh, there's a restaurant. La Bamba. Is that the one you had in mind?"

He looked up and saw the neon beer signs blinking off and on. As they approached, the smell of stale beer assailed their nostrils, and sounds of hard-rock music and raucous voices spilled out to the street.

Her first trip out of the country and he was taking her to a dive. He felt like a creep. "I have a better idea. Let's get a cab and find a nice place."

"WHAT TIME DO YOU PLAN to leave in the morning?" Jillian asked Adam as the waiter led them to a table on the patio. The restaurant, Mucho Macho, wasn't too far, and Adam said he'd heard the food was good.

"Early. At 6:00 a.m."

"You mentioned before that you thought we should team up and go together…and I think you're right. It's a good idea." She hoped he still thought so.

"So if the offer still stands, I'll be ready then, too," she said, trying to sound more upbeat than she felt. On the way to the restaurant in the cab, she'd had second thoughts about this whole venture.

She hadn't fully considered the outcome, and when she did, all the what-ifs frightened her. But she'd come this far, so it would be stupid to turn back now. And every passing minute she spent with Adam made her feel more driven than ever to find out the identity of the man in the photograph.

When Adam didn't respond, her discomfort jacked up a notch. Fortunately the evening was cooler than the day, and a slight breeze brought the scents of tropical flowers.

The waiter took their drink orders—two *cervezas,* the local beer, which Adam insisted she absolutely had to try. The menu of course was in Spanish, but she recognized some of the dishes and decided on *corvina,* fish with rice and vegetables. Adam ordered something with a name she didn't recognize and an appetizer.

"You have to try the *langosta,*" he said. "If you want to get a real feel for a country, you must try the local cuisine."

"When in Rome?" She smiled.

"Something like that. Otherwise, you may as well be in Chicago."

Music with a samba beat played in the background. "Believe me, I *know* I'm not in the suburbs of Chicago anymore. I wish I'd had the opportunity for a little more research on this country, but my plan was to do what I needed to do and go home. That's still the plan."

"It's a good one," Adam said as the waiter brought them their beer. "You really ought to take a little time to enjoy the country and its culture. It's beautiful, *pura vida*—pure life—in its simplest form."

He leaned back in his chair. He looked thoughtful— and sexy in his faded jeans and white cotton shirt undone at the throat, revealing the top of his tanned chest. Sexy with his sleeves rolled to midforearm where she could see the muscles working when he lifted his beer to his lips, full lips that looked inviting enough to kiss.

Stop! She was crazy even to think about things like that. Especially now when she didn't know what the hell was going on in her life.

"You'll have to return for a vacation sometime, when you can appreciate the tranquillity." His gray eyes looked almost silver in the evening light.

"Maybe. But right now, I'm focused on finding this…this man."

He leaned forward. "Why is that so important? If you don't find him, what would be different from a week ago?"

"What would be different?" she repeated incredulously. Looking around, she lowered her voice. "A week ago I was a widow, and my daughter's father was dead. And no matter how many times I tell myself the man is an imposter, I have to be sure. I can't live with this cloud of doubt hanging over me."

She leaned forward, too, elbows on the table. "I need to know, and I'd like to go with you."

He shifted in his chair, his discomfort evident. After a moment he said, "The guy at the car-rental place said it's a hard trip, so I was thinking that since it would be harder on you than me and there's no real need for us both to go, it might be best if I went alone. I can handle it and fill you in later."

Her nerves bunched. Was he just being nice or trying to get rid of her? "I *need* to go. And while I appreciate your concern, I *will* go—with or without you."

He held up a hand. "Okay. I was only making a suggestion because it's a tough trip. Like in any country, there are places off the beaten track that aren't as well developed as this, places lacking in amenities. That's where I'm headed and I thought it would be easier for you to stay here."

"I don't need easy, Ramsey. I need to know what's going on. Before I left Chicago, I found a phone number for a man named Jack Sullivan in Mirador and I called it before I left."

He looked surprised. "And?"

"A man answered and I hung up. But at least I know *someone* is at that number."

His surprise switched to alarm. "You didn't say anything to him, did you?"

As she shook her head in answer to Adam's question, the waiter brought the plate of appetizers. "No, I didn't say anything to tip him off, if that's what you're asking. But I assume your office made the same call, didn't they?"

He snorted a laugh. "You're something else," he said. "We made our inquiries, but not in the same way you did. Because you're right—it wouldn't do us much good if anyone was tipped off."

She felt duly chastised. "Well, I don't think that happened. But if the LAPD had bothered to keep me in the loop, I wouldn't have called at all. And for what it's worth, I'm going to see this man! Tough trip or not. I didn't come all this way to let someone else *handle* it for me."

He held up a hand. "Hey. It was just a suggestion. I was thinking of your comfort. Now, c'mon, forget all that and enjoy yourself. Here, have a taste.'' He indicated the dish with a wave of his hand.

The appetizer looked vaguely like a plate of grubs. She eyed it suspiciously then looked back at him.

"It's a delicacy,'' he said.

"So you've been here before?''

"Once.''

"Oh.'' Suddenly she felt compelled to know more about Adam Ramsey. "Was it a long time ago?''

He looked puzzled at the question.

"That you were here—was it a long time ago? Business or pleasure?''

"Long enough that I've forgotten it entirely, including the person I was with.'' He took her fork, pierced a bite of the appetizer and held it to her mouth. "Try this, I think you'll like it.''

She bit the food off the end of the fork and chewed. A sweet garlicky taste exploded in her mouth. "Mmm,'' was all she could say as she chewed the delicious morsel. He watched her, his smile broadening as she swallowed with obvious enjoyment.

"Oh, that's so good!'' she declared. "Spicy, but not too spicy. It tastes a little like lobster.'' She stabbed another and poked it in her mouth.

"It is, but smaller. Langosta means lobster but these are actually more like crayfish. Langoustines. They're little crustaceans, prepared with garlic and basil. This dish has a bit of extra spice.''

As he spoke, his eyes sparkled with mischief…and suddenly her mouth was on fire. She grabbed her beer and drank most of it down.

He started laughing. "You'll get used to it. Want another beer?"

She nodded, then started laughing, too. After that, they graduated to pleasant conversation, and as the night wore on, the music and party atmosphere rose to a fever pitch, and along with it, Jillian's enjoyment. They polished off the plate of appetizers and then their steaming platters of food, drinking and laughing all through the meal.

By the time they finished and caught a cab back to their hotel, her face almost hurt from laughing so much and she felt light-headed from all the beer. But she couldn't remember ever having such a fun evening.

Adam was a tough man to figure out. On one hand he seemed thoughtful and kind, a man who liked children, but on the other, he purported to be a loner who wanted nothing to do with marriage and family. But so what? What did it matter to her?

As they walked to her room, a sobering thought hit her. If she'd never had such a fun evening, what did that say about her marriage? And the rest of her life?

When she unlocked the door to her room, Adam touched her shoulder, moving her behind him, then he told her to wait while he checked out the room. When at last she went in, she asked, "What was that all about?"

"Force of habit." He shrugged. "Better safe than sorry. Now, lock up after me, okay?" He reached up and lightly brushed the side of her face with his fingertips.

Her heart stalled. She wished he'd stay just a little

longer, wondered how he'd react if she asked him to. "Why? Do you think I'm in danger?"

He smiled. "No, but if I stay any longer, you might be. Now, get some sleep. We've got a big day tomorrow."

JILLIAN AWOKE AT 5:00 A.M. after only a few hours of sleep. She stretched and then kicked off the sheet. It was too early yet to be hot, but the air felt humid and the sheets held the moisture.

Still, for the first time since she met Adam, she'd slept like a rock. She'd so enjoyed their dinner that even her reservations about Adam lying to her had faded. When he'd said she might be in danger if he stuck around, her stomach had fluttered and she'd felt like a teenager wondering if she'd get a good-night kiss.

But when he'd gone immediately to his room, she realized he'd probably just been joking around and she'd read too much into it.

Before getting out of bed to tackle the shower, she allowed herself the luxury of another stretch. Suddenly she was struck by the importance of what she and Adam were going to do today. They were off to confront the man who called himself Jack Sullivan.

Her stomach knotted. She should be relieved that her search might be over soon. But instead she was filled with anxiety and trepidation at what she might find, confused about what she *wanted* to find. On top of that, she was uncertain about what she would do— either way.

She gave herself a shake. Thinking like that was

borrowing trouble. There would be time enough to decide later. If events turned out as she suspected, she'd soon be on her way home and her life would get back to normal. Despite the fun she'd had last night with Adam, she liked normal. She needed normal.

Today, the shower worked as it should, and when she was finished, she towel-dried her hair, combed out the tangles and fluffed it with her fingers. Then she dressed in a pair of safari shorts, a white T-shirt with a small stars-and-stripes emblem on the front and opted for her running shoes, instead of sandals, since Adam had said the trip could be rough.

No point in even trying the elevator, she decided on her way past, and with her wheeled carry-on in hand, she trekked down the four flights of stairs. This time Adam was waiting in the lobby. As she set down her suitcase, she noticed he didn't have his.

He glanced at his watch. "Right on time."

"Of course," she said, as if being on time was normal for her. Chloe had been right on the nose with her comment about her mom's habits.

Adam was wearing khaki cargo pants, the kind with many pockets on the legs, hiking boots and a white T-shirt with Mickey Mouse emblazoned on the front. She grinned. "Cute."

"A present from the nieces and nephews."

"And you actually wear it. That's cool. Not all guys would do that."

"I like it. The kids have good taste," he answered almost dismissively.

He seemed distant this morning and it caught her

off guard. Last night they'd developed a rapport she'd enjoyed and hoped would continue.

"I picked up a thermos of coffee," he said, "and some stuff from the grocery store. We can eat as we go."

So much for a nice leisurely breakfast. After last night she'd been looking forward to a little more relaxation. But he was all business. "Are we in a hurry?"

"I don't want to be searching for a restaurant this early, and I'm not sure what we'll find along the road. I spoke with the car-rental agent, and he told me we could reach Mirador by nightfall if we don't run into any problems along the way. But it's a long haul and it wouldn't be good to be stuck on the road at night."

"Any particular reason?"

"The roads aren't the best. They're not lit up like the highways back home...and there's a safety factor."

Her eyebrows shot up. "You mean, like, robbers?"

"Could be. That's why I suggested you might want to stay here and wait for me. Still can, you know. You might even be able to snag a room at the other hotel if someone checked out last night. You could lounge around the pool, relax and enjoy your first trip out of the country. Would you like me to call the other hotel and check on it?"

"Are you trying to get rid of me, Ramsey?"

"I think it would be safer if I went alone."

She clenched her hands. Gritted her teeth. "There's safety in numbers."

"It'll be faster if I go alone."

"I don't see why. I think you *are* trying to get rid of me."

His eyes narrowed.

Ignoring the look, she picked up her suitcase. "Where's the car?"

Adam started walking. "Around the side of the hotel."

She plodded after him, and rounding the corner, she saw a half-dozen cars parked in a line. She followed as he headed toward a brand-spanking-new white SUV. Her spirits lifted. Whether he wanted her along or not, they'd have a reasonably comfortable ride and, she was sure, air-conditioning.

She stopped at the passenger side, but Ramsey kept on walking.

"Madame, your chariot awaits." He gave her his bright white smile and gestured toward the car behind the SUV.

As she reached it, her heart sank. He stood next to an old Volkswagen bug with a mangled front fender and a passenger-side door that looked as if someone had taken a battering ram to it. Most of the paint, except for the scratched puce-green on the hood, was primer gray.

"So, let me guess. Like the hotel, all the good cars are rented, too?" She glanced inside. Most of the seat padding on the passenger side was gone and what little was left billowed out like dirty hunks of cotton. Through a hole in the floorboard, also on the passenger side, she could see the asphalt.

He shrugged, palms up. "I kind of like it. Reminds me of my first car."

He smiled again, only this time she detected a bit of smugness.

"You want to reconsider?"

Did he think a little discomfort would make her quit? "Not a chance." She grabbed the door, swung it open and was about to chuck her suitcase into the back when she saw the back was already full. She gestured to one of the items, a large box. "What's that?"

"Some stuff I picked up. We'll have to put your luggage in the trunk so I can see out the rear window." He grabbed her bag, went to the front of the VW and pulled up on the hood to the trunk, then tossed her suitcase inside. Unable to close the hood tightly, he finally took a rope and tied it down.

So be it. She climbed into her seat and, straddling the hole with her feet, searched for the seat belt. *Nada.* She should've figured as much. Well…it wasn't likely they'd be going more than a few miles per hour, anyway—if the relic even started.

She shored up her reserves. "I'm ready whenever you are."

Standing squarely in front of the car, he glared at her, then came around, yanked open the driver's door and crammed his big body into the tiny car. She felt a moment of pity. Obviously he wouldn't have rented the sardine can if he'd had any other choice.

Maybe he really *was* thinking of her when he said she'd be more comfortable back at the hotel. But dammit, if he could handle it, so could she. "I'm also ready for that coffee."

He turned the key and got only a grinding sound.

After another attempt, the engine sputtered to life. "The thermos is in the bag in the back, along with some cups and rolls and things."

Junk food. She almost made a face. But her appetite had grown since she'd arrived here. She'd always heard that appetites were suppressed when temperatures rose, but obviously not so for her. "Thanks. I'm starved."

She reached around and pulled a grocery bag onto her lap. Inside she found the thermos and two thermal cups. She wondered if he'd brought them along or purchased them this morning. "Would you like me to pour a cup for you, too?"

He shook his head. "I've had my fill already. You be the navigator and man the map, okay? I circled where we are, where we're going and the roads involved. Just let me know when the next turn is coming up."

"Okay."

He waited until she poured the coffee and screwed the lid back on, then he shifted into First and the car lurched forward. She stashed the cup between her legs, reached for the map he'd placed on the dash in front of her, shook it out and laid it on her lap. Then she rummaged through the grocery bag to see what fat-laden sustenance he'd chosen.

Powdered-sugar doughnuts. She set those on the dashboard where the map had been. A package of sweet rolls with different jelly fillings and white frosting. She took a deep breath. Okay. Doughnuts or sweet rolls. *Bleah.*

He cranked the steering wheel and veered around a

corner as she clutched the bag against her chest and, feeling something weighty inside, dived back into it. This time she pulled out a bunch of bananas and a clear plastic bag with a few other fruits inside, ones she didn't recognize. "Hey, fruit. Great choice." She offered him a banana.

"No, thanks. They're all yours."

"Really? How…nice of you." It was. That he'd thought about her preferences at all gave her a warm feeling inside.

"I think you'd better take a look at the map and let me know if we're getting close to the road that goes to Mirador. That street back there looked familiar."

She shifted the grocery bag from her lap to the back seat, since she didn't want it to disappear down the hole between her feet, and then looked at the map. "We turn in about three inches."

"Oh, man. Now I know I'm in trouble."

"Just kidding. It's about three miles before we turn left, then we take a right, and after that another left, and then we're on the road to Mirador." She gave him a satisfied smile. "'The road to Mirador.' Sounds like an old movie, doesn't it?"

"Thanks," he said, ignoring her attempt at humor.

He didn't sound thankful at all. He sounded cranky and annoyed, and she supposed she knew why. He didn't want her along. But if he didn't want her along, why did he buy the fruit and let her think he was being thoughtful?

She was getting mixed messages. How was she supposed to take him? Well, it didn't really matter, she decided, as long as he got her where she wanted to go.

She had to focus on that. If she could. Focusing had always been an effort for her. She was too easily led astray by other interests and ideas. With her business, however, she'd managed the necessary tunnel vision and then forged successfully ahead.

This was no different. She needed to narrow her scope—stop thinking about Mr. Detective RoboCop and concentrate on her mission. His being along for the ride made no difference. She peeled a banana and, while eating it, took mental inventory of her Mirador to-do list and centered her thoughts on that.

While she was busy narrowing her scope, the road had narrowed, as well. After a few more turns, they were out of town and the paved road was crisscrossed with ruts and dotted with potholes, and the farther they drove, the worse it got.

Fifteen minutes later, the road turned into a four-foot gravel path that looked as if it'd been cut through the jungle by machete. The car dipped into a hole. She flew upward then slammed back down on her tailbone.

"Ouch! Oh, jeez." It hurt like hell. She reached around to cushion the jolts with her hand, but all she succeeded in doing was mashing her fingers. She adjusted herself so she wasn't sitting on the part that was sore, which then faced her toward Adam.

RoboCop just kept on driving, and the car dipped and twisted right along with the road. "What happened to the halfway-decent road we were on?"

He turned his I-told-you-so steely gaze on her. "Want to go back?"

She glanced around, as if looking for someone else, then came back to him. "Are you talking to me? I don't recall saying anything about going back. In fact, I thought I asked what happened to the better road."

"So you did. Well, it went the way of all good roads when they head off into the jungle."

"The jungle?"

"The rain forest. Which is just another word for jungle. Lots of trees, vines, animals, birds, reptiles, snakes and bugs, and the deeper in we go, the worse the roads and everything else gets."

"So, it's a good thing we don't have that far to go," she said, forcing some perkiness to her voice.

He gave a hearty laugh. "That's one way to look at it."

"It's the best way. If there are two or more ways to look at something, why not take the way that makes you feel better?"

"If you can manage that, more power to you. In my business, it pays to be realistic. People get hurt if I'm not."

She thought for a moment. "Okay. I can understand that. But your business isn't your whole life."

"Wrong. My business *is* my life. I forgot that once and I didn't like what happened."

She wondered what he meant, then guessed he'd been hurt by someone—no, not just any someone—probably a woman he'd cared about. That would explain his expressed aversion to relationships or marriage.

They drove a long time in silence, during which the car bumped and lurched almost nonstop. As the day wore on, the heat intensified, and the cloying sweetness of exotic flowers, some of which looked like orchids, made her nose and eyes itch. She was hot and sweaty, her clothes were damp, and she was pretty sure her hair was frizzy beyond recognition.

"How much farther do you think it is?" she ventured about three hours into the trip. "Maybe we should stop and stretch our legs. And if we can find something to cover this hole, I'd be really happy. It's uncomfortable sitting like this, and I'm afraid we're going to hit a bump and I'll accidentally poke a foot through and lose it."

He frowned. "You're right. I should have thought of covering that first thing. I don't know what I was thinking."

She couldn't tell if the remark was one of regret or sarcasm, but preferred the former.

"It's no big deal," she said.

The road was so narrow there was no place to pull over, so they stopped in the middle. Since they hadn't passed another car in all the time they'd been driving, it didn't seem to matter where they stopped. She reached to open the door, but he stopped her with a hand on her arm.

"Wait." He reached behind the seat, pulled out a sack, then dropped a pair of knee-high rubber boots into her lap. "You better put these on first." He reached into a bag and pulled out a plastic bottle. "And put some of this on, too."

"All that just to stretch our legs?"

"Just do it."

She glanced at the bottle. "What is it and why the boots?"

"Heavy-duty mosquito repellent, and the boots are for protection from the snakes. Be careful where you step when you get out."

He opened his door, stuck out one leg at a time and pulled on his own boots. Then he slathered the pungent repellent on his arms and face and, after handing her the bottle, unfolded himself from the VW.

She followed suit, making a face at the acrid scent, hoping it would fade after a few minutes. When finished, she repeated her question, "How much longer do you think it'll take to get there?" Her bladder felt ready to explode. "I think I drank too much coffee."

As she walked around to his side of the car, he stretched his arms above his head and planted his feet apart.

"If the rest of the road is like this, it's going to be a while. I'm just hoping we make it before dinner."

"You're joking, right?"

He shrugged.

He'd said earlier that they wouldn't get back to San José tonight, but she'd had no idea the trip itself would take the whole day. "Well, I definitely can't wait that long."

He studied the landscape. "There are plenty of trees. Think I'll find one myself."

Oh, sure. Easy for him. She cast about for an opening that didn't have multiple layers of thick brush or leaves the size of her living room, and where who knows what might be lurking underneath. At least *he* could stand up.

She went one direction and he went another.

"Watch out for those poison dart frogs, too," he called out.

"Oh, God," she mumbled to herself as she searched for a good spot, yet staying within eyesight of their vehicle, all the while checking for living, breathing, crawling things.

Finding an opening in the bush, she unzipped, and in the forest with the car's engine no longer droning in her ears, the jungle was alive with sounds.

Birds cawed and warbled, crickets made their insistent high-pitched hum, and leaves rustled above her. She looked up to see a bright green parrot and what looked like several parakeets fluttering from limb to limb. A shrill screech rent the air.

She jerked to her feet, nearly falling as she tried to stand and yank up her shorts and panties at the same time. She caught herself by grabbing a tree behind her and immediately felt something soft—and alive—under her hand.

Heart pounding, she jerked her hand back. The tree she'd grabbed was covered with dozens of little brown knots. When she looked closer, she saw they were bats and shuddered with revulsion.

With her breath coming in great gasps, one hand still struggling to fasten her shorts, she sprinted back to the car, swiping aside leaves and branches as she went.

Out of breath when she got there, she noticed that Adam hadn't returned. Her gaze darted about. Something felt different.

She looked up at the tangled canopy of trees above

her, so thick the sunlight barely pierced through. At once the forest seemed dark and ominous, and she had the weirdest sensation—as if someone was watching her.

A shiver crawled up her spine.

That was ridiculous. They hadn't seen a soul on the road since they left San José. She leaned against the car to wait. If she didn't move, she might not feel as hot.

She swiped her hair away from her face with the back of her hand, then checked her watch. A few minutes later, she checked it again. And ten minutes later, he still hadn't returned.

"Adam?" she called. Jeez, she hoped he was all right. "A-A-dam?"

Nothing. What could've happened to him?

It was silly to start imagining the worst, but she was definitely thinking he might've been right. She should've stayed in San José.

A rustling sound behind her made her jump. She swung around, her heart thudding double-time. Between the birds and some other screeching sounds, monkeys no doubt, she heard more rustling, and then…a heavy growl.

CHAPTER SIX

ADAM SLASHED OFF A LARGE hunk of thready bark from the tree with his hunting knife. It was the only thing he'd found that had any substance. He hitched the bark under his arm and then hacked off another piece for good measure. If he layered the bark, it would cover the hole and be too big to fall through.

The forest floor was thick with ferns and masses of roots and flowers, so he'd marked his way and all he had to do now was follow his own trail back to the car.

As he neared the Volkswagen, he saw that Jillian was sitting inside, knees pulled to her chest and her arms wrapped around them. The windows were all rolled up.

When he approached her window and rapped on it, she jumped a good six inches.

Her face was crimson, sweat beaded on her upper lip and forehead, and her hair looked like Little Orphan Annie's. She wound down the window.

"Isn't it a little hot with the windows shut?" he asked.

"I heard something making noise over there—" she pointed "—and then it growled and snarled. I didn't feel like being dinner."

"Did you see what it was?"

"No, and I'm glad I didn't. I thought I heard mewing, too, like kittens."

"Hmm. Could be a momma jaguar and her young."

"You mean, jaguar as in the large-cat species? As in lions and tigers and—"

"Since we're not talking about a car, yes, that's the kind I mean. Could be that or an ocelot. Maybe a mother just being protective."

A look of horror crossed her features. When that passed, she cleared her throat. "Well, if we're going to make it to Mirador by nightfall, maybe we should get going as soon as possible?"

"Right." He sauntered around to the driver's side, chucked the bark on the floor at her feet and climbed inside. "See if that'll keep your feet from going through."

She glanced down. "What is it?"

"Bark from a tree."

"Really?" She stomped on it, first with one foot, then both. A wide grin erupted. "Perfect."

"Good. Now, let's get this show on the road."

He avoided looking at her, because now she had one of those warm smiles on her face, as if he'd done something nice. He started the car, shoved the gearshift into Drive and they were off.

"It won't hurt the tree, will it?"

He glanced over. "What?"

"Won't removing the bark damage the tree?"

He rolled his eyes. "Take a look around. See all those trees with prominent orange roots? That's the milk tree, also known as the cow tree. People have used it for many purposes for hundreds of years.''

Her brows shot up. ''Really? What did they use it for?''

With all her questions, the woman was worse than his nieces and nephews. ''They peeled off the reedy bark and pounded it out to make blankets, they drank the milky liquid produced inside the tree and ate the fruit. And the tree population hasn't suffered at all.''

''Ah, so that's why it's called a milk tree.'' Her blue eyes rounded. ''How come you know so much about it?''

He sighed. ''I was here before, remember?''

''Mmm, that's right. You've forgotten who you were with.''

''Well, that isn't quite true. I was here with my ex-wife, someone I prefer to forget.''

''Oh.'' She seemed surprised. ''Well, thanks for fixing the hole for me. That was nice of you.''

Yeah, he was one helluva nice guy. Except that nice guys didn't use people, even if it was for the greater good.

''It was nothing. Believe me.''

THE CAR BUMPED ALONG at a snail's pace. They could've made better time on foot, but finally, the road evened out and they picked up a little speed. They were closing in on Mirador, she was sure of it.

Adam hadn't said two words since they'd made their potty stop and his attention seemed totally focused on the road. That, or maybe something she'd said was bothering him. Maybe it was her question about him being here before.

He'd made it clear that the subject of his marriage was off-limits, so she hadn't pursued it. But it made her sad that he'd shut himself off like that. It wasn't good to be so alone. Just because one relationship hadn't worked out didn't mean another wouldn't.

Or maybe it was just that he didn't want to get close to *her*. She might've thought so if some of the things he'd done hadn't contradicted that.

In her book, actions spoke louder than words—and Adam's actions, the scowl on his face now notwithstanding, said he liked her. He liked her whether he wanted to admit it or not.

And she liked him, too.

Maybe he was just worried about what they'd find. Lord knows, she was. Her stomach fluttered at the thought. They were almost there, ready to face the imposter—if he was an imposter.

He had to be. She couldn't imagine any other scenario. Well, yes, she could, but every time she did, it made her feel ill and she shoved it from her mind. All she wanted to do was get this over with and go back to the comfort of her home in the suburbs—a place where families lived quiet, responsible lives and people didn't go off searching Central American jungles for crooks and imposters.

Or a dead husband who might not be dead. She didn't know whether to wish for it or hope it wasn't so. But the more she thought about it, the more confused she became. If somehow Rob was alive and didn't know who he was, wouldn't that be good for all of them? Especially Chloe, who really needed a father. Now more than ever.

Whenever she thought about Chloe and home, she was filled with warmth and happiness. Despite being at odds on occasion, she and Chloe managed quite well together. If Rob were miraculously to turn up alive, what would happen to the comfortable world they'd built?

Would he like it that she'd moved to Chicago and had a full-blown career? He'd insisted she work only part-time, but that was because Chloe was a baby and needed her mother at home. Would he like that she'd made many friends in the community? Would he like her best friends, Dana and Logan and Patti?

He hadn't encouraged her friendships with anyone she'd met at hairstyling school, she remembered. And more than once when she'd invited a friend over for dinner, she'd had to cancel. She didn't remember the reasons, just that there had always been one.

But regardless of the little glitches, which all marriages had, they'd had a good life together. Rob was the most caring person she'd ever known.

Adam, she realized, was that kind of person, too. His actions, however at odds with his words, were those of a caring person. He'd been thoughtful enough to buy her fruit for breakfast, he'd brought along a thermos of coffee for her, even when he'd had his fill. He'd taken her to a nice restaurant, instead of a dive, and he'd fixed the hole in the car for her.

He hadn't been forced to do any of that. And knowing he really didn't even want her along, the nice things he did seemed even more significant.

Yes, most assuredly, he was a different person from the one he made himself out to be.

"There, look ahead," Adam said, breaking into her reverie.

Alongside the road was a cabin, made from wooden slats and held well above the ground on stilts. "Dare I hope we're getting close to civilization?" she said. "A shower. And food. Oh, my, I just realized I'm starving."

He laughed. "Don't get your hopes up. It's Mirador, not Chicago. It's not even San José." He glanced over. "And how can you be starving? You ate all that fruit single-handedly. You even broke down and ate a couple of the sweet rolls."

"You said you didn't want any of the fruit."

"Yeah. I need something more substantial," he groused. "Meat. Protein."

"Junk food."

"That, too."

"You think we'll find it here?"

"Maybe. But the only thing I really care about is finding our man."

Right. That was why he was there. Why they were both there. And she'd be wise not to forget it. "I want that, too, so my life can return to normal."

He kept his eyes on the road and made no comment. But she knew what he was probably thinking. If he was right about the man they were looking for, her life might never be normal again.

It was true. If Rob was alive, her whole life would change. Still, not knowing was even worse.

As they drove on, the night descended, bringing

with it swarms of flying bugs that hit the windshield with tiny popping sounds and smeared the glass so much they could barely see the road. She'd expected mosquitoes, but never imagined the hordes of other insects.

A shiver of revulsion swept through her. She hated bugs.

A half hour later, they rolled into a town that she hoped wasn't Mirador. A few tumbledown stores fronted the road they were on and, behind those, a cluster of shacks with tin roofs.

"What's with the stilts some of them are perched on?" she asked.

"It rains a lot," Adam replied tersely. He let out a long breath. "Well, I think this is it."

Jillian cast about for more buildings, but there were none. Her hopes sank. "This can't be Mirador. It doesn't look like there's anyplace to stay. Maybe this is just the outskirts and we haven't hit the real town yet. Maybe there are more commercial buildings ahead."

He snorted and shook his head. "You think we're in suburbia?"

"You know what I mean." She smacked his arm.

"I hope you're right. But don't count on it." Adam pulled up to a house painted in bright parrot colors, red, blue and yellow. A neon *cerveza* sign flashed in the window.

It appeared to be a small bar or restaurant of some kind. She sniffed the air. "Mmm. Smell that. It smells like a backyard barbecue. Steak on the grill. My mouth is watering already."

"It's probably monkey meat."

She wrinkled her nose. "Well, whatever it is, it smells delicious. And at least we know they serve *something*."

"I'll check. Maybe we can get a few questions answered."

She started to get out of the car when he did, but he stopped her. "Maybe you should wait here with our gear."

She glanced up and down the vacant street. "Are you worried someone's going to rip us off? There's not a soul around."

He cast a glance behind her and inclined his head slightly. "Oh, they're around," he murmured, then scratched his chin, which now sported a five-o'clock shadow that was darker than his sandy hair. "On second thought, you better come with me."

He looked worried, though she didn't know why. "I'm fine either way. Do you know something I don't?"

"Just chalk it up to experience and say I'm cautious."

"Maybe overcautious? This isn't L.A., either, you know."

"That's what scares me. C'mon, let's go inside. I'll keep one eye on the car."

He waited until she reached his side, then guided her up the wooden steps with a hand at the small of her back. When they entered the establishment, he pulled her closer.

While the scent of food activated certain glands, the touch of his hand, separated from her skin by only the thin cotton of her top, activated something else entirely. It was the same thing that had been activated the first time she'd ever seen him, that morning at the market, the same thing that had shivered through her last night when he'd taken her to her room at the hotel and suggested she might be in danger if he stayed any longer. Desire, pure and simple and powerful. And in the face of it, all her careful considerations and good sense could fade faster than fog in the sunshine.

As they went inside, a man appeared from behind a bright red-and-yellow floral-printed curtain. The room didn't look like a restaurant, but set near the front window were two small tables, one with four chairs and the other with two. Each was covered in a red-checked tablecloth.

"*¿Habla, usted Inglés?*" Adam asked the man.

He shook his head. "No. No *Inglés.*"

At that, they entered into rapid-fire conversation in Spanish, and the only words Jillian recognized were *hotel, food*—and *Corita Sullivan.* When they finished talking, Adam smiled, thanked the man and then motioned at the tables. "Let's sit down. It's dinnertime."

"Great. I'm starved."

"There's no menu—we get what they have."

"Whatever they're cooking is okay with me, monkey meat or not," she said, and as if on cue, her stomach rumbled.

Adam pulled out a chair for her and took the seat opposite. He adjusted his chair so his back was toward the kitchen, which she presumed allowed him to watch the car.

"Don't expect a banquet," he said. "Ticos typically

eat their main meal at midday and a lighter one in the evening, usually soup and toast.''

"Ticos?''

"From Tiquismos, an expression peculiar to the Costa Rican culture. It's how the natives refer to themselves.''

The man came out from behind the curtain again and, grinning hugely, said, *"Sopa de mondongo. Muy bueno.''*

"He says the soup is good.''

"I know. That much I can understand.''

Then the man asked if they wanted anything to drink. That, too, she understood.

"Dos cerveza,'' Adam held up two fingers to the man before turning to Jillian. "Hope you're up for beer. Our friend here said they have no bottled water or soda.''

"Beer is fine and soup sounds delicious.''

Adam's eyes glinted. "Tell me that later.''

After the man brought the beer, she leaned toward him, lowered her voice and asked, "Why did you ask about the woman and not the man you're looking for?''

"If she's from this area, someone might know where she lives, even if they don't know anything about her husband.''

"And if you find her, you might also find her husband,'' she concluded.

"Right.'' He picked up his beer and saluted her. "To a successful mission.''

Jillian had to remind herself again that was why she was there. That she found Adam Ramsey attractive and sexy had nothing to do with anything. Besides, maybe the only reason he excited her hormones was that she'd been celibate for too long; maybe a touch from any attractive man might do the same. Even the urge to leap over the table and kiss his strong, sensual mouth could be attributed to her deprivation.

In fact, everything she was feeling could be easily explained away.

Still, she could almost hear Dana's voice in her ear. *Do something wild and crazy. Indulge yourself.* Yeah, easy for her friend to say. Not so easy for someone who'd been with only one man her whole life.

Or was it?

Wasn't she the girl who'd struck out on her own at fifteen? Hadn't she thrown caution to the wind and moved with her seven-year-old daughter from L.A. to Chicago without knowing a soul—except a mother-in-law who'd once thought she wasn't good enough for her son? Hadn't she disregarded the naysayers when she'd started her business on a shoestring? And then through hard work and determination, had expanded one store into a profitable chain?

Hell, she was used to wild and crazy—at least when her survival depended on it.

But the urges she was having now had little to do with survival. They had to do with desire and the long-time absence of a physical relationship with a man.

Oh, she'd had platonic relationships with men, such as Keith, her best hairstylist, and a couple of local businessmen who worked near the First Mane Event and with whom she'd become friends. She was comfortable with that.

But her feelings for Adam were definitely not platonic. So why not take Dana's suggestion? Why not indulge herself? Have a fling.

Because a fling is all it could ever be with a man like Adam, who believed marriage and family weren't for him. A man who lived in L.A. for God's sake!

But since she understood all that and was okay with it…why not?

Provided, of course, he was interested.

ADAM, STILL KEEPING a vigilant eye on the car, knew the need for caution. During the 1990s, the area between Puerto Viejo de Talamanca and Cahuita had been a major port for drug runners from Latin America smuggling cocaine into the U.S. It was also one of the routes for smuggling black heroin, which was likely the reason Jack Sullivan had chosen a town nearby for his place of residence.

According to the man who'd rented him the car, the area was now rife with bandits and kidnappers looking for rich American tourists whose families might pay exorbitant ransoms to get their loved ones back. Another reason for taking the tackiest car the guy had— he'd never be mistaken for a *rich* tourist. The rental man had also recommended traveling only during the day, since night travel was especially dangerous.

"Ah, here's the food." Adam watched Jillian as their server placed the soup in front of her. When she snatched up her spoon with a ravenous look in her eyes, he said, "Remember, if you don't eat it, he'll be insulted."

"Well, I'm starving, so there's no need to worry. What's in it? Do you know?"

"Tripe."

The spoon slipped from her fingers into the bowl. "Like real tripe?"

He nodded. "Ever had *Menudo?*"

She shook her head.

"Really? I'm surprised since you lived in California. *Menudo* is the Mexican version of that—" he pointed to her bowl "—and it's great for a hangover."

Adam heard the murmur of voices, male and female, coming from behind the curtain. He couldn't make out much of what they were saying, but heard the name Corita. He reached into his pocket for the photos. Maybe someone could identify Corita Sullivan from the photo.

A dark-haired, middle-aged woman stepped into the room from behind the curtain. Adam got to his feet and crossed to her.

"Buenas noches," Adam said, and quickly explained to the woman that Corita Sullivan had written him a letter because she was ill and needed someone to take care of her son. If he could find her, Adam said, he could help. He showed the woman the photos.

The woman shook her head, then asked who Jillian was. Hoping to avoid further explanation about either of them, he replied that she was the boy's aunt and was there to help. It worked, because the woman said she didn't know about the boy but told them where the hospital was located. Adam thanked her profusely.

Adam returned to the table with Jillian again. "Well, you were right. We're about six miles or so from the town of Mirador, and that's where the hospital is. Apparently the hospital isn't open to visitors after seven, so we can stay in Mirador tonight and check with the hospital in the morning.''

"Fine with me. I wouldn't mind a shower and a nice clean bed.''

"How was the soup?''

She made a face. "I think it's one of those things that you like if you grew up with it, but otherwise…'' She shook her head.

He reached for his soup and took a spoonful.

"Maybe the woman will still be at the hospital,'' Jillian said. "And tonight at the hotel, we can check the directory for addresses, too.''

"Right.'' Though, he was sure finding Sullivan was going to be a bit more difficult than that. Still, they were getting closer all the time, and when he got his man, he'd go back to L.A., and Jillian would go back to Chicago where she belonged.

He felt a stab of regret. As much as he hated to admit it, he liked being with her. She was easy to be around, and she never complained. In fact, just the opposite, sometimes irritatingly so.

He doubted she'd be that cheery once they found Sullivan, though. She'd soon realize her husband wasn't the saint she thought he was, and she'd be crushed. The thought grated.

He didn't like to see anyone get hurt, and he especially didn't want to see it happen to Jillian. Unfortunately he couldn't do a damn thing about it.

When they finished, Adam left some *colones* on the table to pay for their food, and then they were on the road again. Six miles later, they rolled into Mirador. A rather quaint town, it had narrow cobblestone streets and sidewalk stores and cafés. He glanced over at her. Her hair was frizzy and her face flushed from the heat. She looked tired. And beautiful.

She yawned. "I hope we can find a decent place to stay here. I'm—" Suddenly her eyes sparkled with excitement and she smiled. "Listen!"

Marimba music was playing somewhere nearby.

She sat up straighter. "Oh, and look!" She pointed to some brightly colored pottery, baskets and rugs on display in front of several small stores. Her excitement bubbled up like a kid in Disneyland. He smiled, too.

As they drove farther into town, the streets came alive with people walking, shopping, chatting. Some locals stared at them in the beat-up VW, and others ignored them completely. Adam had to swerve to miss a pair of dogs that looked as if it had been a while since their last meal. But he didn't see any hotels. There had to be a *pensión* of some kind.

"I don't see anyplace to stay, do you?" Jillian leaned forward to look out the front window.

He was tempted to say that she should've stayed in San José as he'd suggested, but looking at her, he decided against it. Besides, he couldn't take her back now even if he wanted to. They were too close.

He was too close to getting his man.

He took a breath and another glance at Jillian, all expectant and eager to prove him wrong. She truly believed the man she married would never betray her.

His gut knotted. He got angry every time he thought about it. Even though marriage wasn't for him, he respected the institution. If a man entered into it, he had a responsibility to make it work. And if he was married to a woman like Jillian...

Hell, he didn't want to think about that, either.

Irritated at himself for finding her so appealing, he wheeled into a spot along the street and parked. He should've learned his lesson with Kate. But apparently he hadn't.

Regardless, he had no business thinking like that, especially not with a woman whose husband he planned to take out of commission for the rest of his life. He climbed out of the car, saying, "You stay here. I'm going to ask if anyone knows where there's a place to stay."

CHAPTER SEVEN

"THERE'S THE SIGN. *Pensión*. Right?" Jillian peered out the window. The place they'd been looking for was two blocks off the main drag, and it looked like someone's private home.

Adam parked in front of the small white structure. "Let's check it out."

They exited the car, locked it and walked to the door together. Greeted by a cheerful man by the name of Alfredo with silver-gray hair and deep crinkles around his eyes, they discovered that, yes, he rented out rooms, and they were cheap, too.

Adam paid Alfredo, who handed him a key and said, *"Gracias, Señor Ramsey."* He nodded to Jillian. *"Señora Ramsey."*

Jillian was about to set him straight, but Adam quickly took her by the arm and led her outside to the car.

"You told him we're married?"

"All he has is one room, and I didn't want to take the chance that he wouldn't rent it to us if we weren't married. I don't want to spend the night hunting for other accommodations and maybe end up having to sleep in the car."

She didn't like the alternatives, either. She was tired

and sweaty and thirsty. "Okay. Where do we go? Where's the room?"

"Around back. It has running water, a toilet and a bed. That's all I know." As he spoke, he guided her around the building.

She swatted at the insects buzzing her face. "That's good enough for me. Can we get something to drink, too?"

"The owner is bringing towels and drinks."

The room was a tiny separate building about ten yards behind the man's own home. It was smaller than a single-car garage, but had running water, a place to sleep and a bathroom. What more could she want?

They went inside and flicked on the light—a low-wattage bulb hanging in one corner by the bed. Jillian quickly shut the door so the bugs wouldn't get in.

The bed was supposed to be a double, but looked more like a twin. Hanging above it was a cheesecloth-like contraption dangling from a hook in the ceiling—mosquito netting, Adam said—and beside the bed, a nightstand. The only thing separating the toilet and makeshift shower from the bedroom was a thin curtain. There was little room to even turn around in, much less change clothes.

And how *would* they shower and change if a degree of modesty was to be maintained? Standing at the end of the bed, she crossed her arms and stared at him.

He shrugged. "Hey, I warned you that you'd be better off staying in San José."

She bit her bottom lip and eyed the narrow bed again. "I didn't say a thing. I think it's fine." She waited a beat before she said, "So. Where are *you* going to sleep?"

Without a moment's hesitation, he pointed to the side of the bed nearest the door. "Right there, lady." He walked to one of the windows and threw open the shutters. "Good, there's a screen. That means we'll have a little air." He did the same with the other one. "Ah, cross ventilation. Perfect. Provided there's a breeze."

O-kay. She took another look around. It wasn't that bad. She could adjust. She'd certainly done her share of adjusting in her thirty-two years.

She'd managed fine with the less-than-stellar room in San José, the wreck of a car they were driving, the bad roads, the nasty insects, jungle cats and the *mondo…mondo*—whatever you call it—tripe soup. Primitive accommodations for one night was nothing.

It was sleeping with the enemy that bothered her.

Or was he the enemy? His desire to solve her husband's murder didn't bother her, of course. But his belief that her husband was guilty of something illegal did. Then again, she couldn't really blame him. He didn't know Rob. He only knew what he'd read in the police files, and then he'd seen the photo. He had no reason to believe anything different.

But *she* knew Rob, and Adam would know soon enough. She just hoped she was right.

"Okay. Here's the plan," Adam said as he tossed a small duffel bag onto the bed. "I'm going to pull the car around and bring in the rest of the luggage. You can shower or do whatever you need to do while I'm gone."

She said she'd need ten minutes, so he could come back then. As soon as he left, she undressed and stepped into the coffin-size shower. She felt instant claustrophobia. Still, the cool water was like a caress, and if she closed her eyes, she could pretend she was under a tropical waterfall somewhere—and that Adam was there with her.

She smiled at the thought, no longer surprised she flirted with such ideas. She couldn't help but notice his finely honed muscles, and for a big guy, how gracefully he moved.

Abruptly she realized her shampoo was with the rest of her gear in the car, so she quickly scrubbed off using the bar of soap for both body and hair. She'd have a tangled mess when it dried, but so what. Her ten minutes were about done, but the water felt so good, she didn't want to get out.

She heard a knock. *Adam.* "I'll be out in a minute," she called, turning off the faucets.

Though he hadn't answered her, she now heard rustling in the room and knew he was there. Pulling the door curtain across her body, she peered out to say she'd be only a moment. That was when she saw a man leaning over the bed and rummaging through her small backpack. And it wasn't Adam.

Omigod! She stopped breathing completely, because if this burglar heard her, who knows what he might do. He tossed her backpack aside and grabbed the small duffel bag Adam had left on the bed.

What if he had a gun? Or a knife? Jeez. Where was Adam? Had the burglar knocked him out? Or... Oh, God. She couldn't even think it.

Her heart crashing against her ribs, she silently lowered the curtain and flattened herself against the wall beside the commode. She held her breath and closed her eyes, hoping against hope that the intruder would simply take what he wanted and go. Nothing she owned was important enough to lose her life over and leave her daughter orphaned.

Chest heaving, she heard a click and then a door closing. After what seemed eons, she craned her neck to peer out again. The burglar was gone.

Just then the door flew open. Adam bounded inside with their two suitcases and dropped them to the floor with a thunk. Heart still hammering, she blurted, "Did you see that man?"

He spun to face her. "Man? You mean Alfredo?" His gaze traveled from her dripping wet hair to her toes. She clutched the curtain tighter around her.

"No...no," she sputtered. "A man, a stranger, was in here and he went through our stuff. My backpack. God only knows what he took."

"When?"

"Just seconds before you returned. You must've seen him!"

Almost before the words left her lips, Adam was out the door, but just as quickly he came back and tossed her a towel. "Lock the door after me."

She caught the towel to her chest.

"You should've locked it the first time," he barked on his way out.

He was right. Wrapping the towel around her, she did as asked. Minutes later, Adam was back again.

"No one's out there. Whoever it was knows the

area and knows where and how to disappear. He probably does this all the time.''

She moved to the bed. ''I was just going to see what he took.''

He closed and locked the door and stood with his back against it. ''So, check.'' Once again his gaze flicked over her.

She hiked up the towel and sidled toward the bed. Not wanting to bend over, she sat down by her backpack and what used to be its contents. ''Should we get Alfredo to call the police?''

''Not until we know why we're calling.''

She checked her wallet and found that her identification, money, business cards and passport were still there. ''Odd. Nothing's missing.'' She looked up.

He frowned, then sat down next to her and started going through his duffel bag.

''You sure?''

''Uh-huh. Did he take anything of yours?''

He pulled some small metallic thing from his bag and gripped it tightly in his hand, his shoulders relaxing as if in relief. ''Nope. Everything's here.''

His leg touched hers and her stomach fluttered. From fear or his nearness she didn't know which. ''What do you suppose he was looking for? Drugs?''

''I doubt it. If he was, he'd certainly have taken the money.''

He leaned behind her to reexamine the pile of personal items on the bed, his movement such that he had to place a hand on her upper arm for balance. His hand was warm, and the feeling of it sent a jolt of electricity through her. He stopped midlean, his head next to hers, his mouth near her ear. She heard him draw in a deep breath, as if savoring the scent of her.

She closed her eyes. She wanted him to kiss her. Wanted it badly.

"Did he see you?" he asked softly.

She opened her eyes. "No, I was in the shower when he came in, so I guess he thought I wouldn't hear him.

Another knock startled both of them. "Who's there?" Adam almost growled.

"Alfredo." Then he rattled off something else in rapid Spanish.

"Uno momento," Adam said. Jamming a hand through his hair, he got up and went to the door. Alfredo was carrying a tray with two glasses filled with a red liquid of some kind.

He saw Jillian's state of undress and averted his gaze. Then she saw him raise his eyebrows and smile knowingly at Adam as he placed the tray on the nightstand. Adam handed him some *colones* and he left.

"You didn't ask him about the burglar."

Adam became impersonal again. "The guy didn't take anything, so it's no big deal."

Self-conscious sitting there in a towel and irritated that she was so easily affected by him, she said, more firmly than she'd wanted, "I don't agree. Maybe having someone rummage through your things is an everyday occurrence, but it isn't for me."

"So what would you like me to do? If I bring it to Alfredo's attention and he calls the police, we'll have to wait for them. They won't come till tomorrow, and we won't get started when we want to in the morning.

In addition, there was no break-in, no robbery. Nothing can be done—believe me, I know.''

''I hadn't thought about that.''

He rubbed his chin. ''I'll tell Alfredo in the morning before we go. At least he'll be aware of what happened and can keep watch when he has other guests. Will that make you happy?''

''I guess.'' She shrugged.

''Okay, my turn for the shower, but you're going to have to stay inside. Treat yourself to one of these fruit drinks. They're refreshing.''

Fine with her. Once he was in the shower, she found her nightshirt, slipped it on along with a pair of cotton panties, then placed her silver hoop earrings on the table by the window where Adam had placed some change and things from his pocket. One looked like a medal of some kind.

She picked it up. A Medal of Valor. She remembered that after the terrorist attacks on the World Trade Center, which seemed so long ago now, several officers had received the award for bravery. She'd known then that not all police officers were like her father.

That Adam had received a medal like that for an act of bravery didn't surprise her. But that he carried it with him did. Whatever he'd received it for must've been terribly important to him.

Hearing the water shut off, she quickly took the blanket, which they surely didn't need, rolled it into a tube and arranged it as a barrier down the middle of the bed. She crawled under the sheet on *her* side and was sitting up drinking the fruit punch when Adam came out of the shower.

His hair, wet and slicked back, looked darker. The towel was hitched around his hips, and she had difficulty dragging her gaze away.

"I've got to drop this towel and put something on," he said. "You can either close your eyes or you can watch." He grinned. "I'm okay with either."

She quickly shut her eyes, mostly because she was embarrassed. Embarrassed because she wanted to watch and he probably knew it.

Seconds later he said "Okay. You're safe now."

He was wearing a pair of cutoff sweatpants that hung low on his hips and didn't cover any more than the towel had. Suddenly she found it hard to breathe.

When he crawled into bed beside her, the mattress dipped severely. She had to catch herself to keep from rolling into him.

Getting comfortable in a sitting position, he said, "What the devil?" He flipped up the sheet, then burst into hearty laughter.

"What's so funny?"

He stopped laughing long enough to say, "If I was interested, do you think that scrap of cloth would stop me?"

Heat scored her cheeks.

He chuckled while reaching for his drink from the nightstand. The affectionate smile he bestowed on her caught her off guard. "You're too much, blue eyes, you know that?"

Desire inhabited her body. Could a person be mortified and turned on at the same time? If not, this was a first.

He set his drink down, then lowered the white mosquito netting around them, said good-night and flipped off the light.

ADAM AWOKE FIRST TO FIND Jillian spooned against him, her tangled curls spread out on the pillow. Despite the man rummaging through their stuff last night and his concern about what awaited them here, he hadn't slept so well since his partner was murdered and his marriage had ended.

Now, leaning on one elbow, he watched her sleep. Just looking at her pulled at his insides and sent his pulse into overdrive. He passed a hand over the sheet along the length of her, letting his mind do the touching. Then he picked up a lock of her hair and curled it around a finger. It was just as silky soft as he'd imagined.

But then, he'd imagined far too many things, and if he didn't move away from her now, she was going to know exactly what was on his mind.

He sent his thoughts in another direction—to the man who'd been in the room last night. What would anyone be looking for if it wasn't money or drugs?

Since they'd been asking about Corita Sullivan, it was logical to think there was a connection. Someone wanted to know why they were interested. And who, other than Jack Sullivan, would want to know that?

One thing was clear—they'd probably never know who the guy was unless he came looking again.

Jillian stirred, stretched and reached out. Her hand fell across his chest, warm and seeking.

Man, oh, man. His thoughts could only go one direction with *that* happening. Just as he started to slide away, she snuggled closer, resting her head on his chest.

He closed his eyes, allowing himself a second or two to savor the closeness. She was warm and soft and her scent was delicious.

She moved and her hair brushed his face. He sucked in a deep breath. He could make love to her without a second's thought. But that wasn't going to happen, and he wouldn't be able to walk if he kept this up much longer. He moved to the side and slipped from under her arm. She stirred, then kicked off the sheet.

Her long legs were bare all the way up to her white cotton panties. His blood surged, and for a moment he wondered how receptive she'd be. It was a stupid thought, one he eliminated immediately.

He didn't know her very well, but he was certain she wasn't into one-night stands. Unpredictable though she was, he knew she was the kind of woman who thought about the future.

Hell, he wasn't even sure if *he* could handle a one-nighter. Not with this woman. Because then he'd have to think about other things besides the fact that he wanted her. He'd have to think about how he respected her for doing what she believed in, admired her for her loyalty, even though her scumbag husband didn't deserve it. Worse yet, he'd have to think about how much he liked her.

And that was no good for either of them.

He swung his legs off the bed and stood. At his movement, her eyes blinked open.

She stretched her arms above her head, then when

she noticed he was there and standing beside the bed, she smiled.

"Good morning." Her languid morning voice was low and, to his ears, seductive. *She* was seductive, and she didn't have a clue.

"Good morning."

Still smiling, she trailed her gaze from his face down his chest to his hips.

Instead of averting her gaze, she stared.

Realizing he was in full salute, he turned and started for the bathroom. "Hope you slept well. We've got another big day ahead of us if we're going to accomplish what we came here for."

He closed the curtain behind him. Maybe talking about the job would get his mind and his delinquent body headed in another direction.

Jillian all but flew from the bed when Adam headed into the bathroom. Within seconds, she'd dabbed her underarms with deodorant, pulled on a pair of lightweight jeans and a red tank top, which she covered with a white safari shirt to protect her from mosquitoes. Then she gathered her unruly hair into a ponytail and fastened it with a red-white-and-blue band. Adam emerged from the bathroom and she went in to splash some water on her face and brush her teeth. When she came out, Adam was dressed and ready to go.

Within minutes they were packed up and on their way to the hospital, which wasn't that far from the center of town. She suggested they go there directly and not bother with coffee and breakfast. They'd have enough time for that afterward.

Mostly she just wanted to get it over with.

Adam had balked, not particularly willing to delay his coffee, but in the end, he agreed. She didn't know if he'd acquiesced because he understood her need, or because he didn't want her to discover something without him.

It didn't matter to her. She had her own agenda. She would do what she had to do and go home. Being around Adam was more difficult than she'd imagined. Not because he was a pain in the tush, which he could be, but because she was having a hard time dealing with the feelings being with him aroused. Feelings that upset her equilibrium and set her wondering about her priorities.

Suddenly a safe, pleasant life in the suburbs didn't seem as important as it had been before.

Clouds of dust kicked up behind them as the VW clattered down the small dirt road toward the main part of town. They'd soon discovered that not all the streets were quaint and cobblestoned. Some were hard-packed dirt.

Her nerves stretching tighter with each passing block, they kept driving until they reached the town square, where a statue of a conquistador on a horse stood in the middle of a grassy area. An enormous cathedral was the focal point on one side, and several one-story buildings surrounded the square on the other sides. A side street looked as if it was being set up for a farmers' market.

After parking, Adam got out and inclined his head in the direction of a small white building next to the church. "According to Alfredo, that's the hospital."

Jillian saw a red-cross emblem on one window. "It's so small."

"From the size of the town, they're lucky to have one at all."

With the exception of the farmers' market activity, the streets were quiet. It was 8:00 a.m. but apparently the locals slept late. Her nerves had rendered her almost a basket case as they walked toward the hospital. She walked faster, wanting to get it over with.

Adam held the door for her and she stepped inside. No turning back now. A woman in a white nurse's uniform sat at a desk and smiled as they came toward her. Jillian smiled back, though she felt anything but happy. Why was she so nervous? Did she expect the worst?

Adam appeared to have no qualms whatsoever and steamed ahead. In Spanish, he inquired about the woman named Corita Sullivan. After a bit of conversation, the nurse's face looked stricken. She pressed a hand to her mouth and rattled off another string of words—the only one Jillian recognized was *muerte*. Spanish for *death*.

Jillian's heart plummeted. More conversation between the nurse and Adam, and then he thanked her, took Jillian's arm and led her outside. They crossed the street to a park bench and sat down.

"So, spill. Is she dead?"

He leaned forward, elbows on his knees. "Yes. About four weeks ago."

Jillian sank back against the bench and let out a sigh. "Now what? Did the nurse say anything that could help us? Did you ask where Corita lived? About her next of kin? Where she was buried or if her husband had come to see her? What happened to her little boy? Did her husband—''

''Whoa.'' Adam held up a hand. ''Let me tell you what she said, then you can ask questions.''

Jillian couldn't help feeling impatient. The sooner they got this over with, the better.

Adam leaned back next to her. ''Maybe we should talk about it over coffee. There has to be a café around here somewhere.''

''Tell me now,'' Jillian demanded. ''Then we'll have breakfast and figure out what to do.''

He pulled in some air, obviously reluctant to share. ''She said Corita Sullivan had been sick for a long time and had sent her son to stay with a friend. Corita had no relatives except her son and her husband, who'd apparently run out on her. But Corita didn't believe he'd do that and told the nurse that if her husband came to the hospital, she should give him the directions to her friend's so he could pick up the boy.''

''And? Did he come?''

Adam shook his head. ''No.''

Jillian slumped down in her seat. A dead end. She thought for a second, then said, ''Maybe her husband knew the friend and where to find the boy, or got directions from someone else. Maybe the friend knows where he went.''

''I thought of that. I've got the directions to the friend's here.'' He held up a slip of paper. ''If the kid's father went anywhere, I hope it was to find his son.''

Jillian's mouth fell open. "So that's the plan? Find the boy and we might find his dad?"

Adam looked at her. "You got a better idea, Sherlock?"

"Well, how far is this place? We can try to find the address for the number I called from Chicago and see if anyone lives there or knows where this guy went—in case he decided to go someplace else."

Adam gazed down the street. "Yeah. It could save me some time and a trip that could turn out to be for nothing. I'll have to check the map to see how far Cabacera is."

She noticed he used the first person. Obviously he planned on going alone. They'd see about *that*. "So, shall we try it?"

He cracked his knuckles one at a time. Was he debating about what to do? Whether he should do it with her or not? She couldn't forget that he hadn't wanted her along to begin with.

Finally he said, "Let's find a place for breakfast before we decide anything."

As they walked to the car, Jillian saw that the streets were a little busier. Several children had come to play on the edge of the green in the square, and a couple of women, probably the children's mothers, stood nearby exchanging torrents of Spanish.

She and Adam climbed into the car and drove along the nearest street, stopping at the first café they saw. Again they sat near the window so Adam could keep an eye on the car.

A young girl of about twelve took their orders, then called them out to someone, probably her mother in the back. Hot black coffee came within seconds, and Jillian waited for Adam to take a couple of swallows before she said, "I think you're right. We should go to the village where the woman sent her son."

Adam was silent for the longest time before he said, "Really? I was thinking you should go back to San José and then home."

CHAPTER EIGHT

"IT'S JUST NOT A GOOD IDEA, that's all," Adam said, keeping his eyes on the road. After his stated refusal to take her with him, they'd finished breakfast in silence and climbed back in the car. Now he needed to find a phone.

He didn't like the idea of her continuing on this venture, but it seemed she wasn't about to go home before getting some answers. She'd find a way to get to the village with or without him, she said, but first, she wanted to find the address connected to that phone number.

No way, he thought, would the guy still be staying in the same place if he knew the law was on his tail. The law, or someone else—and his disappearance indicated he knew *someone* was.

But it might be enough to satisfy her, and if it was another dead end, maybe she'd willingly go back to San José.

"I suppose you think it's dangerous?" It was more a statement than a question.

"It *is* dangerous."

"So do you think it's less dangerous if we go together, or if I go alone?"

He gritted his teeth. "That's a stupid question."

Passing a building whose sign on the front read

Tourismo, he jammed on the brakes, shifted into Reverse and stopped in front of the place.

"What are we doing now?"

"I want to use the phone here." He needed to call Rico, but was having a hard time finding any time away from her to do it. He'd tried his satellite phone last night when she was showering—when the intruder paid his visit—but Rico hadn't answered.

"I'm coming in with you."

He didn't respond because what he said didn't seem to matter to her. She'd do whatever the hell she wanted to do, anyway. But he didn't want her listening to his conversation with Rico. His partner had been researching at his end and may have found information that could change Adam's course of action.

"I need a phone, too," she said as they got out of the car and walked toward the tourist office. She walked close, talking the whole time. "I'll call this number and if I get an address, we can check it out. And I should call to see how Chloe is doing and how the shops are going."

During the conversation with herself, she shucked off her safari shirt and tied the sleeves around her waist. But as she kept in step with him, he noticed that her cheeks and nose were a little sunburned and her freckles more pronounced. She had a healthy glow that made her incredible eyes seem even bluer, if that was possible.

But her mouth just kept on flapping. "So, do you want to go first with the calls, or should I? Mine might take a while since I have more than one to make. Come to think of it, I should call Meadow Brook, too, to see how Harriet is. And—"

He stopped in his tracks. "I don't care how many people you have to call or how many things you have to take care of. I'm here on business and that's what I'm taking care of. Then I'm leaving. With or without you."

Her mouth clamped shut, albeit only for a moment. "But I need to see how everything is going. I guess you wouldn't understand that. But just because you don't have anyone who might worry about you if they didn't hear from you doesn't mean other people don't."

He stared at her. He had plenty of people who cared about him. He just didn't need to call them every twenty minutes.

"The people in my life know how to manage their lives on their own. And they do it just fine without me checking up on them. If they need me, they know how to reach me."

It was true. Those who needed to know did. And he was glad he didn't have anyone worrying about his every move or getting upset if he didn't call regularly. It had to be that way in his line of work. Otherwise he'd feel obligated, and that would affect his job. He'd done that once. Better to have no one.

"Well, I don't *manage* other people's lives," she said indignantly. "I truly care about the people in my life and they care about me. If I want to know how they're doing and I want to be supportive and do all the things friends do for each other, I have to touch base. Friendships require a certain amount of participation from both sides. But I suppose if one didn't have friends, one wouldn't have any idea what I'm talking about."

His stomach rumbled. He found it even more irritating to realize that there was probably a smidgen of truth to what she said. He didn't answer her, but turned and marched up to the desk where a woman sat reading a book. *"Buenos días,"* he said.

When he got the information he needed, they went down the hall to the phone. He made his call first. Apparently she understood his need for privacy and went into the small souvenir shop.

He used his calling card, but it still took several minutes to get through.

"Yo, Rico."

"Hey, bud. Thanks for checking in." Rico's tone was dry.

"I was busy."

"You got anything?"

"Zip. But I'm closing in."

"You get the widow to go back home?"

When he'd called Rico earlier from San José and told him the problem, his partner had suggested a couple of ways to handle the situation. But Adam hadn't liked either one. Both would've left Jillian out in the cold, and as she'd said, she was going to go ahead with her search with or without him. And knowing that, all his protective impulses had surged to the fore. It was crazy.

"Nope. But I'm using it to my advantage."

"How so?"

"She's able to get information that I can't." By telling the woman at the restaurant where they'd stopped for dinner that Jillian was the boy's aunt, they'd been given directions to the hospital. But he could tell by Rico's silence that he didn't agree with Adam's tactics.

"She was going to go by herself, anyway," Adam explained. "And I figured it's safer for her to go with me."

"Uh-huh. So, do you know why you got an inquiry from some guy about her?"

"What?"

"I took a call for you from someone asking questions about her. When I asked for details, he hung up and we couldn't get a trace on it. My guess is you've got company."

Adam knew the "company" Rico referred to was either someone else trying to locate Sullivan or someone who wanted to know why they were looking for him. He'd suspected as much. And there was no way to know if that someone was one of the good guys or the bad guys. At any rate, it explained their visitor last night and why he hadn't taken anything. Someone was on to them. Adam just didn't know why—and he was glad he'd said Jillian was the boy's aunt and looking for him. It was the perfect cover.

"Great."

"I figured you'd want a heads-up." Rico was silent for a few seconds, then said, "I thought you'd get in touch before now."

"You worried about me, Mom?"

"No, but I can't get information to you if you don't call."

"I called. You didn't answer. You have something else?"

"Yeah."

Adam heard something muffle the phone. Then Rico all but whispered, "Can you call me later—at home?"

"I can't guarantee that. You got the cell?"

"Yeah."

"Okay, go where you can talk and I'll call you back in five minutes." The conversation disturbed Adam. Whatever his partner had to talk about obviously couldn't be said in front of anyone at the station, which meant only one thing to Adam—and he didn't like the implications.

Jillian sauntered over just as he was hanging up. He gestured to her. "It's all yours."

"I might need a little help with the language."

He grinned. "Are you asking for my help?"

She waited a moment, her forehead creasing in exasperation. She was one independent woman and he knew that asking for help bothered her.

On a deep sigh, she said, "If I should need it, would you please help me make a phone call?"

"I'd be happy to." He folded his arms and leaned against the wall.

After she made a few futile attempts to get through, he held out his hand for the phone. "Give me the number and I'll walk you through it." He did and then turned to go, but she grabbed on to his arm, holding him there.

"Just in case," she whispered while listening to the ringing on the other end. "Besides, I'll need you to help on the next calls, too."

He had to call Rico, but mostly, he didn't want to stay and hear the catch in her voice when she talked to her daughter, or the caring she exuded when she talked to her best friend, the enthusiasm when she talked to her shop manager, or the patience she exhibited when talking with her mother-in-law. But he listened, anyway, and wondered again what it would be like to have someone care about him like that. Wondered what it would be like to have *her* care about him.

He stalked away before she was finished with the last call. He'd helped her. He'd done his good deed for the day. If he could just stop thinking about how great she smelled and how nice her hand felt on his arm, he'd be fine.

He went outside to make his call on his satellite unit.

When Rico picked up, Adam said, "Make it quick. I've only got a few."

"Got it. Your old partner, Bryce, was on an undercover job that joined several federal agencies—the FBI, DEA, U.S. Customs Service and the U.S. Attorney's office, along with binational task forces in Monterrey, Juarez and Tijuana on the Southwest Border Initiative."

Adam knew that already. Bryce had told him the night he left the message.

"SWBI is poised to take down any organized crime syndicate participating in major international drug trafficking. You're right, Sullivan was part of it, but I don't know the details. There's something strange with the whole thing involving Bryce, but I haven't nailed anything down. I'll try again."

Adam spotted Jillian through the glass doors and about to exit. "Thanks. Gotta go."

He stuffed the unit into his duffel bag.

JILLIAN SAW ADAM WAITING by the car when she was done with her calls. She'd just finished talking with

Harriet and then her nurse at Meadow Brook and learned that a couple of men had been there to visit Harriet and were asking all kinds of questions about Rob and Jillian. Also Adam. Then she'd called Information and got an address for J. Sullivan.

Her excitement mounted. It *had* to be him. How many Sullivans could there be in Mirador?

Reaching Adam, she told him about the address and then the gist of the conversation with Harriet.

"Did the men identify themselves?"

She shook her head. "I asked the nurse, and she said they looked official, so she didn't think to ask."

"And they specifically inquired about Jack Sullivan?"

She nodded. "About him and me and you. That's weird, isn't it? I thought they were people you work with, otherwise why ask about you and where you went?"

He frowned. "No one but my partner knows where I am."

"If it's not your people, who would it be? You think someone else is looking for the same guy we are?" She hadn't thought that far, but it was a reasonable conclusion. If the guy was using a dead man's identity, he must be running from something.

"Yeah," Adam said, still frowning. "And if someone else is looking for our guy, that could mean this little trip might get even more dangerous than I thought." He shoved a hand through his hair.

"And you think I'd better go home, right?"

He grinned wryly and nodded, but he didn't look as though he was serious.

"And you *know* how I feel about that, too."

"Unfortunately, yes." The grin disappeared. "C'mon. Let's check out that address."

He glanced around, then pulled the map from inside the car and laid it on the roof to plot their course. "Okay. We'll check out the residence. If we have no luck there, we'll go that-a-way." He pointed southeast toward the ocean. "We should be able to get to the village where the son is within a couple of hours. If we strike out there, too, we'll have plenty of time to make it back here before dark."

Happy to hear that he'd given up the idea of sending her back to San José, Jillian got into the car and they headed out. She glanced at the map again and then at the street signs. They were getting close. "Turn right in two blocks." Her muscles tensed. What if he was there? She couldn't imagine. Just seeing his photo had been creepy enough.

What would she say? How should she react? Would she know immediately that the man wasn't Rob? Every time she'd thought about it, she'd put it out of her head. She realized now that she had, not because she truly didn't believe the man was an imposter, but because she didn't want to face the possibility it could turn out the other way.

And how would she know? There would be recognizable differences—the voice, the eyes, the mannerisms. But what if she couldn't tell? What then? What would she do if he turned out to...

She couldn't even finish formulating the question that weighed the most heavily on her mind. She'd know soon enough.

Once they turned the next corner, the architecture of the houses began to change, and with each block they passed, the homes were spaced farther and farther apart, becoming more expansive, more elegant.

Finally they were out of town and decided that the home they were looking for was located at the far end of the road. The homes now were looking more like estates, and when they arrived at the address on the scrap of paper she held in her hand, her mouth fell open.

Large arching gates led into what looked like a plantation of some kind. "This can't be it, can it?"

"Sure. An American with money can live a life of luxury here."

"You think this…man has a lot of money?"

"If I didn't before, I do now."

She let out a huge sigh of relief. "Well, that eases my mind."

He gave her a quizzical look.

"It can't be Rob," she explained. "How would he get enough money to build or buy something like this?"

Adam didn't answer and just kept on driving right up the curved driveway to the front of the place. God, she was nervous. Was it possible that there were two men with the same name and that they looked identical? No, that was crazy, Jillian decided.

But if the worst was true and Rob had somehow come into a fortune, he would never live in a place like this and let his son be shipped off to some friend of his wife's. But if *this* Jack Sullivan was the same

one who was married to Corita Sullivan, wouldn't he
know that his wife was ill and dying? Wouldn't he
know she was dead and then have gone after his son?
Nothing made sense.

"You coming?"

Adam was already out of the car. "Oh, sure. I was
just…thinking."

"You want to stay in the car? Maybe it's best."

"No, I don't think so." She needed to do this. She'd
come all this way to do this very thing and she wasn't
going to have Adam fronting for her. She had to face
this herself.

What she learned today could change her whole life.
Dread weighing her down, she climbed out of the car
and walked beside Adam up the polished marble steps.
The place was surrounded by flowers of all kinds, and
the sweet scent was cloying. Overpowering. A wave
of nausea hit her.

Adam rang the bell.

Her hands were shaking and her knees felt weak.
She wanted to hang on to Adam, to absorb some of
his strength and his objectivity and his ability not to
feel anything. She wanted to simply do what needed
to be done.

But she wasn't Adam, and her insides roiled and
churned.

One of the massive double doors swung open.

Jillian stepped forward.

A middle-aged black woman stood in the entry.
"May I help you?" Her voice had a singsong Caribbean lilt.

Words froze in Jillian's throat.

"We're here to see Mr. Sullivan," Adam said calmly, as if he was an old friend come to call.

"I'm sorry, but that's not possible," the woman said.

Not possible? What did that mean? Was he there or not? "It's important that we see him," Jillian shot back.

"What she means," Adam said, "is that we have an appointment with Mr. Sullivan. Perhaps he forgot about it."

"Please give me a minute and I'll be right back." The woman shut the door in their faces, leaving them standing on the marble steps listening to the rush of a waterfall in the garden next to the front of the house.

Jillian glanced at Adam. "Do you think he's in there?"

Adam scratched his chin. "We'll find out soon enough."

He looked at her and his eyes softened, as if he understood her trepidation. He placed his hands on her shoulders and turned her so that her back was to him and began gently kneading the tight muscles of her neck.

"One step at a time," he said. "Nothing is going to change while we wait."

The tension in her neck and shoulders melted away, and even in her present anxious state, his hands felt as if they belonged on her. If finding this man wasn't so important, she might wish the woman didn't come back. Or that she'd at least take enough time to allow Jillian to enjoy the pleasure of Adam's strong hands touching her in a way she hadn't been touched for so long. If ever, she realized.

Rob had been attentive and caring, but he'd never sparked the kind of desire she was feeling at this moment. The kind that made her knees melt and left her craving to fulfill her most basic needs.

But that was silly. *She* was being silly. The sooner she got her answers, the sooner they'd both be out of there and they'd go back to their respective lives. She just had to be certain this man was the imposter she hoped he was. Because without that certainty, she'd always be in a state of flux, wondering, questioning.

The door clicked open again, but only a few inches this time. "I can't help you," the woman said. "Mr. Sullivan doesn't live here."

Jillian looked at Adam, then back at the woman again. "This is the address we were given and the number is listed for Jack Sullivan."

The woman gave them a blank look, shook her head and said, "I'm sorry."

I'm sorry? That was it?

"How long has he been gone?" Adam asked.

"He means, did he leave a forwarding address?" Jillian added. "We're here about his son."

The woman's expression softened. "Oh, I wish I could help, but I really don't know anything. I just started working here a few weeks ago."

"Is there someone else who might know?" Jillian pressed, noticing a young girl hanging about close by. "It's very important."

Just then the door was pulled out of the woman's hand. She looked behind her and then stepped away. A tall gray-haired man replaced her. "I purchased the property two months ago," he said in perfect English. "The transaction was through a real estate company.

I didn't ask where the previous owner had gone, and I don't know anything about him. I'm sorry, but we can't help you."

With that, he closed the door with a thunk of finality.

"O-kay! I guess that's our cue to leave," Adam said, his voice sharp with irritation.

"Well, at least we know he's been gone from here for a while. Right?"

Adam scowled. "We don't know squat. Sullivan could've been having breakfast in the kitchen, for all we know."

Jillian started down the steps, and a moment later, Adam caught up with her.

"So how will we know?" she asked.

"Follow up on the real estate lead, I guess. See if the guy is telling the truth. Maybe the agent will know where he went or the bank that conducted the transaction."

"Oh. That'll take a long time, won't it? I mean, we don't know the company or the bank." Her spirits ebbed. It was looking more and more like she was going to go home without the information she came for. "But I guess we're no worse off than we were before."

"I would've liked to end it right here," he said.

"I know. Me, too." Though oddly, she'd felt an immense relief when the man they were looking for hadn't been there. "So now what?"

"Get in. You're going back to San José."

Adam opened the door and slid into the seat. Jillian followed suit, but just as he shoved the key into the ignition, Jillian saw the young girl she'd seen in the house coming toward her.

"Wait." Jillian reached out and placed a hand on his arm. She rolled down her window.

Reaching the car, the girl shoved a piece of paper at Jillian, then turned and ran off. Jillian stared at the markings on the paper. It was a crudely drawn map and some writing. In Spanish.

She handed it to Adam. Watching him read, she saw his eyes light up. "What does it say? What's the map for?"

Adam was silent for a moment. Then he said, "When he left here, our guy was on his way to Cabacera to find his son."

"When?" Adrenaline surged through her veins.

"That's the problem. It doesn't say. Could've been two months ago, could've been yesterday."

"So, let's go."

His expression was uncertain, as if wondering that very thing himself. Then he said, "Yeah. Let's go." He started the car, asked her to get out the map just to double-check the location of the village, then they were on the road again.

She was glad he hadn't made an issue of sending her back, but figured he probably didn't want to waste time. Before long, the road narrowed, this time to little more than a single lane. The foliage around them grew thick and tangled, alive and eager to swallow them up, car and all. The rain forest seemed a primal entity, a living, breathing thing, and she was awed and fascinated by it.

She'd once seen a television program on the destruction of the rain forests around the world, and there'd been dissension between those who wanted more development and those concerned about the environment. What a pity if the forests were destroyed here. Still, with industry came opportunity. A tough choice to make.

"Let me know when you get hungry," Adam said out of the blue.

"And what will we do then? Stop at the nearest fast-food place for a hamburger?" she joked. "Have a picnic with the snakes and poison dart frogs?"

He emitted a hearty laugh. "I think we're stuck with the leftovers I got at our swank digs in Mirador."

She liked the sound of his laughter. It had an honest ring about it, genuine. True.

"It wasn't the Ritz, that's for sure," Jillian said, laughing, too. But she remembered the man rummaging through their things. "I still find it odd that the intruder didn't take anything."

"If he'd ripped off your passport, you wouldn't be able to get home."

"What do you suppose he was looking for?"

"Who knows?" Adam said carelessly, though he knew there was a helluva lot more going on here than appeared on the surface. He jerked the steering wheel to the side to avoid another humongous hole.

"Well, how about hazarding a guess?" She waited a second, then added, "I think he wanted to know who we are and why we're here."

"Oh, you do, do you?" He laughed again. The woman was irrepressible. "And why do you think anyone would care who we are?"

She pondered for another moment. "Because we're looking for a guy who's likely taken someone else's identity. If he'd do that, it's probably not the only disreputable thing he's done, and maybe he's caught wind of it. Maybe *he* has people who keep an eye out for strangers who might come looking for him because of his activities. If he could afford that home back there, he surely can afford a few security guards.''

Adam had thought of that, too.

''Good powers of deduction. You think like a cop.'' He winked at her.

She felt her cheeks grow warm. ''I could never be a cop. And I doubt that I think like one. I'm not that calculating, or that cold.''

''Ouch.'' He gave her a pained expression. ''Is that how you think of me? Cold and calculating?''

She pulled her gaze away and back to the road, her body rigid. ''Of course not. I don't think of you at all.''

He let out yet another howl of laughter. ''Ooh. That hurts. And in case you weren't aware of it, that's a very *cold* comment to make about someone who's only looking out for your best interests.''

She rolled her eyes. ''And if I believed that, I'd be sitting back in San José waiting for you to come back.''

''And if you had waited, I'd have been finished and back by now. And you would have had a few days of R and R.''

''I don't need R and R.''

''Everyone needs R and R.''

''Not me. I thrive on being with people I care about—that and my work.''

''You thrive on being stubborn, impulsive and unpredictable.''

"And you get an adrenaline rush from chasing down the bad guys."

"Hmm. You're probably right about that. I want to see every scumbag drug dealer off the streets."

"I doubt the jails could hold them all."

"There are other alternatives. As long as they're off the streets, that's all I care about."

And he didn't feel the need to explain his reasons for doing what he did. He'd seen too many kids destroyed by drugs, some he'd personally tried to help but had lost in the battle. His best friend and former partner was dead because of drug runners. Getting the dealers off the streets meant more to him than just doing his job. Getting the big guys who sat back and made it happen gave him a cause, a purpose. It gave Bryce's death some meaning.

"Off the streets, dead or alive?"

"Uh-huh. Dead or alive."

That stopped her cold. She wasn't the type to agree with his philosophy and he knew it. Pegged that one right off. Another reason to stay far, far away from this woman.

But as much as he knew what he had to do, his body seemed to think differently. Just massaging her neck, feeling her relax under his hands, had sent his blood pressure soaring, had given him a bigger rush than a dozen two-bit collars. Granted, that was like comparing Viagra with a one-a-day vitamin, but it sure as hell had him thinking twice about touching her again.

So what if she thought of him as a cold calculating SOB? He had only one objective in mind on this trip—

getting Sullivan. "Look." She pointed ahead. "A clearing. Maybe it's the village."

"It can't be. According to this map, we're still an hour away."

"Well, at least it's civilization of some kind. A pit stop, if we're lucky."

"Don't get your hopes up. We haven't been particularly lucky so far."

She turned to look at him, her expression perplexed. "Well, I think we've been lucky. We may not have found what we wanted, but we've found out more than we knew in the beginning. And while we didn't stay in plush hotels, we didn't have to sleep with the animals and insects and creepy-crawly things. I call that lucky. Maybe you should try a little positive thinking once in a while."

"I'm a realist, not a Pollyanna like you are."

She jerked back. "Well, call me whatever you want, but at least I'm happy, which is more than I can say for you."

"Excuse me? How do you know whether I'm happy or unhappy?" The implication annoyed him. How the hell would she know anything about his state of mind?

Her eyes narrowed. "The outside of a person is a pretty good reflection of what goes on inside, except we usually tone it down for other people or try to mask it in some way. We don't want the world to see how we really feel."

"We?" His annoyance kicked up a notch. He didn't need her self-appointed psychoanalysis. He didn't need *her* to tell him whether he was happy or unhappy. He tightened his grip on the steering wheel. "I've found that when *one* is busy mucking around in an-

other person's guts and doling out platitudes about what *one* thinks the other is all about, *one* is usually avoiding looking into *oneself*. I guess that's because it's so much easier to point out other people's flaws than it is to look at *one's* own.''

He glanced at her. He could almost see the steam rising from her skin.

He knew all about avoidance. He was an expert on the subject. It had been easier to screw up his life than to face what was going on inside. And he didn't need her or anyone else to bring it to his attention as if he didn't have a clue.

Just then a little girl appeared in the middle of the road directly in front of the car. He stomped on the brake. Jillian was thrown forward, but got her hands on the dash in time to stop her forward momentum. The engine died.

''Damn,'' Adam said. ''Where the hell did that kid come from?''

Jillian was still leaning on her hands. ''Where did *who* come from?''

Reaching out, he lifted the hair away from her face and neck and touched her cheek with his fingertips. ''You okay?''

She tensed at his touch, then slowly raised her head to look at him. Moistening her lips, she said, ''I'm fine.''

His heart had stopped when he thought she'd been hurt. But she was okay. He looked out, scanned the area. ''There was a girl in the middle of the road.''

''I didn't see anyone.''

Twisting the key in the ignition, he said, ''And if you did, it probably would've been a fairy godmother ready to lead the way.'' The engine made only a grinding sound. He tried again.

''Maybe you need to wait a minute,'' she said. ''It could be flooded and all it needs is a rest.''

''And we could be sitting in a café on the Left Bank in Paris, but we're not. And it's not flooded.''

She smiled, as if she knew he was needling her because he was irritated with himself.

''The child had to come from somewhere nearby,'' she said. ''And where there are people, help might be available. That's a good thing.''

He stopped short. ''Don't you ever get discouraged?''

Her smile widened. ''Rarely. I took control of my own destiny a long time ago.''

CHAPTER NINE

AFTER WAITING FIFTEEN minutes and the engine still wouldn't turn over, Adam had agreed they should set out on foot carrying their gear.

They couldn't just sit in the car on some godforsaken road waiting for help to come, because who knew when that might happen? Act Rather Than React was Jillian's motto, and fortunately, she and Adam had been of the same mind when it came to assessing the situation.

The girl had to have come from somewhere close by, Jillian reasoned, and if they kept to the road, they shouldn't have any problems. Except that it was drizzling and her gear was getting heavy and now the mud was sucking at their boots. With every step, the road got worse and their progress slower.

They hadn't covered a whole lot of ground when Jillian noticed that the usually raucous forest was eerily silent. She saw something large dart through the trees just off the road and a little in front of them. The hairs on the back of her neck prickled.

"Adam. Wait a minute, will you?" she called out as she switched her suitcase to the other hand, then hurried to catch up. Although Adam was loaded down with the rest of their supplies, he looked as if he was on an afternoon hike. He stopped until she reached him. "We have to keep moving. It's already eleven and if we're going to reach Cabacera, get the car fixed and make it back to Mirador before dark, we've got to hustle. Otherwise, we might be spending the night out here—and I don't think you'd like that very much."

"And you would?"

He chuckled. "No. But I guarantee you'd be more uncomfortable than I would."

"Oh, really?" She stopped abruptly.

"Yeah, really. So what's up?" He gave her a nudge to keep moving while they talked.

She hitched up her gear and slogged on, walking faster to stay in step with him. She usually had no trouble keeping up with anyone, but with Adam, she felt like a little kid struggling to keep up with a big brother. She dropped back a step. "Nothing really, except...well, listen."

"I don't hear anything."

"That's my point. It's dead quiet."

He kept on walking.

"What do you think it means? Isn't that a sign of something?" she said to his back.

"I think it means you've seen too many *Rama of the Jungle* movies."

"That's not true. It's just that I...well, I have this eerie feeling."

He stopped abruptly, causing her to nearly bump into him. He turned fully around, crossed his arms over his chest and gave her an impatient, skeptical look, the kind where one eyebrow shot up and she knew he was thinking she was nuts. The rain stopped as quickly as it had started. A ray of sunshine poked through the trees above.

"You have an *eerie* feeling."

She moved closer to whisper, "I have keen senses. I know things sometimes, call it intuition or whatever, but most of the time it's correct. And right now I have this feeling...like we're being watched."

A slow grin erupted.

Suddenly the forest was a cacophony of sound again; blue butterflies fluttered up in front of her, leaves rustled, branches snapped, monkeys squawked, while endless varieties of birds warbled and cawed and swooshed upward in unison, their wings thwapping noisily against the thick leaves.

She pivoted. Her blood pounded in her ears as she searched the landscape for the cause of the disruption.

She looked at Adam, who seemed to be getting immense enjoyment from her discomfort.

"What's so funny?"

He put an arm around her shoulders and moved her along at his side. Then, leaning toward her, said in a hushed voice, "We are being watched."

"We are?" She kept her voice as low as his, her steps quickening with each furtive glance into the bushes. "You know that? Who's watching? Bandits? Natives?"

"The animals whose habitat we're invading," he teased. And on a more serious note, he added, "We're the outsiders here."

"That's not what I meant and you know it."

Just then, she saw another clearing ahead. Thank heaven. As they got closer, the rutted road inclined a bit and the mud quickly disappeared. On a level spot near the edge of the road, several crude tin buildings nestled against a large tree with huge tangled roots that spread like tentacles. A few goats milled around behind a fence made of twigs. A child scurried off behind a building.

Shortly an old man came out from behind one of the buildings. The little child was with him, clutching onto his shirttail.

"Buenos días," Adam said as he grasped Jillian's hand. He engaged in conversation with the old man, who then pointed to the right and rattled off something that somehow seemed important.

Adam turned to Jillian. "The village is down the road less than an hour from here by foot. He doesn't know if the boy is there or not. But there's a mechanic who can help us with the car."

All Jillian really heard was that the man didn't know if the boy was there or not. If he wasn't, that meant his father must've come for him, and the likelihood that they were going to find him was looking slimmer. "If he's not there, then what?"

Adam caught her gaze with his. "Then it's time to go home."

Dammit. That was not the way she wanted the trip to end. She'd come all this way to get answers, and if she went home empty-handed, she would always wonder.

But there was no point in speculating. They'd either

find the boy and his father or they wouldn't. Maybe they'd be lucky.

"Well, so be it. You can't say we didn't try."

MOVING ON, ADAM WAS GLAD Jillian didn't understand what the old man had said. If they got help with the car, maybe he could find someone to take Jillian back to San José while he continued on. He couldn't be this close and not make contact, but there was no question it could get dangerous. She needed to go back.

The old man said he knew Jack Sullivan by reputation, and he'd heard he'd come to pick up his son the week before. He didn't know if he had or not. What confused Adam, though, was the fact that Sullivan had owned the plantation and then disappeared. If he had money, why would his son be shunted off to stay with strangers? Why would he let his wife die alone?

None of it made sense—unless Sullivan knew he was a made man. Unless he knew the police and spooks weren't the only ones on his trail. But Sullivan couldn't know all that unless—and this was starting to seem more likely all the time—someone had tipped him off.

Jillian was one possibility. But if she'd already warned Sullivan, she'd have no reason to be out here with him, Adam. Unless it was her job to keep tabs on him, maybe even throw him off the trail. But whenever he tried to reason that out, he couldn't. There was no sense to it.

Adam didn't understand men like Sullivan. They didn't believe that selling or transporting drugs was a big deal. To them, the addicts were their own worst.

enemy. So what if they overdosed and died? So what if their families were left with nothing but indescribable grief, their lives forever altered?

He'd seen it too damned many times to remain unaffected. And since he'd gotten his act together, nailing scum like Sullivan had become a mission. He and all the other blood-sucking creeps like him who trafficked in drugs were no better than assassins.

"Well, at least the mud is gone," Jillian said, breaking into Adam's thoughts. "It's a lot easier to walk when I'm not getting stuck every other second."

He kept his eyes on the road ahead. "Right." He didn't feel like talking anymore. He had to work out his plan of action. If Sullivan—

"So how about you?" Jillian asked.

He glanced at her. "How about me what?"

Frowning, she marched ahead. "That's exactly what's wrong with society today. No one *really* listens to anyone anymore. Marriages crumble for that very reason. If more people communicated with each other, we might not have the problems in the world that we do toda—"

"Whoa." He stopped her. "How did my not listening land on the same level as the national divorce ratio and the problems of the world in general?"

"Because when a person doesn't listen, it sends a message that he doesn't care what the other person is thinking or feeling, and if we, in general and as a population, don't know what the other person is thinking or feeling, how can we ever solve any problems?"

He smiled. "I think it's best to solve the problems

at hand and leave broken marriages and world peace to those who have the ability to do something about it.''

She huffed. ''You know what I mean.''

He wasn't so sure. And he didn't want to know. Because the more he knew about her, the more intrigued he became. The more intrigued he became, the more he rallied to find out, and when he found out more, he liked her even more. Very simply, he liked being with her—a lot.

But then, there was that whole other thing going on—the more he was with her, the more he *wanted* her.

Not good. Because if there was one thing he knew he couldn't handle, it was another woman who made him crazy. And with all her Pollyanna solutions and platitudes, she made him crazy enough to want to kiss the words right out of her mouth.

Hell, she was right. He wasn't listening to her. He wasn't communicating because he was too damn busy thinking about things he had no business thinking.

They kept on walking. She sulked for the next fifteen minutes or so. At least it seemed that long, and then she finally asked, ''Do you see your family much?''

''As much as I can. Why?''

''I was just wondering. That old man and little girl made me wonder why they were together, and then I started thinking about your big family and how lucky you are to have that. But then, I thought if most of them live in Kentucky and you live in L.A., I guess you don't see them much.''

''We communicate.''

She smiled, but it was a questioning smile. "Except you can't communicate when you're on a job, right?"

"Right. It's tough to mix business with family and personal stuff. It's too distracting."

"I'd find that kind of life very lonely."

"Well, that's where we're different, sweets. I find it easier to focus. I've learned that you can't have it all." It was a fact. He couldn't have it all, not if he wanted to be a good cop. And being a good cop was all he'd ever wanted to be—since he was six and had watched a police officer save his dad's life.

They'd been in a grocery store during a robbery, and his dad was taken hostage to help the thieves get away. He'd watched in horror and in awe as the SWAT team and LEOs moved in to save his dad. He'd thought those cops were the bravest men in the world, and after that, he'd never wanted to do anything else. Still didn't.

Just then he saw what looked like a village in front of them. "Look. We're here."

Jillian stopped abruptly.

"What's the matter?"

"I don't know. I just got the willies. You know... how the bottom of your stomach seems to drop out when something makes you really anxious?"

"Nerves."

"I guess. I mean, even seeing someone who looks so much like Rob will be unnerving." Giving a deep sigh, she added, "And I suppose I'm a little worried I might find out something I don't want to find out."

If that happened, she was going to be hurt. More than hurt. He wished he could spare her from the knowledge of what a scumbag her maybe-not-so-dearly-departed was. But he couldn't.

It was his job to do just the opposite. And, dammit, if she hadn't taken it upon herself to make this trip, he wouldn't have had her tagging along and wouldn't have had to deal with her feelings.

Now he felt responsible for her, and culpable. And there was no reason in the world he should feel like one of the bad guys. He rubbed the back of his neck, hoping a solution would come to him.

"But…what will be, will be," she said softly, and gave a little shrug before moving onward.

She seemed so vulnerable! Was her bravery just a facade? He moved closer, draped an arm around her shoulders and walked with her. "Stay with me, okay?" Yeah, like that was going to help.

She nodded and kept walking. As they neared the village, he could see it was larger than he'd first thought. It wasn't L.A. or Chicago, or even Henderson, but it had shelter and food, and he hoped, a phone and a way to send her back home.

The first street they came upon wasn't really a street at all, but a narrow, dusty road that twisted between small houses built of crude adobe blocks topped with corrugated slabs of tin. But soon the dusty road morphed into a wider road, which he figured was the main street. No buildings of commerce, only a church that loomed at one side of a small square.

"Siesta time?" Jillian asked.

"Could be. In most places siesta time is somewhere between one and five." He glanced at his watch. "It's only a little after twelve but there's not a soul around.''

They kept on walking, but saw no stores, no place they could wander into and ask questions about any of the Sullivans—man, woman or child.

''Why don't we go in the church? Churches are always open and we might find a priest or someone on the premises.''

''Good thought, blue eyes.'' He tapped her on the head, smiled and pulled her along. ''And it'll be cooler inside.''

Jillian gladly followed. His grip on her hand felt warm and solid, as if some of his strength was being transferred to her. In just this short time together, she'd come to believe he was someone she could count on, someone who would be there for her if...well, if things didn't turn out as she wanted.

Didn't turn out as she wanted? The thought surprised her. What *did* she want? She should be happy either way. If the man was an imposter, she could deal with it. If he wasn't, there was a reason and she would be happy that Rob was alive. She would deal with that, too.

But...to her own horrified realization, she knew she wanted something else. She wanted *Adam*. At the very least, she'd like the opportunity to get to know him.

Guilt rose up like a demon inside her. She was lying to herself. She didn't just want to know him, she wanted to make love with him.

The feelings had been there all along—in her subconscious, working on her libido and her emotions. Her wobbly, vulnerable emotions.

That was the problem. Her emotions were all out of whack. And whose wouldn't be under the circumstances? She was susceptible right now. Uncertain. And feeling that way could cause her to think all kinds of things, things that might not be good for her.

Like making love with Adam.

She was vulnerable, all right, vulnerable to Adam's strength. Not only his physical strength, but his strength of character. His RoboCop attitude was a facade. He treated people with caring and respect. The same qualities she'd admired in Rob.

Only her blood hadn't turned hot at Rob's touch. She hadn't desired Rob the way she desired Adam. *Ever.*

She'd never desired anyone like that before. It made her feel wonderful and delicious.

And alive.

Adam, standing in front of the church's ornately carved double doors, did his routine. He scanned the area before he opened the door and then checked out the inside before giving her the okay to enter.

Immediately the air was cooler. There were no windows, except for two large stained-glass ovals behind the altar, which gave enough light for her to see clearly. Compared to the small town, the church was fairly large, with an elaborate carved-wood and gilded interior.

They set down their gear and Adam prowled the inside perimeter, apparently looking for someone who could answer a few questions. Tired from walking, she sat on the end of a pew close to the entry. When Adam finished his surveillance, he came back and sat down beside her.

"What now?" she whispered, even though there was no one to hear.

"We wait. Nothing else we can do." He leaned back, resting his arm across the top of the pew behind her.

"It's pretty, isn't it?"

He glanced around. "Guess you could say that. It would be prettier if they had a few frescoes." He pointed up and to his left. "Angels would work right about there."

"I never would've pegged you for a fresco connoisseur.

Smiling, he said, "My dad was a minister. I used to fall asleep in the pew every Sunday looking at the angels. But even with the frescoes, the church wasn't *this* elaborate."

The son of a minister. What a surprise. "Doesn't it make you wonder why, if there's someone here with the ability and talent to do all this, that they couldn't do more with the town?"

He sighed. "It's all about priorities and resources."

"I can understand that. I guess we all have our own priorities."

He turned to her. "And what are your priorities, Jillian?"

"That's easy. Starting at the top, my daughter."

He nodded. "As it should be. And what about other people in your life? Where do they fit in?"

She sat up, squared her shoulders. "Other people like my employees, my mother-in-law, friends? Obviously they're important, just not as important as Chloe.''

He continued to hold her gaze. ''Other people like a man, someone you date or might have a relationship with.''

''Oh.'' She paused before answering. For some reason she didn't want to tell him she hadn't dated since Rob died. ''Well, if I had a relationship, it would be important because I wouldn't waste time on anything else. And if it was important enough to be a serious relationship, it would be right up there with Chloe on the priority list.''

He broke eye contact first and didn't respond.

''Okay, how about you? Turnabout's fair play.'' Besides which, she wanted to know. She wanted to know all about Adam Ramsey. ''What are your priorities?''

He looked uncomfortable. He shifted in the seat, leaned forward, elbows on his knees, and let out a long breath. ''I suppose I *should* say the people in my life, but the honest answer, at the moment, is my job.''

Something stirred inside her. ''A job should never be more important than the people in your life.''

''Yeah. But since I don't have a wife or kids and the rest of my family live miles away and are involved with their own lives, anyway...'' He shrugged.

''No best friend? Your partner?''

His eyes turned dark. ''My current partner's a great kid, but we've only been together a short while.''

''And before that?''

He looked away. ''Before that, my partner was my best friend. But he...he isn't around anymore. He's dead.''

"I'm so sorry." She had a deep urge to enfold him in her arms like she did Chloe when she felt badly, but instead, she placed her hand over his.

"It was a while ago," he said, pulling his hand away.

"Any special woman in your life?"

Another pause. "No. I was married once and it didn't take. I learned that being a cop and being married is like having two lovers. You can't do justice to either one." Suddenly he jerked upright. "Listen."

She heard a rustling noise behind them and, turning, saw a priest walking toward them—a priest unlike any she'd ever seen before. He had long raven hair and walked so quietly it was almost as if he glided over the floor. As he got closer, she saw he was young, early thirties, maybe, and his eyes were as dark as onyx. He was almost as tall as Adam and just as broad-shouldered, except on those shoulders rested a long white robe with an ornately embroidered purple stole draped around his neck and falling straight down the front of his chest, almost to the floor.

He was beautiful.

Adam glanced at the priest and then at Jillian. "Finally we can get some answers." He got to his feet and started toward the man.

Jillian followed. She hoped he was right.

Adam spoke first and then the two men exchanged a long conversation in Spanish. At the first pause, she said, "Adam, can you ask him if there's a john nearby? I think my teeth are about to float."

Both men grinned. Then the priest said in perfect English, "Of course there is, right around that corner." He pointed in the direction from which he'd come. "You're welcome to use it."

Her ears burned. "Oh! I'm sorry. I didn't— I wouldn't have—" Both men were still grinning.

"It's okay," the priest said. "I've said worse."

When she returned, Adam and the priest were deep in conversation. Assuming the topic wasn't private, she went over to join them.

"Any luck?" she asked Adam.

"Yes. Father Martinez knows the mechanic but says he's gone until late tonight."

"Oh. How will we—"

"And—" Adam stopped her "—he's offered to arrange dinner and a place for us to stay the night."

"Wonderful," she said. "Thank you, Father, thank you so much." She would be grateful just to have a shower and get into some clean clothes.

The priest went to the door, waved a hand and, seconds later, a young boy appeared. They had a brief conversation, and then the boy ran off.

Adam left her with Father Martinez while he went to take care of his own needs.

"I sent Miguel to tell Rosa and Jorge to prepare a room for you," the priest said.

Not knowing what Adam had told him, Jillian simply said, "Thank you." Then she asked, "How did you learn to speak such perfect English?"

"My father was an American," he replied smiling. "I was born in Virginia."

"So how did a Virginian come to live and work in…"

"A godforsaken place like Cabacera?" He smiled

again. "My mother grew up here. She met my father in Virginia, where she was working for an American family. But not long after I was born, he died unexpectedly, and she returned home with me. I spent the first twelve years of my life here, then went back to the States to meet my father's family and ended up staying until I finished college and the seminary."

Adam returned. Father Martinez gave them directions to the place where they were to have dinner and stay the night.

As much as she wanted a shower, she couldn't help thinking that this was another delay. Another delay, and more time with Adam. The prospect of which she didn't mind. Didn't mind at all.

It was true. The man had gotten under her skin. And she didn't know what she was going to do about it.

They said goodbye to the priest, and once outside again, Adam said, "C'mon. It's not far."

She took long strides to keep up with him. "What did he say? Did he know anything?"

"He told me where the boy is staying. We'll need the car to get there."

"Which means tomorrow sometime."

"Right." He turned a corner onto another street, where the homes, she noticed, were spaced farther apart.

During the time they'd been in the church, the little town had come alive. Children scampered in the streets, mothers called out to them, a few scraggly dogs poked around in the dusty alleys, a woman and a young girl hung bright white garments on a clothesline that spanned the length of their front porch, while the men openly eyed the strangers walking down the street.

There wasn't much wealth here, that was evident, but the children smiled as they passed, greeting them with *"Hola"* and *"Buenas tardes."* Life appeared slower, more relaxed. Natural.

"What exactly did he say about the boy? Where do we have to go? Is he still there? Did he know if his father came to get him?"

"Hey, take it easy. We can't do anything until morning. Like I said, the woman the boy's staying with lives out of town a bit, and we'll need the car to get there." Adam squinted, then pointed, "I think that's it, the house at the end of the street with the picket fence."

It looked homey and inviting, and if their hosts were as friendly as the priest, she'd be happy. It would be nice to relax for the night.

Adam held the gate for her and they went to the door together. He knocked on the screen and within seconds a woman appeared. Her dark hair was spiked with gray and held in a bun at her nape. Her round face lit up when she saw them. Opening the door, she introduced herself as Rosa and welcomed them inside.

Jillian greeted the woman in Spanish, then with a surprising sense of pride, watched Adam as he took over the conversation. She heard him mention Father Martinez, at which the woman's face lit up.

Adam was adept with people, smooth and able to coax conversation out of even the most reluctant. But he was different with her. Why was that? And which was the real Adam? This charismatic charmer, or the curmudgeon he sometimes was around her?

Soon both Adam and the woman were laughing and having a jolly old time. She wished she knew the language so she could join in. The woman turned to her and said in halting English, "You are tired, *señora*. Maybe you like to rest before dinner?"

"I'd like that very much," Jillian answered.

"Come," the woman said, and led her guests out the back door. They walked several yards on a small path through dense flora until they reached another house, a very small one, white with a clay tile roof, and nestled beneath a canopy of coconut palms and banana trees with leaves like airplane wings.

The effect was magical.

Just as they reached the door, Adam pulled her back and whispered, "I thought it was safer to have one room."

"There," the woman said, unlocking the door.

Inside, they set their things down while the woman gave them instructions on how to operate the water heater and the ceiling fan, indicated where the towels were and then said she'd see them at dinner, somewhere around seven or eight. With that, she was gone.

Jillian glanced around the room. It was larger than the last place, immaculate and, she hoped, a little more secure. There were two beds, one on each side of the room, and, in the middle, a small table with a mirror on a stand. On the opposite side was the bathroom, which apparently didn't have hot water unless they lit the heater. Fine with her. Hot water was the last thing she wanted.

Adam looked at her and shrugged. "We seem to be striking out on the upscale accommodations, but it's all they had."

Jillian glanced around again. "Well, I think it's lovely. A roof over our heads and a clean bed for the night. It'll be nice to have a shower and a nap," Jillian enthused.

He looked surprised. "So, do you want to go first or should I?" He tested the bed facing the door, bounced a time or two and said, "Not bad."

Jillian dropped onto the other bed with a thud. "Mine feels like a bed of rocks."

"But?" He held out a hand as if she had something more to add.

"But what?"

"But your usual upbeat whatever. Like…but it's better than a bed of nails, or something to that effect."

Jillian stood, went to the small dresser, snatched a towel from the drawer and resisted the urge to snap him with it. "Just because I prefer to see the world in a brighter light than some people do," she said, "doesn't mean I'm not aware of the darkness. Believe me, I'm acutely aware."

His smile faded a little. "I was just teasing."

She knew that. So why had it upset her?

He flopped back on the bed, hands behind his head. "I think it's cute."

Cute. She turned her back to him. *Cute.* Was that good cute or not-so-good cute? Did he think she was a ditz who spouted cheery jingles all the time? That kind of cute? Or was he complimenting her?

At that moment, she understood why the tease had

upset her. She didn't want him to think of her as some ditzy Pollyanna.

But if she didn't want that, how *did* she want him to think of her?

The question already had an answer. She wanted him to like her, be attracted to her. Desire her.

Which was wrong. All wrong. For many, many reasons, of which Rob was only one.

"I'll shower first," she said, then disappeared into the bathroom.

CHAPTER TEN

DINNER TURNED OUT TO BE closer to eight than seven, but Jillian didn't care. After a shower and a nap, she felt refreshed and ready to enjoy the evening with their hosts, Rosa and her husband, Jorge, pronounced hor-hay. They were told to call him George. While she was napping, Adam had gone to make arrangements for the car, buy some extra supplies and see if he could get any more information.

To her surprise, they had another guest for dinner. Father Martinez, whom she subsequently learned was Rosa's son and George's stepson.

Rosa gestured for them to sit, and Jillian found herself sandwiched between Adam and Father Martinez. George sat on the other side of the table, where there was a space for Rosa, who went off to serve the meal.

Jillian thought about moving, but decided this was a better way to be part of the conversation, which immediately went in a direction over which she had no control.

"I imagine your nephew will be very happy to see you, *señora*," Father Martinez said.

Jillian realized Adam must've told him she was the boy's aunt. She shook her head. "This is the first time I've...I haven't had the opportunity to travel to Costa

Rica before to meet him, so this is a first. I'm looking forward to it very much." After a pause, she added, "I hope he feels the same."

Seeming satisfied with Jillian's answer, the priest nodded. Adam had obviously lied to him, too. For some reason the thought troubled her. How could Adam lie to a man of the cloth? Especially as he was the son of a minister?

And the least he could've done was let her in on the ruse so she could decide if she wanted to be a part of it. Now she had no choice, at least not if she didn't want to expose him, which would mean the end of their search, she was sure. She could only wonder what he'd said about *their* relationship.

"It's thoughtful of you to come all this way to help your nephew," the priest said.

Adam grabbed her hand under the table and squeezed it, obviously a signal to play along. "Jillian is all heart, Father. She's always helping others, aren't you?" He smiled at Jillian.

His hand was warm, and the warmth streaked up her arm and through her body, creating an ache of desire deep inside her.

"Given the situation, I'm simply doing what anyone in my shoes would do," she managed to say.

Adam added with a grin, "She's modest, as well."

What had Adam told Father Martinez? What did the priest think she was here to do? Just then, she heard music that sounded as if it came from an old gramophone, a familiar melody, but she couldn't think of the name of the song.

"'Love Is a Many Splendored Thing,'" Adam said with a smile.

"My stepfather likes music from old American movies," Father Martinez explained.

"Really? My dad liked old movies, too," Adam said. "He and I used to watch them together. They were great."

"William Holden is my favorite," George offered in heavily accented English. "William Holden and Jennifer Jones." He gave a big-toothed smile and everyone smiled with him. Strange that a little thing like old music and movies could draw such a diverse collection of people together, Jillian mused.

So Adam liked old movies. He obviously had a softer side. A romantic side. She felt sad that he seemed to have lost it.

Rosa came in bearing plates of food, set them on the table and went back for more. George poured them all some wine, and when Rosa returned with the last plate, he took her hand and seated her beside him.

"George and my mother knew each other as teenagers," Father Martinez said. "Years later they got together again, and as you can see, the spark is still there." He looked fondly at both of them.

Rosa said something in Spanish to Adam and he nodded and smiled.

Jillian leaned toward Adam and whispered, "What did she say?"

"She said we look like we're still on our honeymoon."

"You told them we're married?" she squeaked, barely able to keep her voice down.

He squeezed her hand again. "No, the priest assumed it at the church and told her," he said, talking like a ventriloquist through lips that didn't move, his voice lower than the music so only she could hear. "So you need to start acting like it or we won't get any more information."

Still smiling and sitting closer to Adam than her equilibrium could handle, she hissed, "Would have been nice if you'd told me this earlier."

"Just act like you're crazy about me." Adam gazed at her with loving eyes, lifted her hand to his lips and kissed the back of it. "That won't be hard to do, will it?"

His lips on her hand felt soft and warm, and all she could think about was how they'd feel pressed to her mouth. Struggling to redirect her thoughts, she asked under her breath, "What kind of information are we trying to get, my love?"

He turned to her and kissed her brow. "Anything that relates to your brother, sweets."

Her brother? Ah, she got it. Since Adam had said the boy was her nephew, the guy known as Jack Sullivan would have to be billed as her brother. And if pretending so would help them find him, she could go along with it—even if it meant she had to lie to the priest.

She hated lying. Her mother had lied to her from birth, telling her that her father was a decorated Vietnam war hero who had died for his country. It wasn't until her mother died that she'd found out the truth—and it stung even now. Her father wasn't dead but had simply left because he didn't want them. A fact she'd become very aware of when she went to live with him. He was a cruel, verbally abusive man. Still, her mother shouldn't have lied. A child had a right to know her parents, whatever their flaws.

"Father Martinez says your nephew was staying with a woman who lives about ten miles from here, but he doesn't know if he's still there," Adam told Jillian, his voice at normal pitch now. "And George's brother is the mechanic who will help with the car."

Hauling in a deep breath, she looked to Father Martinez and asked, "Do you know if...my brother's there, too? We haven't heard from him and I've been really worried."

The priest shook his head. "No, I don't. But there's another road that comes into town from the south, so we don't see everyone who travels through."

"Jillian wants this to be a surprise," Adam said.

When Adam said those words, Jillian realized this was it. They may or may not meet Jack Sullivan tomorrow, and if they did, she would know if the man was an imposter or if he was...*her husband.*

She'd put off thinking about it, shoved it out of her mind, telling herself the man in the photograph couldn't possibly be Rob. But now she had to acknowledge the possibility. And the effect it would have on her life and her daughter's.

"More wine?" George asked.

"Yes, please. I'd love some." She was going to need a lot more than wine to get through this night, she thought.

"Adam?" George held up the wine bottle.

Adam declined. He had to stay alert. He noticed,

though, that Father Martinez seemed to be enjoying the grape as much as Jillian and soon they were talking and laughing together.

Apparently George collected jokes during his trips to Mirador, where he worked, and in San José, where he traveled to meet with dealers, American and otherwise, who exported the native crafts he brought to them. Jillian looked happy listening to George's tales interpreted by Father Martinez, and while Adam was glad to see her enjoying herself, he wished it was *him* she was having so much fun with.

Warmth expanded in his chest as he watched them. She had a great smile and a laugh that bubbled up naturally. He liked that she was comfortable being herself. Liked that she said what she thought, even though it was sometimes with little regard to the consequences. He wondered if she was that way in bed, if she'd make love with the same abandon.

The pull in his groin told him it wasn't only his brain that wondered. Hell, he'd wanted to get her in bed from the get-go, that was no surprise. He'd wanted lots of women in the past.

But this, he realized, was different. Not only did he want to make love to her, he wanted to know her. *Really* know her. And that thought was scarier than meeting the end of a gun in a dark alley.

Professionally, that kind of involvement was a disaster. Especially when the woman was married to the guy he was tracking and wanted to see on death row.

A guy she was still in love with.

He gave himself a mental cold shower and rejoined the cheery conversation.

After dinner Father Martinez, who was also staying the night, excused himself. Then Rosa and George left, as well, with instructions that Adam and Jillian stay and enjoy the flan Rosa had brought in.

"It looks delicious," Jillian said to Adam when they were alone.

His gaze caught hers. "You're right. Delicious."

He watched her as she picked up her spoon, took her first taste of the custard, and then another. It was more pleasurable to watch her than eat his own.

"Mmm," she said. "That is *so* good. Try it. It's fabulous."

He smiled. "I was thinking the same thing."

She took another bite and then another until her dessert was gone.

He nudged his plate toward her. "You can have mine, too."

"Oh, no. I couldn't." She shook her head. "Really. I've had enough. And if you don't eat it, Rosa might think you didn't like it."

"Okay." He took a bite and swallowed, then put down his spoon. "So, are you nervous about tomorrow?"

She blew out a breath. "Truthfully, I just want to get it over with so I can get back to my normal life."

He studied her mouth. "And what's normal for Jillian Sullivan?" He leaned back and waited for her response.

"Taking care of Chloe, helping her with homework, spending time with her, going to work, doing things with friends, buying groceries, making dinner, making sure Chloe sees her grandmother and—" She stopped to clear her throat. "I guess nothing you'd think particularly exciting or interesting."

"What *I* think isn't important. It's what *you* think that counts. And if you feel satisfied with your life, that's all that matters."

Jillian looked away. *Was* she satisfied with her life? She'd thought so until last week, but... She reached for his flan, picked up her spoon and took a bite. But being here with him, seeing and experiencing so many different things in the past few days, she'd started to wonder.

He motioned for her to finish the flan, so she kept eating, one spoonful after another. She'd never examined her life so critically before. She'd set goals for the things she had to do, then made decisions on how to reach them, but she'd never really asked herself if those goals were what she wanted. All her life, she'd simply done what needed to be done.

As a child, she'd pretty much taken care of herself. After her mother died and the few years with a father who wanted nothing to do with her, she'd become Rob's wife and then Chloe's mother, a responsible parent, and then a businesswoman with a shop to run. Then she added more shops and a mother-in-law to watch out for.

She'd done what she needed to do to make sure her daughter never had to shift for herself, never had to feel she had no one to count on or that she was alone in the world. Never had to feel unwanted.

And now she had doubts about her *satisfaction* with this life. Being here with a man who made her feel...what? Angry? Challenged? Maybe. But also exuberant. Happy. Desired. *Alive.* She took a deep breath. Being with a man who made her feel all those things had changed her in ways she couldn't describe.

"So, *are* you satisfied?" he asked as she polished off the last bite of his dessert.

She set the spoon on the empty plate, taking great pains to place it precisely in the middle.

"I don't know," she finally said. "I thought I was…"

"I hear a *but*," he said, and ever so softly, touched his fingertips to her wrist. The gesture wasn't a caress, but something caring and tender. *Intimate.* So very intimate.

"But now," she went on, her voice soft, "being here, away from everything that's familiar to me, seeing things I'd only imagined or had seen in the movies or on television…well, it makes me feel as if my world was very small. All of a sudden, I want to experience more. Do more." *Feel* more.

She looked away. "I guess that's pretty selfish of me, isn't it."

He brought his fingers to her chin and lifted it so that he looked directly into her eyes. "I don't think it's selfish at all. And if it's any consolation, I sometimes feel the same way." He took her hand and squeezed it.

Desire hummed through her veins and in that moment, everything she'd wanted to experience a second ago narrowed to right here—to him. Only him.

She hoped that what she saw in his eyes was a similar desire for her. But suddenly he let go of her hand, stood up and cleared his throat.

"We'd better get some sleep. We've got a big day tomorrow." He waited for her to rise, then gestured for her to walk ahead of him.

Adam wasn't sure he'd have been able to retain his self-control if they'd carried on the way they'd been going. He wanted her so badly he could taste it. He wanted to taste *her*.

But morning would come soon enough and with it, he imagined, a whole new set of problems. He wasn't about to go for more.

Outside, the saturated air felt like a warm, wet towel against his skin. He wondered how Jillian's skin would feel against his. Wondered if he could spend the night in the same room without—

"So, how about you, Ramsey?"

"Me? What about me?"

"Are you satisfied with your life the way it is?"

He had to think about that. For years his job had been his life. When he was awarded the Medal of Valor, he'd thought it couldn't get any better than that.

Then he'd met Kate, and she'd changed everything. She showed him there was more to life than a job. He'd made time for her—and had been sorry for it ever since. Because that's when everything went down the tubes.

He wasn't going to repeat that mistake. Ever.

He had to get back to where he was before his partner was killed and before he had a wife. When his life was simpler. And this trip, if he got what he wanted out of it, just might be the ticket. He had more at stake than solving a murder.

"C'mon, I answered your questions," Jillian said

when he remained silent. "It's only fair that you answer mine."

She stopped at the door, turned, and with her back against it, looked up at him. "Unless you're afraid to," she said softly. Sexily.

He laughed. "Blue eyes, the only thing I'm afraid of is the end of a gun. And I'm not even sure about that anymore. I don't know what you think I might be afraid of."

"I think you're afraid to talk about yourself. I think you're afraid to do that because you might reveal something."

He leaned a hand against the side of the building, then leaned closer. "I'm not that deep, sweetheart. There's nothing to reveal. My life consists of work, a friend or two and...sometimes family, but they're so far away, I guess family doesn't count as part of my normal life."

"Yes, it does. Family always counts. No matter how far away they are."

The woman was too honest. Too genuine. He started to reach for the door, but on impulse, he kissed her, instead.

Just like that.

As his mouth met hers, she parted her lips, welcoming him. When she wrapped her arms around his back, his blood surged. He moved closer, wanting her warmth against him. Her arms moved up, and her fingers threaded through his hair at the back of his neck. He'd never felt so aroused.

She knew it. She had to know it. But she didn't push him away. He liked how well they fit together.

He'd never been with a tall woman before and quickly discovered the advantages. Her lips were more accessible, her breasts met his chest in just the right place, her thighs fit nicely inside his, and her hips fit more than nicely against him.

He deepened the kiss, unable to stop from doing what came naturally. Small needy sounds came from her throat, ratcheting up his need even more. He brought his hands to her backside and pulled her closer, grinding against her.

Suddenly she was moving, wildly waving one arm, which hit his shoulder. He heard a loud buzzing sound and then a loud thunk, then another, and she was waving both hands somewhere in the vicinity of their heads.

She pulled away and covered her head with her arms. "Damn."

"What?"

"Bugs. They're attacking us."

He reached for the door and shoved her inside, swatting at the hard-shelled beetles that seemed to be everywhere. He slammed the door and locked it.

"Gross! That was absolutely gross," Jillian spat out, shuddering with revulsion. She thought she probably sounded just like her daughter, but she didn't care.

"Not any worse than snakes or poison frogs."

"Oooh, yes, they are. Much worse."

She plopped down on her bed and crossed her legs, yoga-style, then shuddered again, her skin still crawling.

"You plan on doing a little meditating?"

She laughed. "I should. Maybe it would help."

He stood near the other bed and combed a hand through his hair. "Is there something I can do?"

She paused, then did her best to make her expression and body language convey that, yes, there was something he could do, and it had nothing to do with insects.

She issued her invitation softly. "I'm sure you can."

He paused, his eyes narrowing, as if he were debating the issue. He must know what she had in mind.

"No, I can't," he finally said, then turned, grabbed the top of the bedsheet and yanked it down. "You can sleep here if you want. I'll take the lumpy bed."

Stunned at the rebuff, Jillian just sat there. She'd offered herself to him, and he'd rejected her. She was both mortified and annoyed.

When he didn't say anything more, her annoyance grew. How could he kiss her the way he had and then just stop? He'd been aroused. She didn't have a whole lot of recent experience, but she couldn't miss that.

She remembered her friend Patti's words. *If you make the right moves, who knows what can happen?* She also remembered that she didn't know how to make moves. But she had to start somewhere.

"Why can't you?" she asked.

His hair hung in disarray over his forehead, sunstreaked and sexy. "Because you noticed the bugs and I didn't."

He was certifiable, she was sure. "I don't understand."

"I didn't notice because I didn't want to stop."

Oh, my. She pulled in a deep breath.

It didn't help; her heartbeat tripled.

"Maybe I didn't want to stop, either," she said, suddenly unable to breathe—again.

"Yes, you did. And you should have. I've kissed lots of women, Jillian, in the jungle and otherwise."

She looked away, her cheeks burning with embarrassment.

She didn't want to know his track record, she just wanted...what? To make out? Make love? Have a fling? Hell, a few seconds ago, she knew exactly what she wanted. Now she wasn't sure.

"Well, good for you," she said, unable to conceal her irritation.

"No, not good for me, and not good for you, either." He started for the bathroom, stripping off his T-shirt as he went. At the door, he turned. "Do you want to use the john before I take a cold shower, or can you wait?"

Fire rose in her belly. She wanted to know what he meant.

"You might know some facts about me, Ramsey, but other than that, you have no idea what's good for me or what isn't."

He leaned casually against the door frame, his tanned skin glistening with sweat; his eyes, a smoldering pewter, focused on her face. "That's where you're wrong, sweetheart. I've got your MO. Had it from the minute we met."

He held up his fingers and ticked off each point. "Security. A home in the suburbs. Two point two children. PTA. Little League and family night in front of the television watching Disney movies. Most important, I know you *don't* want a night of passion with a guy you'll never see again when it's over.''

He waited a second, then added, ''Are you going to tell me I'm wrong?''

She wanted to move her lips but they didn't seem to work. Maybe because he was right.

When she didn't respond, he said, ''That's all I need to know.'' At that, he disappeared into the bathroom and shut the door.

AS ADAM LATHERED UP, he heard thunder outside and then the light tick of rain against the tile roof. He hoped to hell it didn't rain into the next day, because if it did, they'd never get out of here. He doubted he could stand much more togetherness.

Mostly, he couldn't stand seeing the disappointment and hurt in her eyes. It shouldn't bother him so much. This was a *job*. Sometimes people got hurt. She was strong, she'd get over it.

But he wasn't so sure about himself. His body told him one thing, his mind another. And the worst part was that he really liked her.

A few minutes ago, she'd looked like a little kid who'd just disappointed her parents. A kid who needed a hug and some reassurance. But if it wasn't for him, she wouldn't have been feeling that way in the first place.

He'd had no business kissing her, no business letting her get under his skin. All he'd wanted was to make her understand that getting involved with him was just about the worst thing a woman like her could do.

She had to know that.

And because he cared about her, he wanted to make sure she thought he was the biggest jerk around, for he was never going to become a nine-to-five guy and live in the suburbs anywhere. It just wasn't going to happen.

He toweled off, wiped down the mirror, took out his razor and opened the door a crack to let out some of the humidity. The light was out, so he figured she must've gone to sleep already. Good. She'd need it.

Another rumble of thunder shook the small hut, then rain began pelting the roof like machine-gun fire. If that didn't wake her, nothing would. When he finished shaving, he used his miniflashlight to see and moved quietly to the side of his bed. He shone the beam quickly around the room to make sure things were okay, but when the light hit the door, he saw it wasn't locked. Strange. He was sure he'd locked it.

He glanced at Jillian's bed. Her mosquito netting wasn't pulled down all the way, so he reached over and peered beneath it.

She wasn't there!

He yanked the sheet aside. Damn. She wouldn't have gone outside alone, would she? Not in the dark, not with all those bugs she hated. But what was the alternative? Another burglar? A kidnapper?

No! Think, man. She probably couldn't wait to use the bathroom and went back to the house—it was only twenty yards away. That had to be it. But he wasn't going to wait around and hope he was right.

He flipped on the light, shoved his legs into his jeans, grabbed his gun and shot out the door into the driving rain.

Shirtless, shoeless, Adam stormed toward the house using his small flashlight to see the path and avoid any reptiles. As he got closer, he saw a light from a room in the back of the house. He hoped to hell that's where she'd gone.

She had no business leaving like that. It was foolish. Dangerous. He'd warned her not to go off by herself, dammit! Two American women had been robbed and killed not far from here a couple of years ago. His anger kicked up a notch with each long stride.

Reaching the front door of the house, he bounded up the steps and yanked open the screen door. The living room was dark, but he heard voices coming from somewhere in the back. His heart pounded.

Laughter. Her laughter. He'd recognize it anywhere. What the devil was going on? He skulked down a narrow hall, passing two closed doors on the way. Bedrooms, probably. At the end was another door, slightly ajar with low light coming from inside. The voices were quieter now and he couldn't imagine who she was talking with, since everyone else had turned in before them.

Standing outside the door, he held his breath and listened. But the voices had fallen to whispers. He positioned himself near the opening by the hinges and peered inside. A large shadow—a man. Movement. A woman's shadow. Shadows blending together. A moan.

Her moan—softly in her throat, just like when he'd

kissed her. Or maybe she was hurt. Pure white rage burned in his chest, and in that split second, he leveled his gun and kicked the door, sending it crashing in splinters against the wall on the other side.

"Get your hands off her, you bastard!"

CHAPTER ELEVEN

TWO HEADS POPPED UP. Jillian's and Father Martinez's.

"Adam?" Jillian's face went chalk white at the sight of his gun.

Father Martinez didn't flinch.

Lowering the gun, Adam took inventory, his gaze darting. "What the hell is going on?"

"I needed a woman's help," the priest said. "I didn't want to wake my mother or get her involved." He smiled. "But—" he looked at the door and grinned "—I think she may be awake now."

"Help?" Adam took a step toward them, tucking his gun in the back of his jeans as he did.

"Look," Jillian said as she stood up and turned to face him. A baby was cradled in her arms. "Isn't she sweet?" Jillian made another cooing noise at the dark-haired infant, a sound that came from the back of her throat. That's what he'd heard and took to be...

He scanned the room, searching for further explanation, *any* explanation.

"When I saw the light on in the guest house, I thought maybe Jillian could help," Father Martinez said. "I went over and got her. Sorry we worried you."

"I *was* worried," Adam said. "I thought something had happened. We encountered a burglar earlier on the trip and..." he sputtered, feeling stupid.

He turned to Jillian, his irritation waning, but only slightly. "It would've helped if you'd left a note," he groused.

Jillian arched her eyebrow, as if to say she wasn't obligated to tell him anything. Especially under the circumstances.

"So, what's with the kid?" Adam turned to the priest.

"Black-market baby smuggling," Father Martinez said. "From here to the U.S. People will pay any amount of money for a baby. Unfortunately some of them are kidnapped from their parents or taken by unscrupulous doctors or midwives from young unmarried girls. Others deliberately get pregnant and sell their own children for profit."

Adam rubbed a hand against his chin. "And what's your involvement?"

"Inadvertent. I heard about it from one of the church members—a young girl was coerced by her doctor to give up her baby because she couldn't pay him. Fortunately she came to me right away. I enlisted some local help who caught the smugglers before they left the country with the baby. And—" He waved a hand at Jillian, who'd just finished giving the infant a bottle. "And my helpers brought the child here tonight for safekeeping. The mother has been notified and should be here early in the morning."

Jillian set the bottle down and crossed to Adam. "She's adorable. Here, hold her. You'll see."

She shoved the kid into his arms. He took the baby and cradled her as he had his nieces and nephews. Having done more than his share of baby-sitting for his older sisters' kids when he was a teenager, he was an old hand at this. A few seconds later the baby sighed and closed her eyes.

Jillian looked at him with surprise. "Goodness, who would've known?"

"You're very good at that," Father Martinez said. "It's an expertise I don't seem to have." He smiled at Adam, but it was more of a smirk. So was the smile on Jillian's face.

Adam rocked the baby a little more, and when he was certain she was fast asleep, he put her in the small basket they were using as a cradle.

"I think I can handle it from here," Father Martinez said as he placed one hand on Jillian's shoulder and one on Adam's. He walked them toward the hallway to go out. "I appreciate your help, Jillian. Yours, too, Adam."

"My pleasure, Father." Jillian glanced at the broken door.

Adam said, "Sorry about that. I'll pay for a new one."

The priest nodded and winked. "They needed a new door, anyway."

Adam and Jillian walked the rest of the way back in silence. The storm had abated to a fine mist, and Adam hoped it would stop altogether or they'd have trouble getting the car. He tried to think of other things he needed to do, but he was still upset about Jillian's leaving like that. He wanted to talk to her, warn her about being cautious, not going off by herself, not scaring the crap out of him, but decided it could wait till tomorrow. What they needed now was a good night's sleep.

Three hours later he was still trying to get it. Finally he raised himself up on one elbow. For safety he'd left the outside light on and now, he was able to see Jillian through the gauzy netting. He was still looking at her when thunder shook the roof.

Jillian bolted upright. "What was that?" she said sleepily.

"Thunder."

She peered through the netting at him. "Don't you ever sleep?" she asked.

"It woke me, too. But it's far away now and the rain has stopped."

Her legs were bare, the T-shirt hitched up across her hip. Yanking it down, she flopped back against her pillow. "I like the smell of fresh rain. Maybe it'll cool the air for tomorrow."

He gave a snort. "It'll be more like a sauna. Go back to sleep." He had to do the same. Because if he cut himself any slack whatsoever, he'd be in that bed with her, and it didn't matter if the temperature was one hundred and twenty.

JILLIAN TRIED TO FALL ASLEEP again, but soon she heard soft music in the background, coming from the direction of the main house, an old song George had played earlier. She wondered if Adam was still awake, heard the music, too.

Adam.

Her awareness of the man lying in the bed across from her was sharp. It had taken her forever to get to sleep the first time, only to awaken in the middle of a dream about him. Asleep or awake, she couldn't stop thinking about making love with him.

As she listened to the music, the heat inside her grew more intense by the second. She rolled over and jabbed at the pillow. One way or another, tomorrow would be a turning point. If they didn't find the man they were looking for, they were going home, Adam had said.

She couldn't argue the point.

The light outside the door cast a low glow through the window, and lying on her back, she could almost see Ramsey's chest rise and fall, could hear each and every breath as if he had a microphone at his lips.

She had an urge to reach out and trace her fingers along the finely sculpted muscles, run her hands down his sides and over his hips. She wanted to leap out of bed and place her lips on his and give in to the cravings his earlier kisses had triggered.

Thinking of them now, she felt a deep ache of desire build between her legs. She hugged her arms close to her chest, willing herself to think about something else. She focused her gaze on the silver hook above her that held up the netting, studied how the white gauzy cloth swirled around the hook like a rosebud and then blossomed out, forming a waterfall of sheer cloth around her.

"Are you asleep?" Ramsey's low voice floated to her like part of a dream.

"No," she whispered.

"The music keeping you awake?"

"No, I like it." She closed her eyes.

"Yeah." He let out a long breath. "It's from *Picnic*."

"I know. William Holden and Kim Novak. George must like that era."

"Me, too. You hungry?"

Yes. For him. She waited a second before answering. "More thirsty than anything."

She heard the rustle of fabric, the slap of footsteps padding across the old stone floor, more rustling. "Ah, what a great selection. Would you like water or water?"

She smiled. "Water, please."

More noise, the sound of air releasing, the dull thud of the cooler lid. Then silence. She waited, listening. Then he was standing next to her and lifting up the netting. Handing her the bottle of water, he sat on the edge of the bed next to her.

She pulled herself to a sitting position.

"Cheers." He touched the tip of his bottle to hers.

"Cheers," she repeated, then watched the muscles in his throat work as he gulped the water down.

Following suit, she sipped slowly, aware that the condensation on the water bottle trickled down her chin and neck as she did. The moisture against her skin helped combat the heat, so she didn't bother wiping it off.

She wished he'd act like the jerk he'd been a few hours ago. But he wasn't a jerk. She knew that. He was a purposeful man with a job to do. Purposeful and intense. Purposeful and sexy.

210 THE MAN IN THE PHOTOGRAPH

"You were good with that baby tonight," she said. His eyes widened. "I've had practice."

She picked at the wet label on the bottle. "I bet it was fun to grow up that way."

"What way is that?"

"With sisters and brothers. A large family. Parents who keep tabs on you, parents who care what you do."

He hauled in a huge lungful of air. "Well, just because we were a large family doesn't mean everything was like a TV sitcom."

"Your parents didn't care about you?"

"I didn't say that," he answered. "Yeah, they cared. Too much, maybe. They devoted their lives to their family, and when we all left, they were a little lost. So don't kid yourself, all families have problems. I don't think there's such a thing as a normal happy family anymore."

"Is that why you're so set against marriage?"

He lifted the bottle to his lips for another swig.

"Partly. Also because I found out just how wrong it was for me. It's a great feeling to finally have control over my life."

"Can't say I blame you for feeling that way. I guess I feel a bit like that myself, though I would've liked it to be different when I was growing up."

He nodded as if he understood.

"I hated the way my mother and I lived and couldn't wait till I was old enough to be on my own," she went on. "I thought I'd be on my own after she died, but that's when Social Services stepped in, located my dad and sent me to live with him. He was a complete stranger. Anyway, I guess he thought having me live with him was better than paying support to a foster parent to house me.''

She took another sip. ''I guess I told you all that before, didn't I?''

''Some of it. And then you told me you'd run away.''

''Yeah.'' She bit her bottom lip. ''The funny part about that was, even though I wanted to be on my own, I wanted desperately for him to want me to stay.''

Again he nodded in apparent understanding.

''Which doesn't mean I don't like my independence,'' she said. ''I'm so used to it now, I don't know how I'd fare if I had to give up even a little of it.''

He smiled. ''I don't know why you'd have to.''

She returned the smile. ''I did for a while when I was married. But I didn't realize it until right this minute.''

He reached out and tipped up her chin. ''You turned out all right, though. None the worse for wear,'' he said softly. With his fingertips, he traced a line down her cheek and across her chin, then lightly over her lower lip.

The effect was hypnotic. She wanted him to kiss her again. He must have read her mind, because the instant she thought it, his mouth was over hers and tasting of fresh, cool water, touching ever so lightly, sensually.

She'd never imagined kissing could be so erotic. And if she'd ever had a reason for resisting, she couldn't imagine what it was. How could she not do something that felt so good?

It was lust, but it wasn't. It wasn't love—or was it? She wasn't sure right now if she knew the difference. All she knew was that she felt it ocean deep within her, and it was like nothing she'd ever experienced before.

Did he feel it, too? If his kiss was any indication, he did. She hoped he did. Even if he couldn't admit it.

She pressed herself to him, her fingers exploring the hard muscled ridges on his back, then moving around to his chest and through the dusting of light brown hair. Desire spiraled through her. She felt compelled to touch him everywhere, and as she did, his breathing became rapid, and his heart pounded against her fingertips as if it were her own.

Then he was kissing her chin, her jaw, her neck, lingering at the soft hollow at the base of her throat.

She tipped her head back. A low moan escaped from somewhere deep inside her as he kissed her breasts through the soft cotton of her shirt.

He blew moist, hot air through the fabric, and before she knew it, he'd lifted her shirt to kiss her stomach. His mouth and his hands were like fire, igniting her everywhere they touched—neck, arms, ankles, legs, thighs—until her whole body was aflame with desire.

When he found her mouth again and kissed her longer, harder, deeper than before, she knew his need was as intense as her own.

"Jillian," he murmured, "are you okay with this?"

Unable even to think beyond the need that consumed her, Jillian groaned, "Yes. Oh, yes."

Even though he'd asked, Adam wasn't sure he *could* have stopped. For the instant she'd kissed him back something wild and reckless had been unleashed in him. Still, he'd had to ask. She was right; he knew a lot *about* her, but he really didn't *know* her at all. Not what was truly in her mind and heart. He didn't want her to regret this, didn't want her to feel he'd forced her or taken advantage.

He didn't want her to have expectations he couldn't fulfill.

Even so, he knew he was about to cross a fine line. He wasn't the man she thought he was. He'd told her the truth, just not all of it. And now the truth was in the urgency of his need—and hers.

He took a moment to find the condom he always carried—just in case. Then he sank into a blissful forgetfulness in which the only thing that mattered was giving her what she wanted at this moment in time. He slid one hand around her narrow waist, pulling her closer, drawing her down so they were both inside the netting. Then he dropped his hand from her waist to the sweet curve of her bottom, pressing her against him, against the throbbing pressure in his groin; she curled a leg around his at the knee and moved her hips rhythmically, providing a friction that made him moan with pleasure.

He eased his hand around her thigh, then lower between her legs, fingers parting her, gently reaching for her most sensitive spot. She was as ready for him as he was for her. He began to stroke her....

Jillian had never abandoned herself to the pure physical pleasure of making love before and reveled in the sensations coursing through her. She felt the tension building, building, building, until an uprush of pleasure exploded within her.

Adam didn't move. He held his hand against her until the throbbing spasms slowly dissipated, and then... she became aware that he was looking at her—that he'd been watching her.

A wave of embarrassment rippled through her, but only for a moment, because his lips met hers and he took her away again, and then she wanted even more. She wanted the pleasure of watching him surrender in the same way she had.

A swell of love filled her till she couldn't breathe anymore. And just then, his breathing deepened, his urgency evident as he stripped off his shorts. She sat up and pulled her shirt over her head.

He reached for the packet she'd seen him take out earlier, and a deep urgency gripped her. She took the condom from his hand and guided it onto him, surprised at the silkiness of his skin. He watched her till she finished, then in one swift motion he brought her around and on top. "I don't want to hurt you," he said, his voice warm and caring. He smiled. "And I weigh a lot more than you do." In the heat of passion, he was thinking of *her*. Her heart melted a little more.

On this one night in a tropical rain forest, she didn't feel like a thirty-two-year-old woman who'd been married for ten years and had a child. She felt like a virgin bride, an adolescent kid who'd never experienced anything so wonderful before. Certainly nothing as wonderful as this.

"Jillian," Adam said, his voice filled with need. He reached for her and pulled her down. Then he turned with her, so that she was on her back. He gently spread her legs and positioned himself over her.

"Please," she whispered, raising her hips. She wanted him now. All of him.

He moved slowly at first, and then, in one swift motion, he was there, all the way. He waited briefly, then began to move, and she matched his rhythm. With her encouragement, he thrust into her again and again, faster, deeper, harder. Just as she wanted.

On a sharp intake of breath, he gave a body-straining shudder, and at that same moment, her muscles contracted and a pure surge of ecstasy rose to its apex and shattered within her.

For the first time in her life, she felt the heady sensation of power. She'd never known such pure unadulterated pleasure—or that she was capable of giving the same to another person. The knowledge was electrifying.

"You okay?" he asked.

"Are you kidding?" she whispered. "I feel wonderful. Absolutely wonderful."

He chuckled. "Then we agree."

Hearing his words sent her spirits to the moon...and yet at the same time, some small niggling thing inside her said she wanted more than that. She wanted their lovemaking to be more than just sexual pleasure, she wanted it to *mean* something to him. Something deep and personal—as it did to her.

Could one actually fall in love with someone after spending such a short time together? She didn't know, but there was no other way to explain what she was feeling. It wasn't possible to have such mind-blowing erotic pleasure without love, was it?

And if all that *was* possible and she *was* in love, she couldn't have picked a worse person to be the recipient of her affections if she'd tried.

But right now, it didn't matter one iota.

She exhaled and shifted her body underneath his.

"Sorry," he said. He eased to one side, resting on an elbow, his other arm still across her chest.

What now? Rob had always rolled over and gone to sleep.

"You were great," he said.

"You, too."

After that, they lay quietly for the longest time.

Finally he said, "What do you say we get some sleep? We've got a big day tomorrow."

It was true. Tomorrow *would* be a big day, but she didn't want to think about it. Not right now.

"You know," he said, "if we don't get the answers we're looking for tomorrow, it's time to head home."

We. A small word with multiple meanings that reminded her they had been at cross-purposes. They needed to talk about what happened between them tonight, she knew that.

But not right now.

"I know. I'm not convinced anymore that finding this man will change anything." In fact, at this moment, she *didn't* want to know.

Rob deserved her loyalty as his wife and as some-

one who had helped her when she needed his help.
She could do no less for him if it turned out that way.
But she couldn't believe—wouldn't *allow* herself to
believe—the man was her husband, because the man
she loved was Adam.

"You still think this man isn't—" He stopped, as
if aware that now wasn't the time to talk about dead
husbands.

She wasn't so sure. This might be the perfect time.
"Yes, I still believe the man is someone else." She
hoped with all her heart he was. "That should be obvious."

"Obvious?" He looked confused.

"Yes, I wouldn't have made love with you if I
thought otherwise."

CHAPTER TWELVE

I WOULDN'T HAVE MADE LOVE with you if I thought otherwise. Dammit! He'd screwed up. He never should've made love with her.

But he had.

He kicked the tire of the VW. He and George's brother, Geraldo, had left early to get the car, after convincing Jillian it wasn't necessary for her to come along.

What he really needed was time to think, because so far, he had no solution. Not any that didn't hurt Jillian. But so what? What was the big deal about hurting one person when the lives of many others hung in the balance?

If by taking out the scum, he could save even one susceptible teenager, wouldn't that be worth it? Wouldn't that make his partner's death mean something?

Yeah. He could tell himself that till he was blue in the face, but it didn't change anything. He didn't want to hurt her if he could avoid it. He just didn't know *how* to avoid it.

"Okay, put a board under that wheel and I'll put one under this side. Then you push from behind while I pull with my truck," Geraldo was saying. After Geraldo fixed the engine, Adam gave it a little gas and the wheels spun in the mud.

"Sure." The sooner they got the car out, the sooner they'd be out of the country altogether. He hated to go home empty-handed, but he couldn't justify staying any longer—not with Jillian along. If he was injured, even killed, that was one thing, but he wasn't going to let anything happen to her.

Forty minutes later, Adam and Geraldo rolled into the yard in their respective vehicles. Adam parked the VW, thanked Geraldo for the work and walked up the path to the guest house to see if Jillian was ready.

He knocked first. No answer, so he went in. The room was empty, all their things gone. He hoped to hell she hadn't done something stupid like striking out on her own again. Damn. His muscles tensed at the thought.

"Forget something?" Jillian's voice came from behind him.

He spun around, relief sifting through him. Relief quickly replaced with annoyance at himself for being so easily affected by the thought that something might've happened to her.

"No," he replied. "Where's our equipment? We've got to go, otherwise we won't make it back by nightfall."

"I've been ready for hours. I brought everything to the main house because I was helping Father Martinez with the baby."

He started walking. "The mother didn't come?"

"No, she did. She came about fifteen minutes ago and she was so happy, she hugged everyone before she left. And just being able to help that little bit made me wish I could do more.''

"I'm glad someone is happy," he grumbled.

"Did you know that in addition to the baby smuggling,'' she said, tripping along beside him, "children who aren't desirable for adoption are sometimes sold and exploited through child pornography and prostitu—''

"I know all that," he interrupted, still irritated with himself. "I've been here before, remember?''

"Well, how would *I* know what you know if you never mentioned anything about it?'' she snapped.

Good. She was angry at him—one way to keep her at arm's length.

"Well, knowing all that, don't you think we have an obligation to do something?''

"Do something? *I* have an obligation to finish the job I came here to do.''

"But maybe we can help!''

"*We* can't do anything right now.'' They neared the steps where their luggage was parked. "Because *we* don't know beans about the situation, the country or what others are already doing.''

He snatched up two of their bags, hauled them to the car and dumped them into the trunk. She grabbed the supply duffel and followed.

When she reached him, he said, "The reality is that people all over the world need assistance in one way or another, and it's impossible to help everyone everywhere.''

She shoved the duffel at his chest. "I'm not talking about helping everyone. I'm not *that* naive.''

"Well, please save the altruistic endeavors for when you're on your own time. Right now, there are a few more important things on the agenda. Unless, of course, you'd rather stay here while I go finish what we started."

If looks were daggers, he'd be dead. She yanked open the car door, climbed in and crossed her arms over her chest.

"Let's go." Jillian was furious. If caring about others was altruistic, then that's what she was. She didn't know why she felt so strongly about it all of a sudden, but she did.

It was almost as if there was a bigger reason she was here than finding out about the man impersonating her husband. Maybe she needed more in her life than work and caring for her daughter, who would, of course, move away one day.

She'd been thinking a lot about all that, especially after being with Adam. Their time together had made her realize there was more to life than work and responsibilities.

There was a time when she'd reveled in the small enjoyments of life. The scent of rain, the sun coming up in the morning, her little girl's laughter, a cup of coffee or a glass of wine with a friend. God, she couldn't remember the last time she and Dana sat down with a glass of wine just to talk. When had she and Chloe really talked?

Being here in this exotic country with a man who alternately enraged and excited her made her feel as if she'd been in a deep sleep and had suddenly awakened.

As irritating as Adam was at times, she had to credit him with her enlightenment. Without him, she wouldn't be here, and she sure as hell wouldn't feel the way she did.

He was a smart man. He'd been right when he said that she couldn't just jump in and do something for a cause she really knew nothing about. But she could do something later, and she made a vow to herself that she would.

Ten miles of silence and several dirt roads later, they drove into a small village, if one could even call it that. Dotting a hillside on one side of the road were a half-dozen small, dilapidated houses that looked as if they'd once been part of a motel. A small child sat on the steps of one, and a second child played happily in the sand nearby.

Adam stopped the car near the edge of the road closest to the first house.

"I've never seen anything like this," Jillian said softly.

"I have. It's just another way of life."

She nodded while her gaze panned the area. Rob would never have stayed in a place like this. He'd never have left a child here. She couldn't imagine *any-one* leaving a child here. Even if the boy's mother was dying, couldn't she have found a better place for her son?

"Let's rock and roll," Adam said, then got out and stood by the front fender to wait for her.

Her legs felt like cement weights. Was she that worried about what she'd find? The man wouldn't be here, she knew that. They'd only come because they might get a lead on where he'd gone. So what was the big deal?

She grabbed the door handle, thrust it down and gave the door a shove with her shoulder. It popped open and she tumbled sideways, landing in the dirt.

Adam turned at the noise. "Need help?"

"No," she said, pulling herself up. She could make a fool of herself all on her own. She dusted herself off and shut the car door. "Where first?"

"Right here." He started walking toward the closest house. She hung back at first, then hurried to catch up.

As they neared, a woman appeared in the doorway. She leaned against the frame, gave Adam a wide smile and languidly smoothed the front of her flowered dress. *"Hola, señora,"* Adam said.

The woman responded in Spanish, to which Adam rattled off something else. Her smile faded and she pointed to the shack on the far end.

"Gracias." Adam took Jillian's hand and pulled her along with him. "Act like we're married. It'll save us a lot of explaining."

She stumbled to keep up. "Explaining?"

"The woman wanted to give me a little pleasure in exchange for money."

"Oh. So what did you tell her?"

Glancing Jillian's way, he grinned. "I said you didn't charge anything."

Jillian slapped him playfully on the arm. "So, where are we going now?"

"There." He pointed. "That's where the boy is staying."

She wondered if the boy's caretaker had the same

profession. "No child should have to live in a place like this," she said vehemently, unable to stifle her feelings.

Adam gave her a puzzled look. "Right. But life is different here, you know. Prostitution is legal if you're over eighteen."

"I didn't know, but—" She cut off her protest. They were here for one reason. He had a job to do and, in fact, so did she.

About ten feet from the last house, he stopped, turned and placed his hands on her upper arms. "I know this is hard for you. Just remind yourself that whatever we find out, it's for the best. Then when you go home, you'll have peace of mind. Which is why you came here in the first place. Right?"

"Right." She nodded. "I'll have peace of mind— one way or another."

"Okay. C'mon." He took her hand again and walked more slowly toward the steps. A woman wearing a magenta flowered sarong came out to meet them. It was difficult to assess her age, but Jillian guessed she was younger than she appeared.

Adam greeted the woman with a wide smile and eased into conversation. As they talked, the woman nodded and smiled. When there was a break in the conversation, Adam turned to Jillian. "The boy is out back, if you'd like to go see him. I'll see what information I can get here."

Jillian wasn't sure she wanted to see the boy. What would it prove? If the woman knew where the child's father was, that was all the information they needed.

Still…

"Okay." She headed around the house, passing a fire pit where several fly-infested pots and pans were scattered in the dirt around it. Dishes, encrusted with old food, lay on a wooden table next to a garbage can that smelled of decay and sewage. Bile rose in her throat. She slapped a hand over her mouth and nose and hurried past.

She'd bet they had no electricity, running water or conventional toilets, which she desperately needed right now. Jillian cast about for the boy and caught movement at the edge of the forest about ten yards away. A head popped up from behind a log.

There. A little boy. Her skin prickled.

Was he the boy in the photograph? Bobby Jr.?

He seemed smaller than a five-year-old, which, based on the date on the back of the photo, was what she'd calculated the child to be by now.

She edged closer.

The boy turned.

She froze, her heart lodged in her throat.

His eyes. Oh, dear God. She recognized those eyes.

"I'LL GET YOU HIS THINGS," the woman told Adam in Spanish, then disappeared inside the shack.

What the hell? She'd said that the child's father had been here nearly two months ago. But then he'd left again. Why hadn't he taken the child with him?

A moment later the woman came out again, smiling and carrying a shoe box with a Nike logo on the side.

"This is everything you need to take him to America," she said. "He will be happy there. And my friend Corita will rest in peace now."

Take him to... Adam's jaw dropped to his chest. "Whoa." He held up a hand. "I think there's been a misunderstanding here."

The woman kept smiling. "No. No misunderstanding. Bobby's father said that someone would come to get him. Someone would take the boy to his home in America. I've put everything in here." She shoved the box at Adam's chest.

Deciding he'd better see what was inside, he took the box and sat down on the rickety wooden steps. The woman disappeared inside again.

He pulled off the cover and set it aside. At first glance, the contents looked to be just a few items of clothing. A T-shirt, one pair of shorts and underwear, a book. He shoved the clothing aside and reached underneath. A piece of tattered paper. He thumbed it open.

"*Robert John Sullivan Junior.* Mother—Corita Sullivan. Father—Robert John Sullivan," it read. Bingo! It was the boy's birth certificate. Before he had a chance to read all of it, the woman returned again. He stuck it in a pocket to look at later.

"When Corita's husband was here, he told me he had to take care of some business, so he couldn't take Bobby. He said if he didn't come back in two weeks, that I should mail the letter he gave me. That someone would come for the boy."

"I'd like to see the letter."

She shook her head. "The letter is gone. After two weeks, I mailed it like he said. My friend Corita, before she died, gave me a letter to mail and number to call, too, and when he didn't come back, I asked a friend who was going to Mirador to mail Corita's letter and make the call for me. But when he called the number he was told it was disconnected." She paused.

Adam pulled out the letter he'd received from Corita Sullivan. "Is this her letter?"

She nodded. "I forgot to do it right away."

That was why the LAPD only received it a couple of weeks ago.

"Something bad has happened to Corita's man. I know it. Because after he left, some men came here looking for him. Men with guns."

"Police?"

"No. Manolo's men. Drug traffickers."

Adam knew of Manolo. Anyone who worked narcotics knew of Miguel Manolo—the man who'd emerged as the new head honcho of the largest drug cartel in Central America. No one had been able to take him down.

"If they find him…" the woman added, then ran a finger across her throat.

Just then, Jillian came around the corner, her expression somber. Thinking quickly, he asked the woman to take the shoe box back inside while he spoke to Mrs. Sullivan. He couldn't tell Jillian everything, not until he sorted out what he needed to do.

He had to know for sure whether Jack Sullivan was dead or alive, and he couldn't take the chance that she'd do something to screw things up. Not when he was so close.

"Hey," he said. "How'd it go?"

Jillian gave him a look he couldn't read. Just then,

the other woman came out of the shack with a piece of paper. She handed it to Adam.

He glanced down. It was a telephone number. No name, no other identifiers. But he recognized that it was a U.S. connection with a familiar area code. A *Chicago* area code.

Jillian moved closer and glanced at the note. Her eyes went wide. She snatched it from his hand and stared. "This is my mother-in-law's old phone number! What's going on, Adam?"

Her mother-in-law's number? Man, oh, man. It was just the evidence he needed to prove Jack Sullivan and Jillian's husband were one and the same. It might not be conclusive in court, but it sure as hell was as far as he was concerned.

But what could he tell Jillian? What *should* he tell her? He couldn't say that her husband had drug thugs gunning for him and who knows what had happened to him. He raked a hand through his hair. "I don't know."

"Then ask her where she got it." Jillian's hands fisted at her sides.

"Maybe you should sit down."

She visibly stiffened. "I don't want to sit. I've just spent the past fifteen minutes with a child who's been shunted around for most of his life." Her voice trembled with quiet intensity. "He barely seems to remember his parents, and the woman he's staying with is a prostitute who doesn't want him. He's dirty and hungry and the saddest little boy I've ever seen."

She paused for a breath, then said more softly, "And his eyes are exactly like my husb—" Her voice cracked and she looked away, but not before he saw the tears form.

"Which means Rob is still alive," she whispered, then closed her eyes. When she pulled herself together enough to look at him, she said, "Rob is Chloe's father, Adam. I need to know what's going on."

His mouth and throat went dry as chalk. She had a right to know. And judging by how she'd held up so far, she could handle it. "Okay," he said, then took her hand and led her away from the house and toward the car.

He physically placed her against the vehicle's door and then leaned close to talk. He'd never been good at telling people bad news. "I don't want to—"

"Just tell me, Adam. Please. Whatever it is, just tell me!"

He took a step back and shoved his hands into his pockets. "The woman told me that the boy's father was here, but he had to leave on business. He told her he'd be back for his son within two weeks, but it's been more than that now and she doesn't think he'll be coming at all. She thinks something bad happened to him because men with guns came looking for him and he never returned."

"Men with guns?"

Adam nodded. "You ever heard of Miguel Manolo?"

She stared at him for a second. Shook her head. "But what—"

"Manolo's a drug trafficker and his men were here looking for Jack Sullivan. And before Corita died, she gave her friend that phone number in case he didn't return.''

Stunned silence was the response. Finally she managed to say, "But that number is old. Harriet doesn't live there now."

He reached out and took her hands in his. The implications were obvious. Jack Sullivan had given Corita the number some time ago—before Harriet moved to Meadow Brook.

The look on Jillian's face broke Adam's heart. He said, "Someone impersonating your husband would probably have all that information, even his mother's number. Maybe he gave the number to his wife just to back up his story. After all, he knew everything else. And remember, if he also looks exactly the same, it would be natural for the boy to resemble him, too."

She heaved a sigh. "Thanks, Adam, but I think we both know the truth. The man we're looking for *is* my husband. I've just been too stubborn and unwilling to admit it. Not to you, anyway." She shook her head. "Drugs. I—I can't imagine Rob ever... But if it's true, there must be a reason for it. Something...beyond Rob's control."

Even with the truth staring her in the face, she still didn't want to believe the guy would betray her. She was that much in love with him. The thought that her devotion and loyalty were wasted on such a creep twisted Adam's gut into knots.

"So," he said. "Despite all that, I think we should follow our plan." She could believe what she wanted, he thought, but she could never be sure until they had hard evidence. And knowing what that might do to her, he didn't want her to know.

She didn't move. "I didn't know *we* had a plan."

"We did. We were going to find out what we could here, go back to San José and then home. It's a good plan."

"But what about…what if he comes back? What about the boy? God, Adam, the child's been here so long without anyone who cares about him, it's heartbreaking. He asked if I had come for him."

"He speaks English?"

She nodded. "A little. His father taught him, he said."

"When did he last see his father?"

"I didn't ask. But he said his father told him he was taking him to America, but that if he didn't come back, he'd send someone else to get him." She looked at her feet. "He thinks that's me. He thinks I'm here to take him home with me."

"So did you set him straight?"

She shook her head. "How could I? He's so pathetic, Adam. And he was so excited. I didn't have the heart to disappoint him like that."

"But he has to know."

Her gaze darted about. "Look at this place. It's a horrible environment for a child." She stopped for a moment, her expression thoughtful. Then her eyes lit up.

"Oh, no," Adam said. "I don't know what you're thinking, but whatever it is, it won't work."

She looked hurt. "You don't even know what I have in mind. Hell, *I* don't even know. I just know we can't leave him here. That woman only kept him as a favor to a dying friend, and because she thought someone was coming for him and would pay her for the effort. If she knows that's not the case, who knows what she'll do?"

"It's not our responsibility."

"It's everyone's responsibility to help where we can."

Oh, man. She still wanted to save the world. "If I took responsibility for every terrible thing I came across, I wouldn't have time to do anything else. Certainly not my job."

"Well, fortunately, I'm not asking you to do anything. But *I* don't have a job that keeps me from helping a little boy desperately in need."

Adam winced. "Despite what you might think, I help people all the time," he said a little more defensively than he'd wanted. Being a cop in L.A., he should be used to disparaging remarks, but hearing it from her stung in a way he hadn't felt before. "But the plain truth is that we simply can't help everyone."

"I'm sorry." She touched his arm. "You're right. I should've said I don't have the same constraints you do."

"Which means?"

"I'm going to do what I can to help him."

"Like?"

"If we can't leave him here, we have to take him with us. That's all there is to it."

Even as Jillian said this, she wondered what they would do with the boy if they took him from here. Put him in an orphanage in San José? Would that be any better? She glanced around. *Anything* would be better.

Adam gave her a look that said she'd lost it. He shook his head. "No way." Then he walked back to the house and went inside.

Several women now stood at their doors watching. One had a baby on her hip, another, two tiny children clinging to her skinny ankles. She looked no more than thirteen. There were no men around. At least, not right now.

Remembering her conversation with Father Martinez, Jillian's feelings crystallized. Older children, orphans, weren't desirable for adoption and were exploited in all kinds of ways. Would that happen to Bobby now that his caretaker believed his father wouldn't return? The thought was abhorrent.

She couldn't let that happen to any child.

So they could take him with them now and figure out what to do later. Maybe Father Martinez could find a good home for him. At the very least, he might know someone who could. The child would be safe with the priest.

Jillian walked back to the house.

"Hi," a small voice said.

Jillian saw Bobby peering around the side of the structure. "Hi, Bobby. C'mon over here, I'd like you to meet a very nice man." She smiled at the boy and held out her hand. Maybe if Adam saw the boy's need, he wouldn't be so reluctant.

Bobby worked his way around the corner of the house, his bare back scraping against the rotted wood. Wearing only a tattered pair of shorts and nothing else, he looked like a small, fearful animal. His hair was the color of dark umber, his eyes a deep rich brown. He was filthy, his ribs poked out, and his knees looked like gnarled tree knots on stick-thin branches. Yet he was adorable. Sadly so.

The boy reached up, placed his hand confidently in hers and walked with her to where Adam stood.

Adam hunkered down on one knee. "Hello, Bobby." He rattled off something in Spanish, and the boy nodded. Adam said something else and Bobby's mouth curved into a wide smile—right before he ran into the house.

"What was that all about?"

"Nothing."

She folded her arms across her chest and eyed him suspiciously. "It was definitely about *something*."

He shrugged, looked away almost self-consciously. "I told him if he was coming with us, he better get his things and say goodbye to the woman who's taken care of him for so long."

Oh, my. Her heart swelled. She threw her arms around him. "Oh, Adam. That's wonderful. *You're* wonderful!" He returned her hug.

Standing in the circle of his arms, she realized how much she needed this. So she just remained there, excited and happy and feeling his heart go *thub-thub-thub* against hers.

He *was* wonderful—and she knew then that she really was falling in love with him.

No, that was wrong. She was *already* in love with him.

CHAPTER THIRTEEN

"I'M READY." AT THE SOUND of the small voice, Adam and Jillian stepped apart. He looked down to see the boy standing next to him and holding a ragged stuffed animal of some kind.

"Well, that was quick." Adam ruffled his hair.

The kid was marginally cleaner than before, still barefoot, but now dressed in a clean pair of shorts and a T-shirt. The woman came down the steps, sashayed over to Adam and handed him the shoe box.

"Can you tell her to please pack his things?" Jillian asked.

He held up the box. "This is everything."

Her mouth fell open.

"Now we have to figure out what to do with—" He cut himself off, remembering the boy spoke English. He inclined his head toward him.

Adam didn't know what Jillian had in mind when she'd insisted on bringing the boy along, but she was right. They couldn't leave him here.

"We can check with Father Martinez," Jillian said, glancing from Adam to Bobby. "Maybe he'll know what to do. He works with children all the time."

Adam nodded. Father Martinez had told him he'd contacted someone at the State Department in D.C.

about the babies being smuggled illegally into the U.S. through the Central American corridor, and when Adam and Jillian had first arrived at the church, he'd thought they were government agents sent to help.

There was another aspect that deserved consideration. If Bobby was with Adam, the boy's father, if he was still alive, might come looking for his son. And if the boy was with Father Martinez, the priest could alert Adam if Sullivan showed up. All Adam had to do was sit back and wait. It couldn't have worked any better if he'd planned it.

And if that didn't happen, at least the priest could find a home for the child. It occurred to Adam suddenly that he didn't care as much about nailing Sullivan as he had before.

Odd. For so long now, nailing Sullivan had been his personal vendetta, but somewhere along the way, the intensity of his quest had diminished. He began to recognize that it really didn't matter who brought the guy to justice. All that mattered was that someone did.

Adam looked at Bobby, then back at Jillian. "Okay. We don't have a lot of room, so I'll shove the box over and you can sit next to it, Bobby." He handed Bobby the small duffel bag. "You can use that as a cushion."

The boy beamed as Adam got the rest of their bags and then chucked them into the trunk.

"So, what's the plan again?" Jillian asked as she leaned against the car on the opposite side. "We go to Cabacera, then Mirador and then we'll drive back to San José?"

"You got it."

"On the same roads as before?"

"Afraid so. Is that a problem?"

She heaved a sigh. "The rain forest is beautiful and all that, but I can't stand to think of that ride again. I'll be a cripple." She narrowed her gaze at him. "And yes, I know I'm whining, and don't you dare tell me again that I should've stayed in San José."

He grinned. "Wouldn't dream of it."

Bobby climbed into the back while Jillian pulled out the map, shook it open and laid it on the roof of the car. "Do you remember when Father Martinez mentioned there was another road that came into Cabacera?"

"Yeah."

"Maybe there's another way to get to San José. Maybe a much longer road that bypasses the rain forest. Anything would be better than the one we took to get here. Or—" her eyes lit up "—maybe we can drive to another city close by that has an airport and we can fly back to San José and not even go to Mirador?"

"That would be great, but first, we have a kid to deliver. After that, we'll see what we can arrange."

Within minutes they were on the road again, and he mentally plotted out their course of action. Once they arrived in Cabacera, he'd contact Father Martinez, who could take the kid. Jillian's idea about getting to San José was a good one if there was another road to a city with an airport, they could fly and save time. He wasn't sure how he would play the rest of it, though.

He could send her home and stay on himself to

finish the job, or he could go back to L.A., attempt to get division approval and extradition papers, then return with help. But that wouldn't happen if he didn't find Sullivan first.

Bobby, he noticed when he checked in the rearview mirror, had fallen asleep, despite the bumpy ride and the roar of the engine. Jillian continued to examine the map.

"There's a road from Cabacera to a town called Puerto Viejo. But—" her words trailed off as she searched the map some more "—no road to San José."

"We'll decide when we get to Cabacera," he said. "It might be good to get input from someone who knows the area."

At that, she folded the map, stuffed it into the visor and then pulled out the Nike shoe box.

"What's in here?" she asked.

"Not much, I guess." He still had the birth certificate.

She opened the cover, poked around, then pulled out what appeared to be a U.S. passport. "Look."

The woman must've added it to the box. He didn't remember it being there before. "Whose is it?"

She flipped it open. "Bobby's. Maybe his mother got it so his father could take him out of the country." Looking at the pages, her eyes widened. "Oh, my." She took a deep breath and slapped it shut. Finally she turned to Adam and said, "He was born in California. He's a U.S. citizen."

"So?"

"*So,* that hadn't occurred to me, and I'm surprised,

that's all." She frowned, then stared at the information in the passport again. "Gosh, a lot of things didn't occur to me." She spoke quietly, talking more to herself than to him. "His father's name is the same as Rob's."

"That's no surprise."

She sighed deeply. "No, I suppose it shouldn't be. It's just that seeing it all...so official—" she held up the passport "—and seeing the boy..."

Adam heard the tears in her voice. He reached over and touched her hand. "Don't think about it."

"I wish it was that easy. But I can't think about anything else. It's...all so surreal, like a dream, and I...I'm not sure of anything anymore. Knowing that Rob is still alive should be wonderful...but the idea that he had another family, that he could have left us..." Her voice cracked. "And then there's this sweet little boy whose eyes are..."

He squeezed her hand again. "Don't start second-guessing, Jillian. Once we get to Cabacera, Father Martinez will find a place for the boy to stay, and you can go home and get your life back to normal again."

"I don't know how it can be normal after all this." Her voice was a whisper. She reached into the back seat and picked up the stuffed rabbit Bobby had dropped when he fell asleep. "Chloe used to have a rabbit just like this. It disappeared around the time Rob died. Do you suppose..." She shook her head and tucked the toy back in Bobby's arms. "What kind of life will Bobby have in Cabacera?"

"He'll have a better life than what he had back where we just came from."

Her eyes came to life. "But we don't have to do that, do we?"

"Do what?"

"Leave him in Costa Rica with Father Martinez. We—I can take him home with me."

Adam gritted his teeth. "Pardon me? This heat must be making me delusional. I'm hearing some really strange things coming out of your mouth."

"I'm his aunt, remember? I'm *supposed* to be taking him to America. And the more I think about it, the more I think it's a good idea."

"You're crazy."

Her expression hardened with resolve. "On the contrary. I'm finally thinking clearly."

He sputtered for words. "You...you can't just decide to take a kid out of the country."

"I can and I did."

"There are laws—"

"There are laws against exploiting children, too. And this is different. His mother wanted him to live in the U.S. Besides, it's the *right* thing to do."

Okay. The woman wasn't rational. He kept on driving, trying not to act as if that wasn't the most idiotic, impulsive, totally irrational decision he'd ever heard anyone make about a life-changing event.

"And why, pray tell, is it the *right* decision?"

"Because."

He snorted. "*Because?* You decide you're going to smuggle a kid into the U.S. posing as his aunt and the only reason you can give for doing it is because?" He jerked the steering wheel to avoid going over a hump in the road. "I don't believe it," he said. "I was right the first time. *You* are certifiably crazy."

She laughed. "Maybe. Maybe I *am* a little crazy, but you know what?" She didn't wait for a response. "It feels good. Damn good. That's why I know it's the right thing to do."

"It *feels* good? Jillian, this isn't…" Glancing at her and seeing the hopeful, excited look in her eyes, he stopped. Hope was infinitely better than the despair that had consumed her less than ten minutes before.

"Okay, I can understand not wanting the boy to stay where he was. I couldn't leave him there, either. But why on earth would you want to take him with you? Wherever he goes, he'll get put into foster care, and he won't be any better off in Chicago than he would be here with Father Martinez. At least the priest can find a family for him in his own country."

"If he goes with me, he'll *be* in his own country. He's an American citizen. Says so on his passport."

"Which doesn't change anything. He still wouldn't be any better off."

"I'll adopt him."

The air left Adam's lungs in a whoosh. He stopped the car, took her hand in his and looked directly into her eyes. "One word. Why?"

"Because—" her voice faded to a whisper "—he's Chloe's brother, Adam. How can I do anything less?"

AS THEY ROLLED INTO CABACERA an hour later, Jillian realized she'd been so intent on finding the man in the photograph that she hadn't really given much thought to the ramifications if the man in the photo turned out to be Rob. Oh, the worry had been there, festering in the back of her mind. But now she had to deal with it.

Her mind reeled with random thoughts. Adam had said she was crazy to consider taking Bobby home with her, and maybe he was right. For how might Chloe feel about it? What on earth would she tell her daughter? Or anyone else, for that matter?

What could she say without telling people that Rob had been a bigamist? Wouldn't hearing that break Chloe's heart? Her daughter idolized her father. How could she knowingly rip that belief to shreds? Especially when she didn't know the truth herself.

Jillian realized then that it didn't matter what anyone else thought. Rob was alive, and sooner or later, everyone would know. And if he loved his son, he'd come looking for him.

The bottom line was, she couldn't leave Bobby here, not when she could give him a loving home with his sister. Chloe would adjust.

Adam drove directly to the church. "We'll see if Father Martinez has any suggestions. We may have to stay overnight again if we can't take a different route out of here."

Once the car had stopped, Jillian leaned into the back seat and gently rubbed the child's arm to wake him up. He'd slept the entire trip, so he must've been exhausted. "Bobby, we're in Cabacera," she said.

Bobby yawned, stretched and sat up. He looked a little confused at first, but then smiled brightly at her. "Is that in America?" Both Jillian and Adam laughed.

"We're still in Costa Rica, kid," Adam said. "And

we've got a few things to do before we go anywhere.''
He shoved open the car door, flipped the front seat
down and reached in to give Bobby a hand.

As the three of them headed toward the church,
Bobby skipped between them, reaching up to hold
both her hand and Adam's. The gesture seemed completely natural, almost as if they were a family.

Inside the church, Father Martinez was standing
near the altar talking with a man in a flowered shirt.
The man looked like a tourist, but something about
him made Jillian think he wasn't.

"Wait here with Bobby," Adam said, and immediately headed toward the priest.

Watching the two men greet each other with exuberant handshakes and then the priest introducing
Adam to the other man, Jillian had a feeling that something was going on that didn't include her.

She nudged Bobby toward an ornately carved
wooden bench near the door and sat there with him.
As before, it was cooler inside than outside. She
scanned the church's interior, noticing things she
hadn't before: a marble basin by the door, a sign in
front of a long narrow hallway on her left that read
Alto, and a stairwell leading up to a tiny archway. A
musty antique-shop scent permeated the air. Farther
inside the church, on both sides, two racks of candles
flickered in the shadows, while refracted light from the
stained-glass windows near the altar glittered like di-
amonds off the gilded statues.

A peaceful feeling settled over her. Everything
would turn out okay, she was certain of it.

Her gaze returned to the men, still deeply engaged

in conversation. Moments later, a smiling Adam strode to the bench where Jillian and Bobby were sitting.

"Who was that man?" she asked.

"He said he was a tourist." Frowning, Adam glanced back at Father Martinez and the man, who were now walking off in another direction.

"And you don't think so?"

He shrugged. "I don't know what I think. But the good news is that there's a fairly decent road to Puerto Viejo, and Father Martinez knows someone there with wings who, for a price, will fly us to San José. With luck, you'll be home by tomorrow night."

Jillian's breath caught and held. Just like that she'd be home. Home where everything made sense.

Here, she felt as if the sultry, exotic surroundings had switched on all her senses at once, stoking up old needs and emotions, dredging up latent desires and unrealistic fantasies that confused as much as excited her. More than once she'd thought about a future with Adam. More than once she'd banished the notion for what it was. Unrealistic.

Yes, it would be good to be home where life was predictable, and she *should* feel happy about that. But she didn't.

As excited as she was about seeing Chloe and helping Bobby get a new start, something was missing.

Adam. Adam wouldn't be there. She'd go home to Chicago and he'd go back to L.A.—and she'd never see him again.

The thought made her heart ache.

Until sanity returned.

What kind of woman was she? Her husband was

alive—if those men hadn't found him and… No. She couldn't be in love with another man.

"Great!" she said, forcing enthusiasm into her voice. "It'll be wonderful to see Chloe. I've missed her so much!"

JILLIAN WATCHED the familiar buildings of Chicago flash by her cab window. Bobby was asleep on her lap and they were headed, unbelievably, toward her suburban home.

The journey from Costa Rico to the U.S. had passed without incident. After a whirlwind drive along a coastal road to Puerto Viejo, where she saw white sand beaches and the turquoise waters of the Caribbean, Jillian had made a vow to return one day. One day when she could appreciate the beauty of it all without yearning for something more. The flight from Puerto Viejo to San José had been in a plane that looked like a battered 1930s crop duster. From San José, another more leisurely flight to Houston, where Adam had departed for L.A. and she and Bobby had changed planes for Chicago.

Gazing now out the cab window, Jillian had a sense that things were different here, but she couldn't put her finger on what had changed.

Maybe *she* had changed.

She'd been surprised at the ease with which they'd been able to reschedule their two flights so they could all travel together. Because Bobby was a U.S. citizen, had a passport and the same last name as Jillian, there had been no problem with Immigration or Customs.

Adam had said he'd be coming back to Chicago the

next day—exactly one week from the day he'd shown up at her door. He wanted to meet with Rob's mother and suggested that Jillian not contact Harriet until they could go there together. Fine with her. How could she explain to Harriet that the son she'd thought dead for four years wasn't really dead?

Considering Harriet's memory these days, the woman might not think it strange at all. The question Jillian had was, should they even tell her? Would she know and remember it? Wasn't she confused enough as it was? Jillian had told Adam they should talk to Harriet's doctor before they did anything.

With so much going on, Jillian was also happy to have a day to get things sorted out. Shortly, she'd need to enroll Bobby in school, kindergarten, probably. Which meant she had to figure out what to do to keep him with her legally.

Dana would be able to give her advice. If one of Chicago's top attorneys didn't know about these things, no one would.

In fact, Jillian might do well to take a cue from her friend; Dana had given up her position as Cooke County's top prosecuting attorney to spend more time with her family. While Dana still worked more than she should, she'd cut her hours down considerably. The Wakefields were a wonderfully happy family.

A sudden ache of longing twisted inside Jillian. She wanted more than anything to experience what Dana and Logan had. She realized now that there'd always been something missing between her and Rob. She didn't know exactly what it was…a connection, a bond between members of a family, something that was felt but couldn't really be explained.

It was a connection she felt with Adam.

After Rob died, Chloe had filled the void. She'd given her all to Chloe. And to her work.

Which brought her back to her problem. She had to think of a way to tell her daughter about Bobby without destroying her father's memory. Jillian let out a sigh. There would be time enough for all that when Chloe came home next Sunday. She was glad to have the next week alone with Bobby. Right now it was important that she help him grow accustomed to his new surroundings—important that she get her life back to normal.

She glanced at the boy. His thick brandy-colored hair was shiny and clean now, and he'd looked delighted with his new Mickey Mouse T-shirt she'd bought at the airport in Houston. It was like Adam's, and Bobby had insisted on wearing it immediately.

His whole life was about to change—for the better, she believed. From the moment they'd left Cabacera, he'd stayed glued to her side, almost as if he was afraid someone was going to snatch him away. Children needed to feel secure and loved, and it was obvious the boy hadn't.

She vowed to do everything she could to make him feel that way. He was a sweet child, and she was certain Chloe would love him, just as she herself already did.

As they neared the house, Jillian's stomach roiled. Soon she'd need to introduce Bobby to everyone, explain who he was and how he'd come to be with her.

She'd have to find care for him when she went back to work, because kindergarten was only half days.

And then everyone would know about Rob.

Still, despite all the unknowns in the rest of her life, she couldn't suppress her excitement about seeing Adam tomorrow.

She'd extended an invitation for him to stay at her place which he'd accepted. They'd spent so much time in close quarters already, she felt as if she knew him better than she'd known Rob. Maybe she didn't know all the details of Adam's life, but she knew the kind of man he was.

He was a caring man, honorable to a fault, loyal to his family and friends, and he didn't give himself enough credit for any of that. He'd never even mentioned that he'd been awarded the Medal of Valor from the LAPD.

He went to work every day, never knowing if he'd return. But he'd never once mentioned the dangers of his job. Never once complained. It took a special kind of man to do that.

Her bias against involvement with a cop was, of course, the result of her experience with her father's brutal tough-cop attitude.

Because of that, she'd lumped Adam into the same category. But it hadn't taken long for Adam to dispel her long-held beliefs. He wasn't like her father at all, and she was grateful to Adam for giving her that insight.

She wished with all her heart that things were different, wished there could be a future for them.

Well…as Adam's dad had apparently said, "Wishes have no substance—it's what you do that counts."

And right now, she couldn't do a thing.

WHEN ADAM RETURNED, he'd gone to the station and immediately begun going through the old files Bryce had been working on before his death. Adam punched in name after name into NCIC, the police database, hoping something would click.

So far, he had pieced together that Sullivan may have been hired by the Manolo drug cartel to transport multi-ton shipments of heroin, methamphetamine and marijuana from Mexico into the U.S. via Tijuana. The only scenario that made sense was that Sullivan had somehow received a tip that the feds were on to him. So he'd done a disappearing act.

But using his own last name didn't make sense, unless Sullivan was too stupid to realize someone might track him down, which seemed unlikely. Obviously there was more to it. From what Bobby's caretaker had said, the guys who were looking for him weren't out to give him a medal.

For Jillian's sake, he hoped they hadn't found him. The thought totally surprised him. For so long he'd wanted to be the one to bring the guy down. Wanted it more than anything. And now, because of his feelings for Jillian, he was in a no-win situation.

"Are you gonna join us at Nick's tonight?" Rico asked. His partner was pulling a weekend shift and Adam was glad to see him there.

"Nope. I'm still on vacation and headed to Chicago in the morning."

"Oh?"

Adam cleared his throat. "Yeah. I think the mother-in-law might shed some light on this." He pulled out the phone number. "The kid's caretaker was told to call a stateside number if Sullivan didn't return. And it just so happens that it's the old lady's number."

He flipped open another file, punched in another number.

"Is that the *only* reason for going to Chicago?" Rico circled Adam's desk, then settled his butt on one corner. "From the goofy look on your face, I'd think you were going to the South Pacific on extended R and R with three hot tens."

"You're nuts."

"Methinks he dost protest too much."

"Cool it, Shakespeare. It's strictly business."

"Right." Grinning, Rico headed for the coffee machine.

Rico knew him too well. Fact was, Adam missed Jillian already. What was that about? Hell, he'd been with more than his share of women and he'd never felt like this before.

He tipped his chair back on two legs and clasped his hands behind his head. Her face formed in his mind's eye. He'd never met anyone like Jillian Sullivan before. Not anyone who made him feel the way he did.

Rico returned with two cups, gave Adam one, then sat on the edge of his desk again. Waiting.

Adam said in a softer voice, so know one else would hear, "The woman is still in love with her husband. I can't compete with that, even if I wanted to. Which I don't.''

"You sure about that? What's it been? Four years? Five?''

"Doesn't matter. Too many obstacles.''

"Yeah. Like geographically undesirable.''

"Right.''

"So, is this an overnighter or an extended stay?''

"Don't know yet. Depends.''

"And you're not in love with her?''

Adam looked at Rico, surprised at the question, yet unable to deny it. Scowling, he turned back to the computer, punched Enter and stared at the screen, waiting for the information.

Rico chuckled. "That's what I thought.''

"Too much thinking can get you into a lot of troub—''

Adam nearly choked on his coffee when he saw the face that materialized on his screen.

CHAPTER FOURTEEN

"Wow!" ADAM BLEW OUT a breath.

"What? You got something?" Rico hopped off the desk and moved around to stand at Adam's side.

"Yeah. A lot more than I bargained for."

"Someone you know?"

"Not by *this* name. The guy I know is a priest. Met him last week in Costa Rica."

Rico and Adam studied the data screen together. Drug charges, hard time in Corcoran, the most brutal prison in California. Damn. So maybe Martinez wasn't helping a young girl get her baby back. Maybe he was part of the black-market operation? The thought sickened him.

"Hey," Rico said. "Any guy who can do that kind of hard time isn't going to end up a priest. You sure it's the same guy?"

Reeling from shock, Adam needed a few seconds to regroup. Then he said, "Not a doubt in my mind. I think I've got a couple calls to make—starting with the prison."

"YOU TAKE CARE OF PATTI for me, okay?" Jillian said to Bobby as the two got ready to leave for the amusement park.

Upon arriving home, Jillian had called the salon to see how things had gone while she was away and wound up explaining to Patti the circumstances that led to Bobby coming to Chicago. Her explanation, however, omitted the part that involved Rob because, until she could discuss it with Chloe, she didn't want anyone else to know.

Patti had readily accepted that Jillian simply wanted to help a child who had no family. And when she'd told Patti that she needed to see Harriet and couldn't take Bobby along, Patti had offered to amuse the boy for part of the day.

"That's right, Bobby. You gotta watch out for me," Patti said. "Especially when I get on those bumper cars."

Bobby smiled and tugged on Patti's hand, obviously eager to get going. Jillian gave him a big hug and the two left for the park. The boy had no idea what a bumper car was, but with Patti's help, he was going to learn.

Glad to see the child happy, she went into the kitchen, then immediately came back out, went into the living room, sat on the couch for half a second, got up and went to stand in the middle of the family room. Adam was to arrive any minute now and she was as nervous as a cat.

She glanced around. The beige carpet was old and spotted, as was the rust-colored sectional facing the brick fireplace where she and Bobby had sat last night munching on popcorn and looking at old photographs. She pictured herself and Adam, Chloe and Bobby sitting there together—an image that warmed her heart.

Despite how distant Adam had become by the end of their trip, her feelings for him hadn't changed. She couldn't deny that hope still lingered in her. But she had to focus on what was important. And most important were Bobby and Chloe.

After the initial surprise of seeing a photo of his father with Chloe and Jillian, Bobby had settled in fairly well. Jillian hadn't yet figured out how to explain to the boy that she wasn't his aunt and that his father was also Chloe's father.

She could tell him that some people got married more than once and that before his mom and dad met, his dad had been married to Jillian. It was the truth. Just not all of it. Later, when he was old enough to understand, she'd tell him more.

A bigger dilemma was what she'd tell Chloe.

Just then the doorbell rang. Immediately her palms got clammy and her pulse doubled. After all she and Adam had been through together, why was she so jittery now? They'd been intimate enough to make love, for crying out loud.

Heading for the door, she realized maybe *that* was the reason for her jitters. That kind of intimacy with someone she was in love with was a totally new experience. While she'd loved Rob for all that he was to her and all that he'd done *for* her, she knew now that she hadn't been in love with him.

She both loved and was *in* love with Adam.

For all the good that might do.

In the foyer, she smoothed her palms down the thighs of her white linen pants, took a breath and swung open the door. Adam stood there looking much as he had the first time he'd shown up on her doorstep. A lifetime ago.

"Hi," he finally said.

"Hi." She stepped back and away from the door. "C'mon in."

She closed the door after him. "Would you like something to drink? Iced tea? A beer?" She paused. "Or do you want to leave to see Harriet right away?"

He shifted his weight from one foot to the other. "Can we talk first?"

"Sure." She led him into the family room. "Why don't you sit while I get some tea?"

As she went into the kitchen, she wondered why he was so somber. After pouring the tea, she returned to find him standing at the fireplace fingering a photo from the mantel. A photo of Chloe, Rob and herself.

"We look like a happy family, don't we?"

"I'm sure you were." He put the photo back and took the tea she offered. "How's Bobby? Is he around?"

"He's fine. My friend Patti is entertaining him this afternoon at the amusement park. I thought it best not to take him along when we visited Harriet." She motioned for him to sit, then sat down beside him on the couch, tea in hand.

The weather in Chicago was still hot and humid, but since the house had been closed up for a while, it was relatively cool inside. "So, what did you want to talk about?"

"I thought, considering all that has happened, you might want to reconsider…" He pulled some folded papers from the inside pocket of his jacket. "I thought you might want to give the okay to have the body exhumed."

A knot formed in Jillian's chest. What had she expected? That he'd come here to pledge his undying love? That he'd ask her to marry him and they'd live happily ever after? How stupid, especially under the circumstances.

When she didn't answer right away, he said, "I thought you might see some advantages to doing that now. Medical history for Bobby for school, knowing about your husband for sure..."

She nodded. She didn't know why it bothered her to be talking about this. DNA needed to be done. It was as simple as that. "Didn't you get a court order already?"

"I tried before I left, but apparently it got bogged down in the process somewhere. It'll go much faster if you agreed to sign off on it. Once that happens, it'll allow me to reevaluate the case based on the findings."

"I suppose it's best, but—"

"And once you know, you can get on with your life."

She nodded. Yes, she could, one way or the other. But there was something terribly final about learning for sure whether Rob was alive or not. Right now, she could assume he was alive, could even hope he was. But if she knew *for sure,* it meant she could no longer imagine she and Adam might end up together. She'd have no hope for the kind of happiness she'd experienced in Costa Rica with him.

And she should feel horrible even thinking like that.

"You're right. Yes, I'll sign the papers." She no longer cared about Rob's wishes in the matter. But what made her feel worse was that Adam was here on business. Strictly business.

After she signed the papers and they'd finished their tea in uncomfortable silence, Adam suggested they leave to visit Harriet. "We can take my car."

She nodded, then got up to slip on her sandals.

On the way out the door, Adam paused, then said, "There's something else I wanted to ask about."

She glanced at him. "Shoot."

"Have you thought about what you'll do if he contacts you?"

He. Meaning Rob. Rob, Jack, whoever he was. Whoever he was…because, while he may physically be Rob, he wasn't the man she'd once been married to.

And of course she'd thought about it. But she couldn't answer Adam's question. "This is like something out of a movie. These things don't happen to ordinary people."

He looked at her, his expression saying, *Yes, but…*

And he'd be right. It *was* happening to her and she was as ordinary as anyone. "I guess that's a bridge to cross when I get to it."

"Will you let me know if he contacts you?"

She couldn't answer that, either. She truly didn't know what she'd do. She doubted she would know until it happened. There were other things to consider. A little boy who missed his father—a father who'd left him in a horrible place with strangers. Chloe, who thought her father dead.

And what about loyalty and trust? And giving her husband the benefit of the doubt until she knew differently? What about standing by his side for better or for worse? She couldn't let her love for Adam color what she should do. She had to do the right thing. She just wasn't sure what that was anymore.

Reason took hold. "If he is alive, why would you think he'd come here and expose himself? If he's the criminal you think he is, that would be pretty stupid, wouldn't it?"

Adam shook his head. "It's just a thought. There's always the chance that he had a compelling reason for what he did."

Jillian pinched the skin between her eyes. "I don't understand. I thought you were convinced that he'd done something criminal." He hadn't taken her into his confidence enough to tell her what crime her husband had committed, other than drug involvement.

"I didn't know one way or the other. I still don't. The evidence indicates involvement in criminal activities. On the other hand, if he is a criminal, I don't know why he'd use his own name. You might be right. The whole thing could be some huge coincidence. But I wanted you to know that if he does make contact, it's vital for you to contact me or someone with the LAPD as soon as possible."

Jillian realized that if he still couldn't tell her what he thought Rob was involved in, he still didn't trust her. "And if I don't?"

He shrugged. "We don't need to get into all that. I just thought I'd let you know it's the right thing to do."

Well, Adam had never taken her into his full confidence. And it looked as if he was still trying to hide something from her. "I might consider it if you'll tell me why it's important to do so."

"I'd like to...but I can't."

"Can't or won't? You don't trust me, do you?"

"That's not true. I wouldn't have asked you to call me if I didn't trust you. I would've had you followed."

At those words, everything became perfectly clear. Whatever moments of intimacy they'd shared, whatever closeness and friendship they'd developed weren't as important to Adam as his job. Getting his man. She'd been stupid to think otherwise.

Her heart ached with the realization.

"Okay." She reached around him and opened the door. "Let's go see Harriet."

WHEN ADAM AND JILLIAN pulled into the parking lot at Meadow Brook Nursing Home, she had second thoughts. What they would accomplish here was a mystery to Jillian. Walking into the building, she said, "I don't think we should tell her anything. She's old and not well. She could—"

"I have no intention of sending her into cardiac arrest," Adam interrupted, then stopped in his tracks and stared at her. "You said a little while ago that I don't trust you, but I think the reverse is true. You really don't trust me, do you? And frankly, I don't think you trust yourself."

Just then, one of the aides saw them and greeted Jillian with a smile. "I'm so happy to see you, Jillian,'' the aide said. "Harriet's been asking about you every other minute, it seems."

"Oh, dear. I told her I was going on vacation."

"Well, the poor thing didn't remember that, just kept asking and asking." The aide led them into the sitting room. "It's not your fault, sweetie."

"Still, I feel terrible." Jillian saw Harriet and waved. "Do you want to wait here for a minute?" she asked Adam. "I'll see how she's doing."

The aide left them alone, and as Jillian started to walk toward Harriet, Adam reached out to stop her. "We should talk to her in private."

Jillian glanced around. "Right. I'll see if we can take her to her room." She skirted the tables and chairs to reach her mother-in-law, who was sitting near the window. "Hi, Harriet."

Harriet gave Jillian a blank stare, as if trying to place her. Finally she said, "Where's Chloe?"

"She's still at the lake with her friend Hallie and her parents. She'll be back next Sunday. I'll bring her to see you then."

"Who's that man you came in with? Is he another doctor? I'm tired of doctors poking me all the time."

"No, he's not, he's just a friend. I'd like you to meet him. How about if we all go to your room so we can chat for a bit?"

"He looks familiar."

"Maybe so, he was here before to talk to you about Ro—Jack."

"He's Jack's friend?"

"You could say that." Jillian went behind Harriet's

wheelchair and placed her hands on the handles. "So let's go where we can talk, okay?"

With that, Jillian maneuvered Harriet's chair to the hallway where Adam had just gone. When they reached him, she said, "Harriet remembers you from before."

"I like Jack's friends," Harriet piped up.

Adam arched a brow and gave Jillian a questioning look. She shrugged, kept on pushing and mouthed, "It's all right."

In the room, she wheeled Harriet over to the window near a small oak table.

"Jack will be here soon," Harriet said to Adam.

"Good, I'd like to see Jack," Adam said. "When was the last time you talked to him, Mrs. Sullivan?"

Jillian noticed that while Adam was talking, another aide had come into the room with some pills in a small paper cup.

Harriet frowned. "I don't remember." Then she said, "I put all his things away. For safekeeping."

The aide, a young woman, smiled pleasantly as if to say, She talks like that all the time.

Jillian exchanged glances with Adam.

Then Harriet added under her breath, "I have everything he gave me."

"Where did you put his things?" Adam asked Harriet.

"In my safe-deposit box. I told him I would keep them there until he came back."

Even though Jillian knew Harriet couldn't help living in the past, she sounded so certain. And she didn't usually fabricate things; what she said was usually something that had happened, but a very long time ago. Now she wondered.

Had Rob given his mother something that he'd kept from Jillian? She'd thought they shared everything. He'd certainly made sure he knew every detail of *her* life. Her stomach knotted.

As the aide handed Harriet the medications she was to take, Jillian said to Adam, "She does have a safe-deposit box, and since I'm the only relative, I have the key and her power of attorney."

The aide finished up and left the room with Harriet, who told her, "My Jack, he'll be home soon and you can meet him. He's a nice boy. The best."

Jillian didn't know what to think. Harriet faded in and out so often, Jillian was doubtful that talking to her about the phone number would serve any purpose, and she told Adam so. He agreed, and soon they took their leave and went directly to Jillian's to get the key.

Adam drove in silence and didn't say a word until they reached the bank. Sitting beside each other at a table in the little room where the clerk had taken them with Harriet's safe-deposit box, Jillian gestured for Adam to open it. He knew what he was looking for. She didn't.

The box wasn't very full, mostly jewelry and old letters. Jillian sat back while Adam put on a pair of surgical gloves, so as not to contaminate the evidence, if there was any, she guessed, and then proceeded to rummage through the stuff.

But when he held up a packet of letters, she recognized the handwriting. Rob's. The top letter was addressed to Harriet at her old address. Had he written to his mother when he was on the road? He'd never once mentioned that he had. Certainly he'd never written to her and Chloe.

Adam held out the packet for Jillian to see. The dates were indistinguishable, but as she looked closer, the postmark was—her stomach seized—Mirador.

She shoved Adam's hand back. "I...I can't do this. Will you?"

He nodded and she immediately got up and left the room.

After a few minutes Adam poked his head out the door and motioned for the clerk to say they were finished. He had the envelopes in his hand as he led Jillian out to the car. "I'm taking you home," he said without explanation.

Whatever Adam had read wasn't good, she was certain. But she couldn't bring herself to ask. Not right then.

Back at her place, they went inside. Adam called his partner, but she was oblivious to the conversation. Still shaken by the letters' existence, she didn't know what to do next. She wanted to know what was in those letters, but at the same time she didn't.

When Adam came out of the kitchen, where he'd made his call, she was curled up on the couch in the family room. He sat down on the ottoman across from her. She stared at him and asked, "What's going on?"

"I don't know yet. I'll need to have the lab examine the letters for authenticity."

"Authenticity? You mean you think the letters aren't from Rob? Why on earth would anyone fake something like that?"

He shrugged. "I don't know. But I've learned it's best not to assume anything."

"What did the letters say?"

Adam cleared his throat. He was obviously avoiding something. "I need to know, Adam."

"Yes, you do," Adam said. "It has to be tough not knowing whether the person you love is dead or alive. It's just that this is truly sensitive information, and if it gets into the wrong hands..."

There it was again. Distrust. "I don't know what you think I'd do with whatever information is in there, Adam, but I assure you my interest is strictly personal," she said as she snatched the packet from his hands. "I have two children who need to know if their father is dead or alive. And if you won't tell me, I'll read them myself. I need to *know*."

He chewed on his bottom lip, watching her. What did he think she'd do, rip them to shreds?

Finally he said, "If you must, at least wear these." He reached into his pocket and took out the latex gloves, then set them atop the letters in her hands.

She turned her back to him and walked to the end of the window beside the fireplace. Standing there, she put on the gloves and pulled out the most recently dated letter first.

Dear Mom,
This is the letter we talked about before. If you receive this letter, it means that the worst has happened. I know that's going to be a shock to you, but remember, I knew this could happen from the beginning. The important thing is for you to give

the key I sent you to the LAPD. Then you must find someone to go to Mirador to bring my son home. Please take care of him for me or find someone who can.

Jillian's world started to spin. She'd just reached out to clutch the window ledge when a pair of strong arms supported her from behind. Adam led her back to the couch.

"You okay?" From the look on Jillian's face, he knew she wasn't. Who could be okay after seeing in his own handwriting evidence of her husband's duplicity? The sleazebag had been alive all along, and now, presuming the note wasn't a fake or something meant to lead the law off track, he was dead.

It made Adam's job easier in a sense, but gave him little satisfaction. Nothing in his life had been more difficult than seeing the despair in Jillian's eyes. She'd lost her husband, the man she loved, not once, but twice.

He realized then that her happiness meant more to him than any score he'd wanted to settle. If he could've changed her husband into a hero, he would have—just to see her happy.

But he couldn't do that. He couldn't even soften the blow. The guy was a rat who'd sell his family for a buck. And Jillian was still in love with him.

He crouched down beside her and eased the packet from her fingers. "I don't think you need to read all these right now."

"Adam...he was alive all along," she said incredulously. "He was alive and his mother knew it. I can't believe it. That's...it's...it's inconceivable that he could simply drop out of our lives as if we meant nothing to him.''

She looked up at Adam. ''You knew, didn't you?''

He shook his head. ''I suspected, but I didn't know for sure and I still don't.'' God, he hated saying that.

He hoped to hell she wasn't going to cling to the hope that her husband was still a good guy, because if Jack Sullivan wasn't dead— He stopped the thought in motion.

''Like I said,'' he went on, ''I need to have the evidence checked out, because all this—'' he gestured at the envelopes in his hand ''—could be a ruse to throw off the law enforcement officers. Make us think he's dead. I'd like to take the letters with me, have the DNA done and go from there. That okay with you?''

She nodded. ''Well, at least one of us got what we were looking for.''

He felt the bite of her words. ''Well, if it's any consolation, I wish it hadn't been me.''

''Why? You wanted your proof and you got it. Everything else was just part of the job.'' She shook her head. ''God, I can't believe I was so stupid. First with Rob and then...'' She ran a hand through her hair and flipped it back over her shoulder and away from her face. She turned away as if she couldn't even look at him anymore.

''Then what?'' But he knew what she meant. She meant that making love with him had been stupid, a mistake. Maybe so. It had been a mistake for him, that was for sure.

Because if he hadn't, he might not be in love with

a woman who was still in love with a dead man. Or if Sullivan wasn't dead, he might as well be because he was going to spend the rest of his life in jail.

But none of that made Adam feel any better. And it served him right for getting emotionally involved while on the job in the first place.

"Nothing," she said, her words laced with bitterness. "Take the damn letters. I don't want to see them again."

He bowed his head, wishing he could do or say something to make her feel better. Hurt less. But nothing came to him.

When he didn't respond, she waved him off. "Just go."

"I'll go. But not before I talk to Harriet again and find out about that key. Will you come with me?"

Jillian raised her gaze to his; the hurt in her eyes was almost palpable. "I took her to the bank just a few weeks ago so she could put some things in her box. That's when she must've put the last letter in. Maybe the key is there, too?"

Adam shook his head. The key hadn't been in the box. A lump formed in his throat and he reached out to take Jillian into his arms to comfort her. She stiffened, pulled away and shot to her feet. He got up, too, and for a moment, they just stood there, face-to-face.

Then she said, her voice unnaturally calm, "I know you have a job to do, Adam. I know it's important to you. My problems are my own and I need to deal with them. So you're right, let's find out about the key, then you can finish up whatever it is you have to do."

"And what about you? What will you do?"

She shrugged. "Life goes on. I have a job and two children to raise. If—" her voice cracked "—if something else comes up with all this, I'll deal with it when I need to. You've got my signature on your papers, and all I ask is that you, or someone, let me know the outcome of the DNA testing."

He nodded. "Of course. I promise. Now, let's go find out about that key."

CHAPTER FIFTEEN

As ADAM HANDED THE search warrant to the bank manager, he could feel a renewed rush of adrenaline.

They'd found the key in Harriet Sullivan's jewelry box, but there was no way to know if it was the same key given to her by her son or what it was for. Harriet couldn't remember.

A couple days of investigation to determine that the key came from a California bank, another day to get the warrant, and he was in Chula Vista, a small town just north of Tijuana.

The manager asked him to follow her to the back of the bank, where she unlocked a set of barred doors. She used a master key to pull out a safe-deposit box about two feet long and then led him into another room where he could view the contents in private. When the woman left and closed the door behind her, he pulled on his latex gloves and shoved in the key.

He tensed in anticipation of what he might find. Slowly, he turned the key, and the box clicked open.

Inside was a manilla envelope that contained two floppy disks, two CDs, some photos and a note from Sullivan that said he'd prepared the information as his safety net. There was also a small packet addressed to

Jillian Sullivan. The back of Adam's neck prickled. Even in death this guy had a hold on her.

But he couldn't think about that. As he read Sullivan's note and the words slowly hit home, he sank back in his chair.

Stunned. Shocked. Blown away.

He had in his hands all the information needed to take down the leaders of the largest drug cartel, and some major players in the largest crime syndicate, in the Western Hemisphere.

Damn.

But where did Bryce fit in? In the message he'd left on Adam's machine, Bryce had mentioned a covert operation, the biggest ever. He'd also mentioned Manolo.

Bryce's voice had been frantic, and it'd been hard for Adam to understand half of it. He'd mentioned an organization but Adam didn't recognize the significance of it at the time. He'd begged Adam to meet him that night. He needed his help. No details beyond that. Adam would've dropped everything and gone to meet him if he'd only known in time.

By the time he'd come back from vacation, the funeral had already been planned. Everyone knew before he did. Everyone, dammit. It still galled him that the chief hadn't called to let him know. So what if he was off trying to save his marriage?

Then he'd only connected Sullivan to Bryce after the photo and letter from Sullivan's wife number two had come in. Based on the letter, he'd done a casual search on the police database for Sullivan and discovered the cold-case file. When he'd picked it up, he'd felt as if he'd been whacked in the gut.

On the same night Bryce had died, not far from where his partner had asked Adam to meet him, Robert Sullivan's truck had gone over a cliff and ended up incinerated at the bottom of a ravine. Sullivan's wife's photo was in the file, and he remembered the woman he'd seen in the interrogation room the day Mac had transferred him to Vice.

Based on that little bit of information and a hunch, he'd gone about investigating the case on the sly. And when he saw that the investigation had holes as wide as Montana, he knew he was on to something. He just didn't have all the pieces.

And now, everything he'd been looking for, and more, had fallen into his lap. Like magic. The puzzle was still incomplete—but not for long. He hoped.

On a high he hadn't felt since his first arrest, Adam picked up the packet to view the photos. He recognized a couple of guys he'd busted before on minor drug charges, as well as several names, big names, that were well-known to law enforcement agencies. Many others were new to him. No surprise, since he hadn't worked Narcotics in several years.

But when he reached the last two photos, the faces he saw leaped off the page. Father Martinez. And, more jarring, *Bryce*.

What the hell? Martinez he could understand, since Adam had gone to the prison and discovered that Martinez's cellmate had been Manolo's brother. But Bryce? He was undercover and he'd been murdered because he'd been made. It didn't make sense that Sullivan had *his* data along with the others.

Three hours later and still reeling from the impact of what he'd found, Adam was back in L.A. He'd gone home, scanned the disks and CDs and was now at the station barreling into Chief MacGuire's office.

"Ramsey." Mac greeted him as if this was like a normal day and Adam hadn't just found his best friend's photo lumped in with a powerful and dangerous crime syndicate.

Adam knew he shouldn't be upset. Bryce had been undercover for a year before he died. So there was an explanation. There *had* to be.

He slapped the folder on Mac's desk. "I want to know what this is all about, Mac. What the hell is going on?"

The chief weighed two-fifty and stood six-five. His bald head gave him a further aura of menace. If Adam didn't know the man, he wouldn't want to meet him in a dark alley.

Mac picked up the folder and drew out the photos. "Where did you get this?" Mac's voice was even, but the hand that held the folder visibly tensed. The other balled into a fist at his side.

"That's not an answer to my question."

A muscle in Mac's square jaw twitched. "Leave it alone, Ramsey. It's not your gig."

"You're wrong. If it involves the Sullivan case, it is my gig. If it involves my former partner, I'm involved."

"You've already overstepped your authority by going out of the country without approval."

"I was on my own time."

"With a suspect's wife."

Adam glanced through the glass at Rico's desk. "Who told you that?"

"Not your partner. And that's not the point, anyway. The point is that you need to leave it alone. You're off the Sullivan case."

"Just like I was off Bryce's."

"If you have a problem with that, stuff it or I'll put you on suspension."

Adam raised a hand and took a step back. "Okay. I get the picture."

He swung around to go out, yanked open the door, then stopped. He turned to the chief. "But I can't leave it alone, Mac. I'm going to find out about Bryce. Suspend me if you want." He went to his desk and grabbed his coat, then stormed out and down the hall toward the elevator.

He got the picture, all right. He was digging too deep, but into what, he didn't know. If Mac had said the department had an investigation going that he might screw up, that was one thing.

But *this,* he didn't understand at all. Mac should've been grateful for the information. Instead, he'd told him to butt out. It didn't make sense.

Just as he was stepping into the elevator, two suits came up behind him and physically directed him down the hall to one of the interrogation rooms. He didn't recognize either of them, but they had *feds* all but tattooed on their foreheads.

"What's going on?"

Mac entered the room. Adam glared at him. "Tell me what's going on, Mac."

"We're having company. You'll know soon enough."

UNABLE TO CONTAIN HER JOY at seeing Chloe, Jillian swept her daughter into her arms. "Chloe, I missed you so much."

"Mo-om." Chloe wiggled from her mother's tight embrace. "I missed you, too. But we had *so* much fun, I want to go again next year. For even longer."

Jillian hugged Dana and Logan, then kissed the top of little Remy's head while Hallie struggled to get the boy out of his car seat. "I'm so happy to see everyone. I missed all of you."

"Right," Logan said. "I doubt you had any thoughts of us when you were lying on the beach in Costa Rica."

"Well, I was busy, that's for sure." Jillian had many things to tell them all, but first and foremost was telling Chloe about her brother. That had to be done in private, so she'd asked Patti to watch Bobby for a couple of hours while she got Chloe settled in and gave her the news. She so hoped Chloe would be excited.

Later when Chloe had unpacked, Jillian went to her room and peeked in. Chloe was flopped across the bed with earphones on, listening to a CD. When she saw Jillian, she smiled and took off the earphones.

Sitting down on the bed next to her, Jillian said, "Hey, sweetie. I've got some exciting things to tell you."

Chloe perked up, her blue eyes widened. "You went on a date?"

Jillian couldn't help but smile. She'd done a lot more than that, but it wasn't the kind of thing one discussed with one's eleven-year-old daughter. "No. Something else." After an uncomfortable moment, she launched into it, why Adam had come to the house, why she'd gone to Costa Rica, but she played down Rob's part in it, explaining that something bad had happened, forcing him against his will to leave Chicago and his home.

"So he went away but he didn't want to?"

Jillian nodded. "That's my belief."

"And is he really dead?"

"The police believe so. And so do I. In fact, because of that, some other things have come up that I need to tell you about."

Chloe sat up and crossed her legs. "Hallie and I were talking about our dads, and when I started to talk about mine, I couldn't remember anything. Just the stuff you've told me. I only remember what he looked like because you have pictures of him. It made me really sad. It's like I never had a dad."

Jillian took a deep breath, then gave Chloe a big hug. "You had a father, honey, and he loved you very much. No matter what, you need to remember that. You need to remember him as the wonderful person he was when he was with us. Whatever happened after that happened for a reason. We just don't know what that reason is."

"But if he left us like he did, and he wanted to, that's mean."

"I can't imagine that he wanted to, honey. I'm sure there was a really good reason. We have to be positive and not let negative thoughts color our feelings. If we do, then we'll suffer for it, we're only hurting ourselves. And so far, I think we've done pretty well together, don't you think?"

Her daughter nodded, but Jillian could tell something was still bothering her. She lifted Chloe's chin so she could see her eyes. Eyes that brimmed with tears. "What's wrong, sweetie?"

Chloe's chin quivered. "I guess being with Hallie and her mom and dad and little brother made me think about what I'm missing. And now I find out all this other stuff and it makes me feel even worse."

Jillian's heart broke. She'd tried to dilute the truth as much as she could, but it hadn't worked. Now, she realized, if she hadn't brought Bobby home with her, she wouldn't have had to explain anything to her daughter and Chloe wouldn't be feeling like she was.

"I won't ever have a family like theirs, either, because you won't get married again."

"I never said I wouldn't get married again, did I?"

Chloe shook her head. "But you won't. You don't even date."

Oh, my. Should she say something? Would that make Chloe feel better, give her some hope? She hauled in a long breath. "Well, that's not exactly true. I did date a little while you were gone."

And that wasn't exactly a lie. Dinner with Adam was almost like a date. And certainly making love would have to be considered something.

Chloe's eyes brightened. "Really?"

Jillian nodded. "Well, sort of."

Her daughter's blond eyebrows met in the middle. "Sort of? How can you sort of date?"

"Well, it started out not as a date and then..." Shoot. She'd have to do this delicately.

"You remember Adam and what I told you earlier about why I went to Costa Rica?"

Chloe nodded, her eyes wide with expectancy.

"Well, I didn't go alone. I met Adam on the plane, and while we started out as just friends, it ended up a little more than that."

"Oh, wow!" Chloe jumped up on the bed and started bouncing. "You're going out with Adam. That's so cool. Really, really cool. He's such a hunk."

Jillian raised her hands in a time-out gesture. "Uh, slow down, missy. I said we ended up a little more than friends. That doesn't translate into anything major."

"But it could, couldn't it?" Excitement rang in Chloe's voice.

"I don't think so."

"Why not?"

"He lives in L.A., for one thing."

"But if he comes back here, you'd see him again, wouldn't you?"

As much as she'd like to, as much as she wished things could've been different between them, she wasn't going to give herself or Chloe any false hopes. "I don't think he'll want to. He has a job and commitments. We're very different...." Her voice trailed off.

"But if he wanted to, if he came back and he

wanted to see you, you'd want to see him again, wouldn't you?''

Jillian thought for a moment, felt her heart squeeze. Then she said, "Yes, I would. I'd like that very much."

Chloe took one last bounce, came to a sitting position again and gave her mom a hug.

"So, there's hope for me yet, don't you think?" Jillian said, feeling a little better herself. Nothing was going to happen, but realizing she was open for it if it did was exciting in a way. "And there's something else I have to tell you. Something very important that will *really* change things around here...."

Fifteen minutes later, she and Chloe were on their way to pick up Bobby. Chloe'd had no qualms whatsoever, and in fact, was quite ecstatic about it. She'd have a brother. Her family was growing and her mother wasn't hopeless, after all. The things she'd learned about her father had seemingly left no scars.

Maybe it was a good thing Chloe didn't remember her father very well. It would've hurt more if she had. God knows, her own heart still ached.

As much as she thought she'd known her husband, she hadn't known him at all. What did that say about their happy marriage?

ADAM WAS STILL SITTING in the room two hours later—pissed off as hell. No one had explained a thing. Mac had left to make some calls. The suits had left to do who knew what. He would've gone back to his desk, but the door had been locked. It was as if he'd been collared and was awaiting interrogation.

He understood now what Jillian must've gone through four years ago. The difference was that she'd been in mourning for her husband at the time. Sometimes his job just plain sucked.

So what was the alternative? A few retired cops that he knew had gone into P.I. work, started their own businesses and only took on the jobs they wanted. Could he do that?

If he worked in Chicago, he could be closer to his family and Jillian at the same time. But then, if being close to Jillian was his objective, he could do the same thing by joining the Chicago police.

But what would be the point? So he could pine after a woman in love with another guy? That wasn't his gig, either.

So why couldn't he stop thinking about her, wondering if she was okay, wondering what she was doing. Had she gone back to work? How was she getting along with Bobby added to her family? How was Bobby getting along with them? He wondered what explanation she'd given to her daughter, but mostly, he wondered if Jillian thought about him at all.

And every time he thought about her, he got this hollow feeling inside. He'd gotten used to being around her, but hell, that was one week out of a lifetime. How could he miss someone he barely knew so much?

How could he have been so stupid as to fall in love with her?

Just then the door opened. Mac came in with two guys following on his heels. One Adam pegged as FBI, even before the introductions, and the other, he learned, was part of the binational task force in Mexicali. Mac said a special agent from the DEA would be joining them shortly.

All were part of SWBI, the Southwest Border Initiative, and were there to debrief him—because even though he hadn't been involved in their operation, he'd managed to jump into the middle of it. Mac hadn't been able to convince him to forget the case, so now he was bringing him in.

"We need to know everything that happened down there, Ramsey," one of the feds said. "We need to know where to go from here."

They launched into a discussion, and by the time they finished, Adam had learned that the DEA had a former special agent who'd taken a few months in the slammer with Manolo's brother and was currently doing a stint in Costa Rica. He had good cover, he knew the language and the people. In fact, Adam had met him. Father Martinez.

Relief swept through Adam. He'd liked the priest and had been utterly disillusioned and filled with disgust when he'd thought the guy was dirty. More surprising was his realization that all his old values and beliefs, all his ideals, still lived someplace deep inside him. He'd thought them long gone.

Matt Stryker, the DEA agent, said, "The southernmost area of Costa Rica on the Caribbean side has been a mainline for drug trafficking from South America, the islands and Europe for years. The goods are transported up through Mexico and into the U.S. at various points along the U.S.-Mexican border, including Tijuana."

Adam knew that already from working narc for two years.

"Father Martinez," Stryker continued, "is one of our civilian contacts in Costa Rica. He was brought in temporarily on the first leg of the operation."

Just then Mac shoved a picture under Adam's nose. It was the Hawaiian-shirt guy he'd met the last time he'd seen Father Martinez.

"What's his role?" Adam asked.

"He's DEA."

"Yeah." His instincts were still good. He'd known the guy was no tourist.

"How'd the priest get tapped?" Adam asked.

"He's a former agent. He went through the seminary, couldn't decide if that was his real calling, so he did a stint with the agency before deciding to go back to the priesthood. The department thought it necessary to enlist the aid of a few influential private citizens in the country, and he was a natural for the job. Especially since he'd done time with Manolo's brother when he was with the agency on another job. Sometimes private citizens are our best contacts, since they know the country and the people."

"So where does Bryce come in?"

Mac sat on the edge of the table. "Bryce was assigned to the task force on the Tijuana end, the last leg on the route. Bryce was deep inside, working as Sullivan's contact to get across the border. The nearest we can figure out is that when Sullivan found out the feds were on to him, he staged his own death and left the country.

"The Corita woman had been part of Sullivan's

cover for a long time, and since he had to leave the country fast, the wedding was one way to make it work. With no time to get a new identity, he had to use his own name. Which apparently didn't matter to him once he'd left the country, because the law here thought he was dead.''

The Southwest Border Initiative was huge, and the number of agencies involved was enough to boggle anyone's mind. But none of the explanations, none of Sullivan's information, had mentioned that Bryce had been made or why he was killed. From the FBI reports, it looked as if his cover had still been intact.

''So, who made Bryce?''

The men looked at each other. Mac had everyone leave except him and Adam. When they were alone, he sat on a chair next to Adam.

''There's no easy way to say this, Adam. Bryce was working with Sullivan. When Sullivan realized he was in trouble...'' Mac stopped, then said, ''We don't even know that he was made. He could've just been unlucky and been in the wrong place at the wrong time. All we know is that Sullivan needed to leave and he didn't want anyone to know he was still alive. He needed a body.''

Adam swallowed. He felt as if he'd been poleaxed. He took a breath and blew it out noisily. ''The one in the truck?''

Mac nodded.

Adam shook his head. ''All this time you knew. And you covered?''

Mac shook his head. ''We didn't know. SWBI had lost contact with him. Word from our source in Mexico confirmed he was dead and then his bloody clothes turned up in a Dumpster at a motel near Tijuana. Bryce's body was never found," Mac said. "The operation would've been blown if we'd done anything or let it be known he was missing. There was no body in that casket—that's why it was closed. I couldn't let you work on the case back then because you're too good. You would've uncovered something. The operation was too important to take that chance."

Adam let Mac's words sink in for a moment. Then he asked, "How long have you known about the body in the truck?"

"We didn't know until you brought in the information and the DNA came in earlier today."

WITHIN THE HOUR, Adam had left the division and spent the rest of the day on the move, walking, driving, running—it didn't matter where as long as he kept moving. His shock had quickly shifted to anger. Anger at Bryce for dying on him, and at himself because he hadn't been there for him.

He hadn't been there for his partner because his marriage was on the rocks. Ironically, his marriage was on the rocks because of his job, and his focus had been on saving his marriage. He was too involved in his own personal life to see that his partner was in trouble.

At home later that night, Adam paced the floor in his living room. Bryce had died for nothing. He'd died so some scumbag drug dealer could live the good life on a plantation in Costa Rica. It didn't make sense.

The only thing that did was that his partner had died for something he believed in.

As Adam thought back, he realized there were plenty of signs that should've triggered suspicion that his partner needed help. But, like Adam, Bryce could never admit when he needed help.

But dammit! If Adam had been aware at all, he should've known. The signs were there. Bryce had stopped joining the guys at Nick's Place after work, his attitude had changed from outgoing to moody, and he'd become defensive, guarded, remote and secretive.

Just as Kate had become before he found out she'd been cheating on him.

Both times, he should've known something was wrong. But he hadn't. He hadn't even suspected. What made him think he could ever have another relationship with anyone? What made him think he could be a good cop?

Jillian's image formed in his mind. He'd actually fantasized about a future with her, even thought about changing jobs. Which just went to show how far off the mark he was.

The only good thing that had come of it all was that with the information Jack Sullivan had provided, SWBI would be able to attack the command and control functions of the crime syndicate behind the international drug traffickers. So far three different prior operations had resulted in the seizure of more than twenty-two thousand kilos of illegal drugs and thirty-five million dollars. The operations had also helped reduce corruption, violence and alien smuggling associated with drug-trafficking activities along the border.

Now with the assistance of the Mexican government and the Costa Rican government through the bilateral Maritime Counter-Drug Agreement, it was possible to nail the cartel's leader, the elusive Manolo, which would leave the organization in disarray, without leadership and unable to conduct business in the U.S. It wouldn't last forever, but it would be a while before a new organization could take over.

Still, he couldn't close the Sullivan case until he knew for sure what had happened to the guy. What he didn't know was whether all this was part of Sullivan's plan, or if he'd crossed Manolo, too, and the cartel had finally caught up with him.

Mac had assured Adam he'd know as soon as he did.

CHAPTER SIXTEEN

JILLIAN EXITED THE SALON and waited outside the First Mane Event for Patti to come so she could lock the door. The kids had been in school for a few weeks and life was getting back to normal.

But there wasn't a day that went by that she didn't think about Adam.

She'd heard from him only once. He'd called to say they'd received the DNA results and that the man in the truck was definitely not Rob. He'd said he hoped to have more information for her later, but couldn't say any more right then.

Even though she'd expected the DNA results, the news had still thrown her and she'd barely said two words to Adam before hanging up. She still couldn't get used to the idea that the man she'd lived with for thirteen years, been married to for ten, the man she'd loved and trusted above all others, had led a double life.

And he was still out there somewhere.

For the better part of that week, bitterness had consumed her, and she despaired that she'd never trust another man again. How could she have been so blind?

She'd trusted Adam, too, and he'd used her for his own gain. But hadn't he let her know from the beginning that he wasn't the kind of man she should fall in love with? That she had was her own fault. But knowing that didn't make her feel any better. Just more stupid. Naive.

Patti came out and Jillian closed the door and locked it.

"So, tomorrow is the big day," Patti said.

Jillian stared at her. "Big day?"

Patti looked at her askance. "Hello. I'm meeting the e-mail guy. The one I've been corresponding with for two months, remember?"

"Oh, right. I'm sorry, Patti. I guess I'm just preoccupied these days."

"I guess. Jeez, Jilly, you gotta snap out of it. There's more to life than pining over some guy."

"I'm not pining!"

"Oh, sure."

"I'm not! I'm just…pensive. I have a lot of things to think about. I've got two children…."

"Who are happy as little clams, they're both excelling in school, and they think the sun rises and sets on their mom, who just happens to own three businesses and doesn't have to worry about where her money is coming from. Y'know, I wish I had your troubles."

Patti was right. Her life was going along smoothly—at least on the surface. It was her emotions that were all screwed up. She'd felt so vulnerable lately, and the least little thing seemed to bring on the tears. Aside from the fact that her husband was a bigamist, and the man she loved didn't want anything to do with her, her life was a breeze.

She missed Adam. Missed him desperately.

For so long she'd been without a relationship, without someone to share the little things with, without someone to hold her and love her and make her feel special. Adam had made her feel that way. She'd never known how important those things were.

Adam had made her realize how important it was not only to love someone as she did her children, but to share her love and life with someone who filled all the empty places inside her, someone who made her feel…complete.

"You know, you could call *him.*" Patti came to an abrupt stop by her car. "You don't have to wait for him to call you."

It wasn't as if the thought hadn't occurred to her, Jillian thought. But what was the point? What would she say? "He lives in L.A., Patti. He works there."

"So?" Patti shrugged, palms up. "My e-mail guy lives in Nebraska and he's coming to visit."

Now Jillian looked at Patti askance. "That could be dangerous, you know."

"Not any more dangerous than meeting a guy at a bar, or at church, even. Remember the 'sermon serial killer'?"

Jillian had to laugh. "Yes."

"Just living is dangerous, kiddo. You can't live in a vacuum. You gotta take a few chances."

"I went to Costa Rica."

"You did. And wasn't it worth it? Even if you never saw the guy again, I bet it was worth it. So why not take a chance on love?"

"I don't think that's one of my options, at least not with Adam."

"How do you know? Maybe he's at home thinking the same stupid things you are."

"Even if he was, and I took a chance, it could end badly."

Patti shrugged. "Life ends badly. We die. But at least we can live a little before that happens."

Jillian and Patti made plans to take the kids to the fair on the weekend, said their goodbyes, and then Jillian headed home. The kids should be there by now.

Instead of enrolling Bobby in kindergarten for half days, she'd enrolled him in the full-day schedule, which started later in the morning and ended at the same time Chloe's classes did. The teacher had thought it best since he needed to catch up, and the time worked well with Jillian's new schedule, too.

Since Costa Rica, she'd vowed to spend less time at work and more time with her children. More time appreciating the world around her.

Chloe was a great help at home and had taught Bobby the alphabet and all the slang words kids her age knew. She'd also taken it upon herself to walk Bobby home from school every afternoon. Chloe had recently taken on several responsibilities as if she'd been born to them. Definitely a radical change, and while Jillian liked the new Chloe, she knew teenagers and didn't hold much hope that it would last forever.

In the few weeks Bobby had been there, the boy's English had improved dramatically. Best of all, he'd fit seamlessly into their little family as if he'd been there all along. Even if there was a void in her love life, the rest of it was good.

She was immensely thankful for that.

As she rounded the corner, a candy-apple-red SUV with a Californian license plate came into view. Could it be…? Her heart fluttered. Could it be Adam? But then she realized that if it *was* him, he was there on business.

That was it. He'd found out something that he felt required a personal trip. Dread swept over her. Oh, God. What now? Had they found Rob? She didn't know if she could handle that.

Opening the side door and going into the kitchen from the garage, she heard soft voices in the family room to her left. Taking a few steps down the hallway, she heard Adam's voice, then Chloe's.

She could see their reflections in the mirror over the built-in oak buffet. Chloe was sitting on the ottoman and Bobby in the chair. Adam was pacing the floor as he talked. Jillian couldn't make out the words, but then she saw him hunker down.

She inched closer to hear.

"Since my mom's not home yet," Chloe said, "can I ask you some questions? Some things I can't ask her?"

Jillian jerked back in surprise. Chloe could ask her anything. Why did she think she couldn't?

"Sure, but I can't promise I'll know the answers."

"Did you know my dad?" Chloe asked

"No, I didn't. Not personally."

Jillian caught her breath, praying he wouldn't tell them everything. She thought about making a noise to let them know she was home, but if Chloe had questions she couldn't ask her own mother, she wanted to know what those questions were.

Adam cleared his throat before he went on. "Even though I didn't know him, I know he did some very good things."

Chloe's eyes brightened. "I thought maybe he did some bad things, because he went away and didn't tell us. Then he met Bobby's mom and they had him."

"Well, sometimes, when we don't know why things happen, we start looking for answers. That's when the imagination can run amuck. Like yours just did." He ruffled her strawberry-blond curls.

Jillian pressed her hand against her mouth to keep from crying out, then heard Adam's voice again.

"I do know that your dad helped put some bad guys in jail."

Jillian froze.

"Wow!" both Chloe and Bobby said simultaneously. Chloe's eyes flashed with excitement when she asked, "Was he a hero?"

Adam fidgeted, as if uncomfortable with the question. "That's what they give medals for, isn't it?"

"He got a medal? Did you see it? Did they give it to him after he died? Hallie's dad said they do that sometimes."

Adam reached into his inside jacket pocket and Jillian craned her neck to see what he was showing her. She couldn't see it, but heard him say. "This is it. It's called the Medal of Valor."

"What does that mean?" Bobby asked.

Adam paused slightly. "Valor means courage and

bravery. And this medal is only given to those who exhibit both, usually in times of danger.''

Chloe's eyes almost glowed she was so proud. Her chest literally puffed up. ''That's really, really cool. Can I hold it?''

Adam handed Chloe the medal and she stroked it like a precious gem. Jillian's throat cramped. Tears welled up in her eyes. Chloe had needed that. She needed something of her father to hold on to, something good to cherish and keep close to her heart.

''Sometimes,'' Adam said, ''when you feel very lonely and you think you're doing everything wrong, it helps to have something like that. Something to remind you that you can be brave and have courage.''

Chloe pressed the medal against her chest, her eyes rounding like full moons. ''Can I keep it?'' she breathed.

Without hesitation, Adam said, ''Of course.'' And then Jillian watched as he gave her little girl a big hug. ''Your father would want you to have it. But you have to share with your brother.'' Then he gave Bobby a hug, too. ''Take good care of it, okay?''

Jillian thought she heard his voice crack, and felt tears moisten her own cheeks. She wanted more than anything to go to him and hug him and thank him for his wonderful gesture.

He'd given Chloe the one thing he had that made him feel he was worth something, and knowing how important that medal was to him, she didn't think she could let Chloe keep it.

She slipped back into the kitchen, went to the door

and opened and closed it again, noisily this time, to let them know she was home. "Chloe, Bobby, where are you two?"

Chloe came on the run. "Look! Look what Adam brought. It's a medal for my dad because he was brave and had courage. That's what *valor* means. Isn't it cool?"

Jillian hugged both kids and, looking over their heads, saw Adam standing in the archway between the kitchen and family room. Chloe pulled away and ran toward the stairway. "I'm going to put it in my room. I can take that little doll out of that shadow box and put it in there," she said. "Then it'll be very safe. C'mon, Bobby. Let's see where it should go." And with that, the two children raced up the stairs.

Jillian straightened, smoothing the front of her tank top and jeans as she did. "Hi," she said. Her voice quivered just a little.

He raised an arm to lean against the archway. "Hi."

Self-conscious, she glanced around. "Would you like some—"

He cut her off before she offered him something to drink. "No, nothing. I'm fine."

"That medal. I don't think..." She trailed off, unable to find the right words. Finally she said, "I really appreciate what you just did. Chloe needed something...something like that. But I know how important the medal is to you and I don't think she should keep it, especially since the reason is...well, since it's not true."

"It is true—in a way. What he did allowed us to

take out some of the most dangerous criminals around."

"But he only did it to save himself. It wasn't honorable and certainly didn't have anything to do with courage or bravery."

Adam looked down. Shook his head. "Well, there still could be a reas—"

"No! There isn't. I appreciate that you slanted the truth for Chloe and Bobby's sake, but you don't have to do it for me." She turned away, unable to look at Adam, afraid he'd see how vulnerable she was.

"I really hate all the lies," she went on. "They're so incredibly hard to live with. My mother lied to me about my father, everything I thought Rob and I had together was a lie, and it seems everything between *us* was a lie."

Tears stung her eyes, and swallowing the lump in her throat, she added softly, "So please don't tell me more lies just because you don't want to hurt my feelings or think I can't take it. Tell me the truth, Adam. Why are you here?"

Adam was stunned. Did she actually believe that everything between the two of them was a lie? "I came here to tell you they found his body," he said quietly so the children wouldn't overhear. "And to give you this." He handed her an envelope with her name on it—in Rob's handwriting. "It was with some other things…and I'll need to return it after you look at it."

Her hands shook when she opened the envelope and pulled out a one-page letter.

Dear Jillian,

No matter what you might think of me now, I want you to know I loved you. I always loved you. I got caught up in something bad that took over my life, and I wasn't strong enough to get out of it. I never planned for it to go as far as it did, and then I was afraid I'd hurt you and Chloe—or that someone else might. Things got worse and I couldn't come back. I wanted to, but it was out of my hands. Please forgive me. I never wanted to hurt you or Chloe. I love you both.

Rob

She clutched the counter for support.

Adam went to stand behind her and put both hands on her shoulders. She stiffened at his touch. After a moment her shoulders relaxed.

"You all right?"

She nodded. "Yes. I think I've known all along. But even so, this makes it real. Final. How long have you known he was…"

"A couple weeks. The DEA were on it—the blond guy at the church in Cabacera."

She looked surprised.

"Sullivan had gone to him long before we arrived and asked for his help to get out of the country. He'd sent his wife and son into hiding before she got sick because he feared for their lives and his own. Apparently he offered information on the cartel in exchange for safe exit for him and his family, but Manolo's henchmen got to him first. His body was found buried near one of the strongholds that got raided by the covert organization working on this case. There was a positive ID."

Jillian sucked in a deep breath. "Why didn't you tell me earlier?"

"I knew how much it would hurt you."

She swung around. "Dammit, Adam. It's not up to you to decide what I should hear and what I shouldn't. And here." She shoved the letter into his jacket pocket. "You can have your damned evidence back."

He winced at the anger in her voice. Anger at him. And it hurt.

He wasn't one of the bad guys and he didn't want her to think he was. Her opinion of him meant more than anything.

"You didn't tell Chloe everything because all it would do is cause her more pain," he said. "I did the same thing for you, that's all. I wanted to protect you, blue eyes, and I'm sorry if I judged that wrong. I'm sorry if I took advantage of you when we were together, but don't lump me in with the people in your life who've lied to you. I never lied to you about things between us, not once. And don't ever think that what happened between us wasn't meaningful. It was to me."

She looked at him incredulously as she stepped away from him and reached to shut the kitchen door.

"Meaningful? What the hell does *that* mean? I didn't make love with you because I wanted to have a meaningful experience. I fell in love with you, Adam. I wanted to make love with you because I was in love with you, and I wanted more than anything for the feeling to be mutual."

He gave a start of surprise. Words stuck in his

throat. She was in love with him? *She* was in love with *him?* Had he heard that right?

"But what about— I thought you were still in love with—"

She stopped him with a hand in the air, hauled in a great gulp of air, then, looking down at her hands, said softly, "I loved him. I loved the person he was when he was with me. He took care of me when I needed someone. He helped me get on my feet. He deserved my love and my loyalty.

"But when I met you, I realized I was never *in love* with him. I didn't know what that kind of love was like, how it felt. I was fifteen when I met Rob, and I'd never been with anyone else." She whirled around, anger and pain, love and hate, want, need and desire all roiling inside her.

"And I'm sorry if that's a total surprise, and I'm sorry if it makes you feel even more guilty and more—" she waved a hand in the air "—more whatever it is that you feel. But I'm not like you, Adam. I can't shut off my feelings, I can't stifle them or pretend I don't even have them, and—"

"The feeling *was* mutual."

Her head came up.

"And meaningful means I love you."

She looked at him as if she hadn't heard him right. "What?"

"I said I love you. The feeling *was* mutual."

"Oh."

"Oh?"

A tentative smile formed. Her eyes brightened, then the smile broadened. "Really?"

"Really."

"But you said…you didn't ever want to get…you said marriage wasn't—"

He shushed her with a finger over her mouth. "I said it, and that was how I'd felt since…well, for a few years. But with you it's different. I want different things. It's just that—"

He stopped, not sure he could admit the truth to himself, much less to the person he loved. But more than anything he wanted her to believe him, to believe that what he felt for her was real, not a lie.

"I've always considered myself a strong guy, and I've never failed at anything in my whole life—except at my marriage."

His throat closed. Damn. This was one of the hardest things he'd ever had to do.

"My marriage failed because my wife found someone else, Jillian. She left me for another guy, and I can't seem to get rid of the fear that sooner or later, the person I fall in love with will find me inadequate in some way and then leave."

He took a huge breath, then forged on. "You made me realize that I was using my job as an excuse. It was easier not to get involved than to face failure again. But it didn't stop me from falling in love with you. Even knowing that you still loved your husband didn't stop me from doing that. But I—"

Jillian placed a shushing finger over *his* mouth and locked gazes with him. He was so fearless and so proud, and she knew the incredible courage it must've taken for him to admit what he just had to her. And he'd told her because he wanted her to know the truth. He wanted her to trust him, believe in him.

And she did. She truly did. Her heart was so full of love it felt ready to burst.

"I'm in love with *you*, Adam Ramsey. No one else." She sighed. "And I don't know what to do about that."

"What do you want to do about it?" His gaze stayed glued to hers and for the longest time neither said a word, as if talking might somehow shatter such a fragile moment.

Finally she whispered, "What are you thinking?"

"Geography."

"Excuse me?"

"We've got to do something about that. Me in California, you in Chicago." He leaned forward, his forehead against hers.

"We can work on it."

She felt his warm breath against her lips. "*Now* what are you thinking?"

"I'm thinking about your mouth—about kissing you."

"And after that?"

"I have a hundred other ideas. One of them includes a wedding."

When his lips met hers, she had a hundred other ideas, too, and they all started with him.

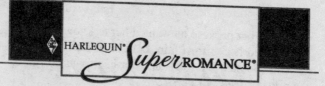

Princes...Princesses...
London Castles...New York Mansions...
To live the life of a royal!

**In 2002, Harlequin Books lets you escape to a
world of royalty with these royally themed titles:**

Temptation:
January 2002—*A Prince of a Guy* (#861)
February 2002—*A Noble Pursuit* (#865)

American Romance:
The Carradignes: American Royalty (Editorially linked series)
March 2002—*The Improperly Pregnant Princess* (#913)
April 2002—*The Unlawfully Wedded Princess* (#917)
May 2002—*The Simply Scandalous Princess* (#921)
November 2002—*The Inconveniently Engaged Prince* (#945)

Intrigue:
The Carradignes: A Royal Mystery (Editorially linked series)
June 2002—*The Duke's Covert Mission* (#666)

Chicago Confidential
September 2002—*Prince Under Cover* (#678)

The Crown Affair
October 2002—*Royal Target* (#682)
November 2002—*Royal Ransom* (#686)
December 2002—*Royal Pursuit* (#690)

Harlequin Romance:
June 2002—*His Majesty's Marriage* (#3703)
July 2002—*The Prince's Proposal* (#3709)

Harlequin Presents:
August 2002—*Society Weddings* (#2268)
September 2002—*The Prince's Pleasure* (#2274)

Duets:
September 2002—*Once Upon a Tiara/Henry Ever After* (#83)
October 2002—*Natalia's Story/Andrea's Story* (#85)

 **Celebrate a year of royalty with
Harlequin Books!**

Available at your favorite retail outlet.

HARLEQUIN®
Makes any time special ®
Visit us at www.eHarlequin.com

HSROY02

A
BETTY
NEELS
Christmas

What better way to celebrate the joyous
holiday season than with this special
anthology that celebrates the talent of
beloved author Betty Neels? Bringing to
readers two of Betty's trademark
tender romances, this volume will
make the perfect gift for
all romance readers.

Available in October 2002
wherever paperbacks are sold.

International bestselling author

SANDRA MARTON

invites you to attend the

WEDDING *of the* YEAR

Glitz and glamour prevail in this volume
containing a trio of stories in which
three couples meet at a
high society wedding—and
soon find themselves
walking down the aisle!

Look for it in November 2002.

HARLEQUIN®
Makes any time special®